W9-BSI-839

lightning on the sun

also by robert bingham

pure slaughter value

lightning on the sun

a novel

robert bingham

DOUBLEDAY

New York   London   Toronto   Sydney   Auckland

PUBLISHED BY DOUBLEDAY
a division of Random House, Inc.
1540 Broadway, New York, New York 10036

DOUBLEDAY and the portrayal of an anchor with a dolphin are trademarks of
Doubleday, a division of Random House, Inc.

Book design by Lynne Amft

Library of Congress Cataloging-in-Publication Data
Bingham, Robert.
Lightning on the Sun : a novel / by Robert Bingham.—1st ed.
        p.   cm.   I. Title.
PS3552.I496 B56   2000
813′.54—dc21
99-047900

ISBN 0-385-48856-4

Printed in the United States of America

May 2000

First Edition

1   3   5   7   9   10   8   6   4   2

For Vanessa

I implore you—a knock on the door may not allow me to finish this sentence, so take it as the last request of a dying man—if you have abandoned one faith, do not abandon all faith. There is always an alternative to the faith we lose, or is it the same faith under another mask?

—GRAHAM GREENE,
The Comedians

lightning on the sun

·

chapter one

ASHER WAITED FOR the bats. The little rats, he thought, where the fuck were they? All day long the bats took shelter in the eaves of the National Museum, waiting for dusk, waiting for the heat to die. Asher paced. The bats were late, and to be late on this particular evening was unsettling. Bad luck, bad karma, bad what? He did not know. He paced his porch, sweating. Asher's porch had a commanding view of the National Museum. It faced east and received good light in the late afternoon. At around six o'clock, give or take twenty minutes depending on the season, the bats took to the local skies in a great cloud of squealing motion.

When it came to his life in Phnom Penh, there were few things of which Asher was proud. One was his third-floor porch with its view of the museum and its back gardens; another was his Honda Dream; and the last was a rule he'd never broken: no drinking until the bats flew. He checked his watch. It was a little past six-thirty.

"Fuck," said Asher.

This evening was of considerable consequence for him and he badly needed a drink. It was late March and windless. The dry heat of January and February had intensified into stupefying weather, and though they were more than two months away, already he'd begun to pray for the rains.

Asher had originally arrived in Phnom Penh as part of a UNESCO restoration team. His first assignment had been the thankless chore of cleaning bat shit off Khmer statues housed in the National Museum. Back then he had been no friend to the bats and their shit. He'd quickly fallen into the camp of "preservation experts" that wanted to see the bats driven from the rafters. His ally in this camp was a Pakistani who would smoke anything handed him, and who like Asher had washed up in Phnom Penh for easy UN money and to get away from a woman.

It evolved that the French preservation community was quite fond of the bats and their shit. From their UNESCO compound computers they spewed memos in nearly perfect English arguing that to rob the bats of their "indigenous setting" would be cruel and unusual. Apparently the National Museum bats weren't just any bats. They were a rare species. Besides, the French argued, it was charming how a handful of the natives were making a good living selling organic fertilizer derived from the bat shit. The debate raged for nearly eight months and engendered a surprising amount of ill will and accusatory letters to the editor in the two local English-language newspapers. The French eventually prevailed, and Asher and his ally Alex were kicked up north to the town of Siem Reap, where they helped reconstruct the earthquake-damaged Elephant Wall, an infuriatingly complicated Khmer bulwark that had fallen into several hundred pieces some centuries ago. The pay was better in Siem Reap, but eventually the two friends, Asher and Alex, fell out with their project supervisor, a pedophile from Rotterdam with a yen for his young Khmer employees. Alex went into the hotel business and Asher into almost nothing at all.

Through his Nikon binoculars Asher watched a lovely Khmer woman he'd nicknamed Lovely Lane Lily sweep the pathways that meandered through the museum's gardens. Ordinarily this view of Lily would be standard enough but tonight he needed her more than ever because her serenity was a powerful antidote to the transaction upon which he was about to embark. Lily was as stunning as ever. She wore a baby-blue dress and looked like a sexy nurse. It had white buttons down the front and was cut fairly low to the breasts by Khmer standards. It had a nice slit at the back. Asher watched Lily sweep. Unlike Asher and the country at large, Lily was at peace, at peace with herself and her work. Asher wondered if she'd ever slept with one of King Sihanouk's many offspring. The Royalists and their FUNCINPEC party—oh, how they'd blown it. It was really kind of sad to see how that murderous bastard of a fascist dictator Hun Sen had muscled them out of power despite the Royalists' victory in the UN-sponsored election. The only ministries FUNCINPEC now controlled were Tourism and Culture. The National Museum was one of the few undisputed bastions of Royalist patronage. The employees were said to be hired for their looks and nepotistic connections to the royal family. It was considered a good job.

Asher put the binoculars away and wiped the sweat from his brow. He walked into his kitchen, drew a bottle of Stolichnaya from his freezer, and returned to the porch. Tonight it would be necessary not to get drunk. He poured a measure into his water glass and waited. The city was nearly silent but for the distant hissing of street stalls and the clattering yelps of his landlord's children playing soccer on the street below. Heads of green palm trees were catching the orange light from the river. It was a windless dusk.

Nervous and impatient, Asher lit a cigarette. The day had dragged horrendously. He'd had breakfast at a noodle stall at the foot of Wat Phnom, where he'd been harangued by street urchins and amputees. An elderly man had offered him an elephant ride. The elephant of Wat Phnom was drugged and lumbered around the circular hill occasionally carrying intrepid tourists.

Asher had arrived at the Bank Indo-Suez five minutes before opening. Standing in the blinding courtyard light he'd felt stupid and criminal. The guards had eyed him suspiciously. Phnom Penh was a secretive town, and when hungover, Asher was susceptible to the distrusts and paranoias that informed the place. The bank had been his only errand of the day, and with it over well before noon, he'd had nothing to do but return to his apartment and wait—wait and try not to drink. When he stood up to put something on his stereo, the bats suddenly took to the skies.

"There you are, you little rats," he said, draining his glass. "I don't know what I see in you."

The bats rose up black against the vermilion roof of the National Museum, a Halloween pictorial, a horde of flying freakery, kinetically connected, swooning above his head before they disappeared in the direction of the river. With three hours to kill he paced and refilled his glass. A massage; he couldn't believe he hadn't thought of it before. Of all hours this one was tailormade for a massage. He lit a stale, two-day-old joint and listened to the seeds crackle and pop. The marijuana in Cambodia was as legally bountiful as it was weak. It was necessary to wet one's papers with hash oil if one wanted to get high, but Asher's hash oil had run out months ago. No matter; it would be necessary to balance drugs tonight. Balance was the theme. Nimbleness and balance. If he wanted to come out on top, nothing must dominate. He stubbed out the joint and went inside to change. His bedroom smelled of himself, of his sweaty socks and months of compounded cigarette smoke. On his bedside table sat a high-end tourist replica of the four-headed statue that guarded the ancient city of Angkor Thom. Four Buddha faces in the likeness of God King Jayararman VII stared in four directions.

"North, south, east, west," said Asher. "Watch it."

Typically Asher took his four-headed Buddha bust as a discourse on perspective. It was a reminder, this bust, that most problems could be solved if approached from varying perspectives, from the perspective, say, of one's enemy. "Know thy enemy, know thy self," that kind of thing. Tonight, Asher touched the lips of the God King and went with a more literal translation. He went with vigilance. The heads had been used as watch towers to guard the sacred city. There were unreliable people in Phnom Penh, people to watch out for in all directions.

His bed was a mess, sheets crinkled and soiled. It occurred to him that it had been months since anyone but himself had frequented this room. White, or what the Khmers referred to as *barang*, Phnom Penh society had begun to bore him with its predictability. It was dominated by journalists who indulged in all the clichés of their trade. Asher was friendly with a handful but collectively called them "journos" behind their backs. These journos seemed primarily to interview one another, and drank at the same bars. If desired dead, they would be easy to find. He pulled on his jeans and took a gray button-down shirt from a closet hanger. Then came athletic socks and a navy-blue windbreaker. From beneath his bed he took out a worn leather satchel that had been left behind by a Flemish World Health Organization field coordinator, a terrible house guest. In the bag was three thousand dollars in cash, wrapped in three equal bundles.

At the top of the stairs he slipped on his sneakers and clambered down to the street-level workshop of his landlord, Mr. Hang. Mr. Hang specialized in the mass production of canvases depicting iconic Khmer landmarks for the burgeoning hotel trade. Asher suspected Mr. Hang for an opium smoker but had no evidence to back up his suspicion. Tonight Mr. Hang was swaying softly in a hammock listening to Khmer music on the radio. One of Asher's arrangements with Mr. Hang was that he was allowed to keep his Honda Dream parked in the landlord's workshop. It cost him a few thousand extra riel a month, but he was glad of the security. He wheeled his bike out the front door, kick-started it, and was shortly on the move.

The evening, as usual, calmed him. There was something special in the night air, a feeling of lassitude and excitement that endeared him to the city. You made your own arrangements here, and the outcome was your personal pleasure or problem. It was a city of twists, a town of secrets, a wonderfully lawless place, a good city for a motorbike. He took a right along the river. The Foreign Correspondents Club was alight from above. He could hear the din of chatter. The journos and their dates were in high cocktail hour, going at it again. Asher shook his head. The female AP correspondent was said to be dating the new Reuters guy. They gave each other scoops, so to speak. Asher took another right onto the road fronting the Royal Palace. It was a wide, low-lying boulevard that got swamped in the rainy season and was often impassable. Tonight it was dry and uncrowded. Guards in khaki uniforms stood idly at intervals, leaning on their guns, biding time by the palace wall. On his left Asher passed the Renakse Hotel, which had recently opened an outdoor restaurant he had no interest in frequenting. Gaudy high-wattage Christmas lights were strung up over the bar, illuminating the ads for Angkor and Tiger beer.

At Independence Monument he hit a crowded roundabout. The French and their former colonies. . . . This was Phnom Penh's equivalent of the circle surrounding the Arc de Triomphe. Built in the Haussmann style, it was a heavily trafficked affair with a tall, honeycombed monument in the middle. Asher found it difficult to manage. There were no rules at Independence Monument. He was nearly sideswiped by a white Toyota with tinted windows. Asher cursed the vehicle and was glad to finally be heading down Norodom Boulevard, one of the major thoroughfares off the circle, which led to many things, including Mr. Hawk's massage parlor.

The lobby of the Apsara was furnished with black leatherette love seats. Unzipping his windbreaker, Asher felt goose bumps from the air-conditioning. A fresh breeze had perhaps never visited the Apsara. There were mirrors on doors, mirrors on the back walls and on various tables. There was a full-length mirror behind the bar. A few of the ladies of the establishment looked into their own handheld mirrors. They were all huddled together inside a Plexiglas box at the far end of the room. Mr. Hawk greeted Asher with his usual obsequious affability.

"You have come later than usual but still you have come," he said. "It is good to see you, Asher. Would you like a beer?"

"Perhaps afterward, Mr. Hawk."

A massage, after all, is a banal enough private moment for a man and not terribly worthy of exploration. Asher chose number 36, a good running-back number, and disappeared into one of those soiled little windowless rooms.

Upon hearing the good news that UN personnel were to be given $120 per diem, Nuon Hauk, known as Mr. Hawk to the Westerners who knew him, flew to Saigon, where he spent several days recruiting country girls off his cousin, a pimp from Cholon. As luck would have it, his cousin was in debt to a consortium of Chinese businessmen who'd lent the man a considerable sum of money to acquire virgins. When word got around that many of the so-called virgins were not virgins at all but had instead used pig's blood, the cousin considered suicide. Not only had he lost much face, but his loan was shortly called due. And so Mr. Hawk, who had nothing but secret disdain for the extravagant falsities of the virgin trade, picked the girls up on the cheap. Fortune had smiled on him, and before he returned to Phnom Penh, he paid a visit to the Phung Son pagoda in Cholon, where with trembling hands he lit stack after stack of votive dummy money in thanks.

And so in those halcyon days of the UN presence in Cambodia, the Apsara prospered. A trickle of overweight Finns and Danes were the first regulars. They were the most disinclined to the heat and seemed to take just as much refuge in Mr. Hawk's air-conditioning as they did in their fifteen-dollar massages. They were followed by Russian helicopter pilots. The Russians were known for their criminal sociability and saw their stay in Cambodia as a financial boondoggle. They were thieves, and the UN was a great unguarded henhouse for the fox. No one seemed to own anything. All of it, the Land Cruisers, the video cameras, the demining equipment, the mobile phones, the cases of canned goods, the frozen steaks—they were all up for grabs. Sometimes Morris

Catering, the UN's food supplier, could be a difficult institution from which to thieve but, Morris aside, pilfering from the UN was like taking candy from a baby. For the Russians the only problem was unloading what they had stolen, and this is where the Apsara came into play.

The local Cambodian powers-that-be in the black market distrusted and feared the Russians. Perhaps they were resentful of the imperial attitude the Russians had taken toward Cambodia in the wake of the Vietnamese invasion. In the 1980s Phnom Penh's streets were filled with drunk Russians, patrons of the occupying Vietnamese. The Russian pilots took a dim view of the indigenous Khmer population and the feeling was returned. Yet the Russians needed a broker they could trust to help them unload the stolen Land Cruisers and other UN paraphernalia. They went to the Tamali Tigers, a close-knit group of Sri Lankan separatists who'd taken up residence in Phnom Penh in order to trade arms. Quantity not quality was what Cambodia was known for in the arms department. There were American grenades and M-16s, Chinese handguns, Vietnamese armored personnel carriers, Russian mines, a wonderful bazaar of Cold War armaments augmented by more modern UN equipment. Supply greatly outstripped demand.

They were a Masonic lot, the Tigers, and for three years every Thursday evening at eight o'clock sharp they met with the Russians at the Apsara to discuss business, and later get a massage. Mr. Hawk was paid handsomely for his discretion, service, and silence. In the space of three short years he acquired a fortune. He became happy and fat, but like most businessmen with Chinese blood, his portliness befitted him. His belly rounded into a satisfactory, Buddhalike protuberance, and he purchased silence from his wife about the lovers he took on by buying her quantities of jade jewelry.

When the UN pulled out of Cambodia, business at the Apsara plummeted. Other massage parlors opened up. The Apsara was still visited by journalists and the occasional Australian contractor, but the money certainly wasn't what it used to be, so Mr. Hawk became a loan shark. He had to do something with his UN capital. On the streets of Cholon, where he'd grown up, Mr. Hawk had been a firsthand witness to the power of usury. His father had run a restaurant that had neither been an outright failure nor a success. It leaked money, and one day Mr. Hawk's father was forced to take a loan off the street. At the time, banks were state-run affairs in Vietnam and largely closed to the entrepreneurial Chinese, who were much resented by the more Communist-inclined Vietnamese in the north. Mr. Hawk's family, unable to get a bank loan, underwent systematic persecution when his father could not withstand the outrageous interest payments required by the loan sharks. It was a terrible family trauma. His father's mental state, always closely aligned with his financial well-being, went into a free-fall. He spent hours at the pagoda but no amount of incendiary prayer could help. One night a Molotov cocktail was thrown into the kitchen. A young Mr. Hawk had been the first to get to the fire but could not save his family's home and business. His mother was a Cambodian with a relatively wealthy brother in Phnom Penh, and so the family fled to the nearby capital, where Mr. Hawk's father shortly died of a stroke.

And that is the thumbnail on Mr. Hawk. He'd recently hired a small squad of young men from the national kickboxing team to help him out when people played truant on their loan obligations.

Under the mildly erotic strokes of number 36, who hummed
to herself a Vietnamese lullaby, Asher's thoughts returned to Julie.
Why had she contacted him again? It was maddening. The same
tide that had swept her out to sea had pulled her back in again.
Oh, Julie G-Spot, Julie G, why, why, why? He banged his fist on
the mattress, causing number 36 to stop her humming.

"Me no good?" she inquired.

"No, you're fine, sweetheart. You're fine. She was just too
good, much too good in bed for me."

Just as the physical distance he had put between them had begun to register mentally and emotionally, just as the door was
about to close on their relationship, it had opened again. Somehow, she had gotten her hands on his e-mail address. Julie G-Spot.
It was what he called her in bed. He remembered her so well, on
top, writhing to the twisted sounds of her own pleasure. Things
hadn't worked out in L.A., and now she was back in New York
working behind a bar at a strip joint. There was a tinge of venge-
ful satisfaction in knowing things hadn't gone so well since him.
Julie G-Spot. She was the reason he'd fled to this country to begin
with, and now she was back again with her schemes and deals.
They'd been feverishly e-mailing, Asher screaming when his server
crashed. But they'd cut a good deal. If things worked out, it would
be very lucrative for all involved.

Number 36 raised him up and got hold of his neck. This was
his favorite move. She cracked every vertebra. Then she placed

her little feet in the middle of his back and pulled his arms toward her. The cracking went down the line of his spine. She lay Asher back down on the bed. A great tension, like a held breath, escaped from his body. I can do it, he said to himself. I can handle Mao and come out at the other end. I can do it. Then number 36 asked in her way if he wanted a handjob. Number 36 was good, but she was a wicked negotiator when it came to the extra amenities of her trade. It was always a drag, this haggling, a humiliation, really. Anything short of five bucks and she could get mean and start bitching in Vietnamese. Asher didn't need it. You don't have to go there, son, he told himself, not tonight. Tonight you are going to Mao's house. He looked at his watch. Perfect. He got up and tipped number 36 three red five-hundred-riel notes. It was about 55 cents.

"You no like me," said number 36, shaking her head. She was going for the pity party. It was always step two in the game, professional hurt, followed by the pity party, followed by malice.

"You're good," he said, reaching for his wallet. "I mean really good, a hell of a change-up pitcher."

He gave her a two-dollar bill. He didn't know why. It must have been the night. This two-dollar bill had been in his wallet for nearly three years, ever since UNESCO. It was his lucky two.

"Tonight," announced Asher to himself. "I've got to give it away. You got to give it away to get it back. See, here's what it is, Thirty-six. You're the highest number on the roulette wheel, so wish me luck."

He threw his satchel over his shoulder and was about to leave, when number 36 blocked his way. But of course, she hadn't seen the two before. It didn't make any sense. He watched as her confusion changed over to a glaring distrust. The mighty two, it held no currency with her. It wouldn't translate at the Central Market currency stall. Asher pictured the confusion and distrust the presentation of such a strange bill might provoke. The woman who ran the stall would have to run and get her husband. There would be a prolonged conference behind the gold scale and rubber-band-wrapped wads of money. After all, the bank might not accept such a bill, didn't she have any of the other, more standard denominational fare?

"No," said number 36, holding the bill out for Asher to take.

"*Ba, ba, ba,*" said Asher. It meant "five, five" in Vietnamese and "yes, yes," in Khmer. Like a goat Asher bleated out the words.

"Young lady," he said. "That man on the bill is Thomas Jefferson. He might have copulated with his slaves, but he was a great man, a pillar of eighteenth-century American thought, an architect."

"No," said number 36. She shook her head. It was more of a twitch, a Vietnamese eye blink. Bad news.

So, thought Asher, tonight will not be the night of the lucky two. He took the bill back and handed her two singles. That seemed to satisfy her.

In the lobby Mr. Hawk was talking to clients Asher hadn't seen before. They were lounging expansively in the love seats. Definitely loaded. They were Malaysians possibly, thought Asher, Malaysian or Singaporean Chinese. They were putting out big-money vibes and smoking Benson & Hedges.

"On top of it all," said Asher, placing his hand on the proprietor's shoulder, "she's a hell of a chiropractor, Mr. Hawk, but she needs a history lesson."

Mr. Hawk's shoulder was shaking. He was giggling at something his new clients had said. He had no time for Asher tonight, which was fine with Asher. He exited the Apsara, only to find a child sitting on the Dream. Asher sighed. This country could be so exhausting. Little hustlers, burgeoning extortionists were what these boys were. They made you pay them to get off your bike in the name of protecting it.

"*Blah, blah, blah,*" bleated Asher, holding out a filthy note for the child.

As he made his turn onto Norodom Boulevard he realized he'd forgotten to pay Mr. Hawk the base massage fee. That was unlike Mr. Hawk. The new guys in the lobby must have really been heavies.

He stopped at a Caltex gas station to fill up. He was headed out to the outskirts of town and he didn't want to get caught at night without enough gas, not out there. Back on his bike he passed the Troika, a pleasant Russian restaurant. The poor Russians, thought Asher, the poor Russians. They were descending into chaos, those people. The embassy was a shadow, a ghost of its former self. The so-called businessmen went about threatening to kill low-level embassy figures. All of it went down at the Troika. Last month there'd been a shooting. The Russians were . . . He couldn't exactly decide what they were. They kept changing the game rules. They wandered around in dangerous, pecuniary moods desperately trying to be the newly anointed captains of the changing game. The thing with that country, thought Asher, who had never been there, the thing with that place was the punks had arrived. The kids were sticking the knife in.

Up ahead he saw they'd thrown up a roadblock.

"Motherfucker," said Asher.

He tried to take a right. He couldn't. There was a car. Someone was blowing a whistle at him. There was a cop with an evil baton. It was lit red by something sinister within. The cop waved it at Asher. If he kept going they might shoot him, but maybe they wouldn't. Asher considered not stopping. It was a golden rule of the country roads; don't stop unless you have to. The whistle went off again. The whistle. It was a monster. He pulled over.

The extortion had a semblance of bureaucracy. There were two cops going through people's papers. They had flashlights. One cop was pointing his flashlight into the face of a motorist and explaining to him how it was going to be. Asher had no papers. Asher had nothing to account for himself but three thousand dollars. He waited his turn.

"Never stop," he hissed to himself. "Never fucking stop. Never."

It had all gone down so quickly, and now the wait to be stolen from infuriated him. There were two people in front of him. Everyone was male but one. There was a prostitute one-hipping her way off to the side, waiting for her john to pay up. Asher couldn't really make her out. The cops had control of the light. It was hatefully boring waiting to be stolen from. Hateful. He put his leather satchel in Position Two. Position One was the most secure, with the strap across his chest. Position Two was more ladylike. It hung off his shoulder. That's what has happened to you, he thought; you lived inside these paranoid systems. Position Three was between the legs or under the table. He didn't have a five yet. Four was give the bag to a trusted friend. Make sure he kept it under his arm. Asher badly needed a friend. Position Four. He didn't have it. Now he was next. The only identification he had was frankly funny. It was a gym card from L.A. Asia had made Asher weird about his wallet. He only kept symbols in it. Symbols of a lost life, very little money, folly. This would have been a good time to have his Youth Club papers. His Youth Club papers—fuck, they were in his room. They would be good here but he didn't have them. They looked official. The Youth Club; it could be a good defense against extortion. This flashlight was evil. The first cop actually had it in his mouth. Now he had his L.A. gym card in his hand. He flipped it over. He flipped it over. The flashlight was bearing down on this senselessness. The cop shook his head. This would not do. He would have to visit the next man, the superior. He pointed to where Asher had to go. It was very elemental. You go there, the cop said. Now. He had to go. The superior turned out to be a fat man.

"Follow the fat man," said Asher, presenting him with his gym card. "And never stop."

His L.A. gym card was terribly unimpressive. It only had a photo and a few numbers. The fat man shook his head, and then suddenly took the satchel from Position Two. It was a strike against its entire raison d'être. Position Two was supposed to be *languid*. It was supposed to have some savoir faire. Position Two was a fake-out they hadn't bought. Now the cop had a knife out.

"I didn't come here," said Asher, "to be insulted."

The cop extended the knife and cut the strap of his satchel. It was his now.

"Here's what you don't understand," said Asher. "The contents of that bag are in my legal possession. But you don't get that, do you?"

He was a sinister extortionist, the daddy of the roadblock. Asher made a lunge for the bag but the fat man deftly moved from his stool and tripped him up. A whistle sounded in his ear. The first cop, the one with the baton, had drawn his gun and was pointing it at him. As Asher picked himself up, the fat man began talking to his inferior in quick, clipped Khmer. No, it would not be advisable to shoot the *barang*. It would be enough to take his money. If he took his life, there would be paperwork, an investigation. The fat man wasn't having any death. It could be expensive.

"Fuck you," said Asher. "You fuck."

Now the cop was beaming his flashlight into the contents of the bag.

"You asshole, give that back to me."

The cop shook his head. It wasn't happening. He waved him on. He wanted him out.

"I'm never, ever," said Asher standing before the fat man. "I'm never going to go away. That's why I'm here, man."

Asher stood. The cop continued to shine his flashlight into his leather satchel. Then he reached into the bag, grabbing one of the three wads of money, and handed it to Asher.

Back on his bike he was strangely relieved. It was a counter-intuitive moment. He felt light with loss. At a dark residential corner he lit his Zippo and counted what had been taken. Exactly two of the three thousand was gone. Now he did not feel so light. He looked at his watch. He had an hour to come up with two grand before his meeting with Mao.

Asher considered Chicago. If he didn't get back home soon, he might not get back home at all. The problem now was paying Mao.

"Come up with something," he said. "Come up with something now."

He rode back toward Mr. Hawk's, cursing the night. Mr. Hawk was in an expansive mood. The Malaysian or Singaporean heavies were getting massages.

"Young man," said Mr. Hawk, "you look lost."

"Thank you," said Asher. "I am in the middle of a bright darkness. I should probably just go home. It would be better for everyone concerned."

"Home? Where do you find home?"

"Inside," said Asher. "Not out."

"Mr. Asher," said Mr. Hawk, "I will not . . . how do say it English? I will not . . . I will not undertake your crazy."

"My crazy is what's keeping me going, baby."

"Who is the baby? What baby?"

"I need some money."

Mr. Hawk reclined in his chair. Money. He understood that. It was not insanity.

"When?" he said.

"Yesterday."

"It will have to be tomorrow."

"Why?" asked Asher.

"Because."

"Look, I need some money now. Phnom Penh's finest took me down. They stole from me. I've been stolen from."

"The finest what? I do not understand you."

"The police, Mr. Hawk. The cops. The Cambodian People's Party, the man."

"How do you know they were CPP?"

"I was in CPP country. They run this town."

"Yes," said Mr. Hawk. "Yes, they do. They probably looking for Taiwanese. How much do you need?"

"Two thousand dollars, what they stole from me. They were surprisingly accurate."

Mr. Hawk thumbed his chin stubble.

"I will give you two thousand at ten percent a week."

"Do you have two grand now, because I'm going to be late for a rather crucial appointment."

"Yes."

"Where?"

"Here."

"Where," asked Asher, "is here?"

"Wait," said Mr. Hawk. "Young man, you must wait."

"Okay," said Asher. "I'll wait. Will you please give me a beer?"

"You didn't pay tonight."

"Tonight," said Asher, "is all in the past. We are going somewhere else now."

"You are crazy man," said Mr. Hawk, getting up to go to the bar. "Ten percent a week. We keep it simple."

"Simplicity," said Asher, standing up to accept his Angkor beer. "I've never been an enemy of it."

"Good," said Mr. Hawk, kneeling down behind the bar. For a moment Mr. Hawk was canceled. Asher couldn't see him, but he could hear a key. So that's where you keep it, he said to himself, you bastard. Mr. Hawk wrapped two bundles of money in a copy of the *Cambodia Daily*. Then he secured the bundles with a rubber band and placed them in a white plastic bag.

"Two thousand," he said, "at ten percent a week."

"Ten a week?" complained Asher. "How about ten a month?"

"Ten percent a week, Mr. Asher. I will not haggle with you. Ten percent a week. Now you must say it."

"Ten percent a week."

"We have nothing more to speak."

"Fine," said Asher, clutching the plastic bag.

Standing in the middle of the Apsara, the two men looked into each other's eyes. There had been a kinship there inspired by years of massages and banter. Now money had come between them.

"You," said Mr. Hawk, "need a woman. You need a child."

"I've got this problem, Mr. Hawk. Want to know what it is?"

"No."

"I dislike children. They're a burden. They're too heavy and right now I'm into lightness."

"What?"

"Lightness."

"You need a woman, a wife," said Mr. Hawk.

"Look, I can't refute that. But I don't have one. I had a woman in sunny California but she left me. It's an old story; perhaps even *you* have heard it. Woman leaves man for another man. I'm lacking, you see. I'm lacking in that department. Right now I'm looking for action and light, for money. If I don't return home to my native land, I might die right here in the Apsara."

"Crazy," said Mr. Hawk, shaking his head.

Asher took Mao Tse Tung this time. It was a large, poorly lit industrial boulevard that crossed Monivong Boulevard a few blocks east of the roadblock. Waiting for one of the few traffic lights in the city, idling there at the intersection of Monivong and Mao Tse Tung, Asher considered the political geometry of the city. Vietnam was the key, the pull. Vietnam to the east. The Cambodian People's Party, or CPP, were patrons of the Vietnamese. Hun Sen's compound, known as "the Tiger's Lair," wasn't far from the border. The CPP ministers lived on the east side of town, not far from the ministry buildings which they dominated. Strange that another country could affect the layout of a city, but there it was. The farther west one went, the less obvious the CPP presence.

The French embassy, the human rights offices, FUNCINPEC headquarters, they were all in the west.

Fearing large boulevards, Asher took side streets eastward. He traveled the dusty grid that is residential Phnom Penh. Corrugated-steel doors fell in nearly unanimous verticals to the street, which was empty but for potholes. The light was bad. Finally he saw the circle at the end of Monivong. The circle that led to the bridge, the circle that led to the bridge which led to the road with the slaughterhouse which led to the turn to Mao's house. He stopped his Dream on the dark street and considered his situation strategically, militarily. He could scrap the deal, get a job, and earn the money back. If he didn't get a job he could freelance some computer work. He didn't have to do this. But then there was Mao to consider. He'd given Mao his word. He'd given Mao his word about the night on which he'd arrive, the time, and the amount. He couldn't be sure, but in all likelihood Mao hadn't paid for what Asher was to buy off him. He'd stolen it from the Ministry of Interior, where he worked as a middling bureaucrat. In a way Asher did owe Mao for taking a gamble with his position at the ministry. Perhaps there had been a hefty bribe to get into the storeroom at night. But hold on. Perhaps Mao hadn't even bribed a colleague. Maybe Mao had a key, or a friend with a key with whom he had promised to split the profits. Asher enjoyed and was fascinated with Mao's company almost as much as he disliked and was bored with himself.

"You are a Merchant Prince," said Asher. "Push on."

He restarted the Dream and was not stopped by the police guarding the bridge. A breeze came off the invisible river below. On the other side there was yet another circle, where sleeping taxi drivers lounged in their reclining seats, dreaming of money, dreaming of gold. Someone hissed at him. He hated that about Asia, the hissing. He didn't hiss at people; why did they hiss at him? Perhaps it was this part of town. *Barangs* were not expected to be found out here at night.

The spoke road off the circle began to muddy and deteriorate. It was a hectic street. He passed a sawmill and then came the oncoming lights of the slaughterhouse, the biggest pig-killing factory in the country. Shortly Asher was in squealing range. On the near side of the building a pig farmer in knee-high rubber boots was heaving his animal by the ass, trying to push his pig through a side door. Suddenly the squealing pitched upward in tone, filling the night. Was this awful sound simply a function of his growing proximity to the slaughterhouse, or was it a singular pig somewhere in the depths of that deathly operation meeting its final moment? It was difficult to tell. Asher could feel the commotion inside. The generator rumbled. The slaughterhouse doors fronting the street were closed but had tiny ventilation slits. They must be up to their knees in it, thought Asher, up to their knees.

Now the sound of the slaughterhouse began to ebb. This part was tricky, this final turn to Mao's. There were plenty of little rutted paths that dipped down into obscurity. Was it two or three turns after the Angkor beer sign? Asher could never remember. Each time he came out here the light was different. He took the third turn and was glad of it. He recognized the path. He was carrying Mr. Hawk's money wrapped in a plastic bag inside his shirt. The bumpy road shook the money, and Asher secured his girth with one hand.

"A lump sum," he said.

The path broadened as it descended from the main road, giving out onto a wide open field. Asher was amazed to see that it wasn't quite dark here. The last line of sundown, already extinguished in the city, was just hanging on in the fields. The horizon was a pencil-thin line of diluted red, barely illuminating the green of the distant rice paddies. Weak blood, thought Asher, a late-innings sundown.

"Last light," said Asher. "Right on time."

Mao had built a makeshift corral around his property. The chickens clucked and pecked at Asher's arrival. A water buffalo eyed him as he kicked up his bike stand. Madame Mao was downstairs. She stood on a straw mat eyeing him suspiciously.

"Good evening," said Asher. "Is your husband home?"

Mao spoke very little English but Mrs. Mao spoke none at all. She took out a broom and began sweeping. Overhead Asher could hear the floorboards creak. Mao was rising. Now he was on the top of the stairs looking down on him, smiling.

"Smoke," said Mao. It was his favorite word.

"Certainly," replied Asher. "*Toujours.* Smoke. The principal, the alpha of life."

Mao waved for him to come upstairs. Asher took off his sneakers and climbed the narrow ladder. It was a sturdy ladder but not designed for a man his size. He took each rung slowly, methodically, thinking, Here we go, this is where it unfolds. When he got to the top floor, he bowed his head and entered. Mao stood in the middle of the room. He wore no shirt or shoes, only a pair of olive-green army pants and a belt that passed through a cheap bronze buckle upon which was printed an eagle. He had thin black hair, black eyes, and a slightly concave, caramel-colored chest, a shade lighter than his face. A smoker's chest, thought Asher.

Confiscated drugs were Mao's speciality. The Golden Triangle, being landlocked, required an outlet. Cambodia was like gravity, drawing the drug down the Mekong to Phnom Penh. The country was a smuggler's paradise, but face and the American DEA required that there be the occasional bust. Most of the drugs confiscated were taken from men with unreliable connections to the CPP. The confiscated stash ended up at the Ministry of Interior for eventual redistribution minus a few kilos for the press to watch burn. The journos liked these drug photo ops. They liked to watch the drugs burn, especially if it was marijuana, because that provided a more spectacular pyre, a better visual. Only a small percentage of the confiscated drugs was actually destroyed. The rest was dealt by the CPP. Mao was very CPP.

"Smoke," said Mao.

Slowly Asher lay down on the mattress. A trail of black fumes snaked upward from a small oil lamp burning by the bed. Mao was ready for him. On the floor not far from the pillow were his smoking utensils. There was a thin nail file, pipe cleaners, a Swiss Army knife, tweezers, three steel utensils slightly thinner than a knitting needle, and tinfoil. Mao's gun lay next to the pillow on the floor. Asher had a thing for Mao's gun. It was called a T.T., a Chinese-manufactured eight-millimeter with a serrated black plastic handle grip. The T.T. was modeled after an American Colt .45. It sat there on the worn teak floor looking dangerously idle and very American.

Mao got down into his crouch and began cooking. He took his utensils out of the beaker and applied a small ball of opium partially wrapped in an olive leaf to the oil lamp, twisting and turning it for a short time until it reached Mao-ideal malleability. Then he put it in the hole in the center of the round wooden bowl. He handed Asher the end of the wooden opium pipe. Asher took several breaths. Then he took a large one and slowly breathed out until his lungs were as empty as he could get them. Mao lit the opium with a Bic lighter.

"Smoke," he said.

In the movies smoking opium was supposed to be a languid, relaxing experience. Asher didn't see it that way. In Mao's house one had to keep the ball of opium bubbling for what could be an excruciatingly long period of suction time. Mao was a miser about his opium and if one ran out of breath before the ball was burned up, then what was left was wasted. Mao didn't like that. He would shake his head.

"Smoke," said Mao.

This meant pull harder. Asher increased his intake.

"Good," said Mao. "Smoke."

It was bubbling along, bubbling along; for a good while he had the thing going quite well. Briefly he exhaled out his nose. He could feel Mao beside him, pleased with his smoking ability, but what Asher knew and Mao didn't was that he was running out of breath a little early in the game; he began to feel the need to exhale again. It was like running out of breath while swimming under water. Now in the middle of the ball Mao was twisting with one of his delicate stainless-steel utensils, now when he needed his strongest pull, he didn't have it. He was going to go for what he called the reverse saxophone routine, breathing out from the corner of his mouth so that he could suck back in again. This was always dangerous as it momentarily dissipated the power of the flame. He did it. He quickly breathed out.

"No," said Mao. "No, you smoke."

He sucked in again but it was too late. Mao had taken the flame away and was shaking his head. He'd blown the bowl. Asher exhaled. Even though he paid Mao for his opium, he felt ashamed when he didn't get down to the end of a ball and wasted the drug.

"Fuck," he said. "I'm sorry, Mao."

You needed strong lungs to smoke at Mao's house. Now Mao was scraping the bowl clean of the half-burned, useless opium. From downstairs a radio came on. It was the CPP evening news in Khmer. Mao barked something at his wife and shortly the channel was changed.

"Make a small one, Mao, tic tic," said Asher.

He put his thumb and index finger nearly together, signaling a small amount. Mao nodded his head. He understood. This was his fifth or sixth session at Mao's house. Usually he did three bowls but tonight, since there was business to conduct, he decided that this ball would be his last. Asher went into his breathing routine as Mao fixed the opium. He imagined himself standing at the edge of Uncle Bob's pool outside of Chicago, hyperventilating so that he could make the distance under water in one breath. A soft Asian droning drifted upstairs, gently filling the room with its strangeness. Mrs. Mao could just be heard humming along. Now the new ball was ready and in place. It looked a good size, and Asher summoned all the spirits of his lungs to take it.

"Smoke," said Mao.

Asher came out of the gate a little too gently. He wasn't getting it bubbling.

"Smoke," said Mao with emphasis.

He pulled a bit harder. It began to bubble.

"Good," said Mao. "Good smoke."

He kept it going at a consistent, sustainable pace, watching out of the corner of his reclining eye as the opium ball transfigured itself. About halfway through, he realized it would require a greater effort to keep a consistent pull on the flame and so he reached for what it would take. He had it this time. He sucked and sucked, Mao adjusting the distance of his flame according to his own hidden knowledge. There would be no need to come up for breath this time. He was going to do it. The ball began to diminish. It was like seeing the other end of the pool come into sight and knowing it would be reached in one breath. Mao pulled the flame away.

"Good smoke," he said.

Asher rolled onto his back and looked up at the ceiling slats. He held on to the lungful as long as he possibly could. Tiny white stars crackled before his inner eyes. He blew out. No, he did not blow out. He bellowed out a heavenly cloud of opium smoke into the Cambodian night.

"A perfect pipe," he said eventually. "Professionally executed by all parties."

Mao handed him the Tootsie Roll–shaped pillow as was his custom. Asher propped it up under his neck and considered how high he might shortly become. The radio was on a fine number. It was neither one of those ghastly Asian covers of "MacArthur Park" nor a shrill indigenous menace. It was, thought Asher, a lullaby. The wonderful relaxation amid mild nausea arrived. The nausea was a good sign. It would pass. Mao remained in his crouch, his tailbone nearly touching the floor. Bad opium ingested orally was the problem. That, considered Asher, was a drag. It could make one sick for days. Asher rolled over on his side.

"So," he said to Mao. "Shall we? I'll show you mine if you show me yours."

From the foot of the bed he kicked Mr. Hawk's plastic bag toward the pillow. The plastic bag was from the Lucky Market, a high-end import-driven store filled with various extravagances from the West. Asher bought Pringles and vodka there. Inside the bag were bundles of fifty- and twenty-dollar bills. Mao took the dirty rubber bands off all the bundles and spread the bills over the floor as if they were a huge hand of cards.

"Three thousand dollars," said Asher. "As promised."

Mao stood up and barked something to his wife. Shortly her head poked over the floorboards. She had a frown on her face and glared at Asher. Then she thrust a bamboo pole into her husband's hand and disappeared. Now, this is unusual, thought Asher. Only a very paranoid Cambodian man would trust his wife with the goods. The Chinese were different. Their women were in on the action. They sat on the couch that hid the life savings. A hen on the golden egg was a Chinese woman. Mao handed the pole over to Asher. Both ends were stopped up with a piece of plastic secured with electrical tape. Asher pointed to the tape. Mao, without getting out of his crouch, moved laterally. Asher heard the click of a switchblade. Smiling to himself, Mao ran the blade across the flame of the oil lamp. Then he cut open one end of the bamboo shaft and slowly inserted the blade into its contents. Withdrawn, the blade was barely visible. Mao placed the knife on the floor for Asher to examine. It was a brilliant amniocentesis Mao had performed, and even through the opium, Asher could not hide his excitement and fear. With his pinkie nail, he worked a bit of powder off the tip of the blade and hit it. No burn. Its lack of strong sensation in his nose was a good sign. Then he went for a bit near the handle and through a different nostril. Mao clicked his tongue and shook his head.

"Don't worry, Mao," said Asher. "My hope is that you will shortly be fetching me a bowl."

Asher considered the consistency. It was a shade lighter than putty, not a brilliant white but a dull, caked one. He was dealing with the pure or virtual pure. You could step on this three times over in New York and it might still be considered weight. It would still not be ready for retail. He should have asked for more than seventy-five grand from Julie's boss. Asher put his head back on the pillow. A wonderful wave, a gentle pressure drop, an increased nausea, a departure. He was departing from care.

"Mao," said Asher. "Get me a bowl."

With his hands Asher pantomimed a bowl and then feigned puking in it. Mao barked something downstairs at his wife. She arrived in the nick of time. When he was through puking, Mao tossed the contents of the bowl out of the back window for the chickens. Asher reclined. He looked at Mao standing in the doorway and looking down on him, smiling. He was a wonderful man, Mao.

"Everything," said Asher, "is going to be fine tonight."

chapter two

THE NEXT DAY Asher woke late and signed onto the Internet. Luckily the phone lines were working and he got through. There was a message from Julie. In Julie's "Subject" head was a David Bowie lyric that went, "My mother says to get things done you'd better not mess with Major Tom."

Hey, went the message, *I suspect you and Major Tom have by now become acquainted. By all accounts Tom is a mercurial man given to wide swings of weight loss and gain. His marching orders are to arrive at the residence of my employer as my employer is a man who trusts me not with Tom, feeling I will seduce him and lead him down the path of weight loss. My employer is also quite interested in method of Tom's travel. Will you be personally escorting him or will there be another, hopefully more reliable mode of transportation?*

Once on a sunny summer day before their move to L.A., they'd walked along the banks of the Charles and smoked a joint. The sailboats and crew shells seemed postcards written to one another in a loving hand. Then they'd lain down on the grass and groped each other. The early days, oh, the early days. These were no longer the early days. Asher put his hands to his face. He was getting old. There were so many things he would never be now. Next to him there sat a pile of drugs. He had $175 in his bank account. What was he doing? He pressed his right palm into his left eyeball. The early days. The Boston summer sky. Julie in his hands, in his hands, his hands. They'd sprung for a room in the Hyatt, the pink pyramid with all the glass. Stoned in the giant atrium, she'd collapsed in a fit of laughter with jokes about stones thrown in glass houses and the Jacob Javits Center. She'd gone on about how it looked as if Martha Stewart's interior designer had gotten together with the folks at the Jacob Javits Center. They'd just barely gotten a room whereupon entering she'd gone after him with such memorable avidity, oh, fuck . . . the early days with her splendid body up against his, her thick rings on weird fingers. The early days. What had they been doing in Boston? He couldn't remember the year, and this annoyed him. It was well before L.A. He sat at his computer screen and desperately tried to come up with the month and year he and Julie had visited Cambridge. L.A. was fucking things up. L.A. was the problem. How long had they lived in L.A., he could not remember. Other appetites, other weeds in the garden had strangled their relationship. The early days had been a long time ago. Their love had risen, then fallen like a dead cat thrown from an apartment building. Now with this deal in play, the cat had hit the pavement. Their new lift on life was a dead cat bounce. He was a drug dealer now.

Asher returned her message.

Hey, Major Tom and I have met and he's taken up temporary residence with me and is eating well. He spoke of a wonderful trip from Laos and even a helicopter ride with the President of the Cambodian Chamber of Commerce. In fact, he's sitting in my apartment right now keeping me company with his songs of forgotten lands. Trans-

*portation with Tom is still an issue. I will not be traveling with him.
I'll find someone, don't worry.*

*By the way, do you remember that summer day we had in Boston?
I loved you then. Me.*

Then he signed off, put on his tennis outfit, and took his
Dream out to the Youth Club. The fact that he had no partner and
was therefore forced to hire one of the Youth Club's teenagers to
hit with him was a source of secret humiliation. Still, he enjoyed
tennis and his bloodstream badly needed the oxygenation. He
chose a kid he'd played with before, a wily youth of happy coun-
tenance given to slicing the ball. Because he was a slicer and because he was paying him three dollars for an hour of his time,
Asher stuck the kid in the sun, taking the shaded side of the court
for himself. Asher disliked serving into the sun and had already
predetermined that there would be no court changes. It was a typical *barang* move, neoeconomic colonialism at work. As they began
to hit, two ball boys joined the equation, scurrying around the
court in earnest. Asher had not requested the ball boys and would
now have to tip them. No matter. The ball boys looked mangy and
underfed. The money would mean a lot to them.

Asher had a pretty good top-spin game and, lacking any per-
formance peril, he went after the first few balls with vigor. The
teenager was crafty and had a good backhand which he used to
slice down on Asher's deep top-spin returns. The kid never came
to net, never. None of the Cambodians he had played with came
to net. It wasn't in their game. As the balls flew Asher wondered
why. It had something to do with trauma.

Asher was halfway through his first set when he noticed a man
on the next court he'd seen around town but had never spoken to.
All he knew was that he was a journalist, and it looked like he had

a decent game. He too was playing with the hired help. He was quite turned out, this guy, all in whites and with a racquet of his own. At the service line Asher paused to watch his game. He had good, steady ground strokes and a reliable haircut. A citizen, thought Asher, a man with his own racquet. Now that was something to ponder, arriving in Phnom Penh with a tennis racquet. A man with a passion or a splendid illusionist? Delusional, thought Asher, definitely delusional. But you had to admire the shirt. It was white with blue trimmings and the famous Boast marijuana leaf on one breast. Now that was very nearly old school, thought Asher, impressive. This *barang* tennis player looked like the drunk American in *La Dolce Vita*. He was even wearing the same horn-rimmed glasses and, unlike Asher, he was adhering to the etiquette of the court change. When they were beside one another, Asher decided to engage.

"You want to hit?" he asked.

"What?" said the steady American, punching a backhand into the net.

"I was wondering," said Asher, "if you wanted to hit."

"Sure," he replied. "But what do we do with these guys?"

"We tell them to go play with themselves."

"Okay."

There was vast confusion among the ball boys and the two pros about interrupting the as-of-yet-unpaid-for hour. Luckily Asher had plenty of singles and after ten minutes of negotiating in pidgin English sent the two pros packing and kept one ball boy. While all this was going on the steady American stood in the shade of the far court drinking water.

"I knew that would be more difficult than you bargained for," he said, once Asher had taken up position opposite him.

"Well," said Asher. "Isn't everything?"

"I've seen you around," said the American. "Someone said you used to work for UNESCO. Is that right?"

"Yep," said Asher. "And I suppose you're a journalist, right?"

"Right."

"What's your name?"

"Reese," he said. "And you're Asher. Katherine Coats told me about you."

They hit in silence. Now Asher vaguely remembered seeing this man at the Foreign Correspondents Club. He'd been packed in with all the other journos, standing out only in that he was taller than most and didn't make as much noise. This journo was a fine tennis player. He had a two-handed top-spin-heavy backhand and a solid forehand that landed the ball deep in the court. They were well matched, the journo perhaps a shade better. It had become a good time to play tennis. The sun had dipped below the treetops, casting splinters of orange light on the red clay courts. Asher loosened up and began to enjoy himself immensely. It was rare finding someone with near-reciprocal sporting skills in Phnom Penh. He was wearing cutoff khaki pants and a T-shirt that said DON'T LOSE on the front and THE RIGHT TO CHOOSE on the back. He'd picked it up while trolling for women during a pro-choice rally. The journo's crisp returns were bringing out the best in him. They rallied hard for a good twenty minutes in silence. It was better than any conversation he'd had in months. Tennis, thought Asher, it was a language.

"Right," said the journo, "first ball in."

His second serve was in and they were off. Asher liked how he'd taken the initiative to get the game started. It showed journo balls and breeding. The journo won 6–4, and drenched with sweat they retired to the bamboo bar off the pool. They talked shop. At Agence France Presse the journo had taken the place of a tragic Irishman. Asher filled him in on his predecessor, Stephen, a lesson in hepatitis. Stephen had fallen in love with a much younger American journo and stupidly followed her to Los Angeles. Asher, who knew both Stephen and Los Angeles, hadn't seen the fit. It was a mistake to abandon a wire-service job to follow a capricious young lady to the City of Angels, a town where, Asher had assured Stephen, his specialty would carry very little water. Stephen had been the master of Phnom Penh politics. He knew the players in and out and had reported well on the power plays between the Royalist FUNCINPEC party and Hun Sen's CPP. Asher told Reese all this, leaving out the drugs. But of course drugs were essential to Stephen. He'd become a terrible junkie and part of his rationale for leaving Phnom Penh had been to kick. But he hadn't kicked, not in L.A. Instead he'd come down with hepatitis. What strand of hepatitis depended upon with whom one spoke.

"I tried to tell him he was giving up his career for a piece of ass," said Asher. "I said, 'Stephen, mate, you're being irresponsible,' but he wouldn't listen. He would only shake his head. He was going. He was sick of this country. He loved this girl. Ah, but the man could quote huge sections of Shelley and was even better with Dylan Thomas. L.A. has no need for him."

"I heard he had a drug habit," said Reese.

"There was that, yes," said Asher gravely.

So the new journo *had* heard. He'd heard and he did not sound sympathetic to drug problems. Poor Stephen, thought Asher, he'd really liked the guy. A good journalist, a fascinating drunk, a friend. Asher had counted the man as his only real journo companion because when it came to journos, Stephen simply had the most style and romantic flair for the self-destructive. But he told none of this to Reese. All he told Reese was that he and Stephen had had an off-the-record relationship, and to come over to his apartment because a friend working at the World Bank had faxed him an interesting document concerning a study the organization had done on Phnom Penh's banks. The document confirmed what everyone suspected. Phnom Penh's banks were awash in counterfeit and drug money. The journo agreed to come over and Asher gave him his address.

"You can't quote my friend, though," he said. "He only sent it to me for fun."

"Fine," said Reese. "I'll come over to your place once we're through here. Is that okay with you?"

"Sure."

"To Stephen," said Reese, raising his Angkor beer. "And the City of Angels."

They touched glasses. The beer was strong and local, an Angkor stout, something like a Guinness but with a touch of carbonation and higher alcohol content. Asher was feeling lightheaded, overly solicitous, and crazy. This was the most exercise he'd ever had in Cambodia. His body was having a difficult time cooling off. He could just see how his face might look to the journo; beet red and crazy. His stomach was empty, and the beer was making for a peristaltic problem in his bowels. He found himself having to clench down on his innards so as not to humiliate himself. He finished his beer and ordered another.

"You see that pool?" said Asher. "April, May seventy-five, that pool was empty of water and filled with bodies. It's where the Khmer Rouge threw all the monks they shot or bludgeoned to death. Red on saffron."

A lone man was doing laps in the pool.

"Yeah," said Reese. "And now the Australian embassy flack has it all to himself."

"Is that who that is?"

"That's who that is."

"Is he new?"

"Fairly fresh, yes. They brought him up from Canberra something like two months ago."

They watched the Australian embassy spokesman do laps.

"Well," said Asher. "He certainly has a routine."

"That he does."

"Everyone needs routine or they'll go crazy here."

"That they do."

"What day is it?" asked Asher.

"Thursday."

"You want to start a routine?"

"Sure."

"Good," said Asher. "Let's play tennis every Thursday night at five."

"You're on," said Reese. "Here's my card."

Two nights later there was a swarm of *moto* and cyclo drivers outside the Foreign Correspondents Club. Asher, who intended to drink heavily, had left the Dream at home. He scanned the gaggle for familiar faces. He'd be moving on from the FCC and would need a reliable *moto* driver. They were hormonal guys, merry in their larcenous pecking order. Most sat on their bikes outside the FCC stairs. Others hunched down, slamming playing cards on the pavement. Tonight Asher recognized Dada, Smiley, and Hat, all favorites of the journos. Asher tipped Smiley 500 riel and said, "Stay here. I'm coming out one half hour," and then ascended the stairs, where he passed a wealthy Khmer man whose name escaped him, a man of uncertain royal blood and president of a company known as the Power Investment Group, or PIG. PIG had recently taken a bottled water concern public in Bangkok. The president of PIG thought Asher a lowlife and the feeling was mutual. On the staircase the two men squeezed past each other in silence.

At the third-floor bar the journos were in high form, engaging unreservedly in a great cluster fuck of ribald prognostication. Asher pushed his way to the bar.

"That weakly little carpetbagging bastard, Mr. PIG, doesn't stand a bloody chance in hell of getting another contract," said a journo beside him.

"If you want to play, you got to get in bed with the big boys, kiss some serious Hok Londy ass," said another.

Reese walked up and patted Asher on the back.

"How is it we never see you here?" he said.

"Because," said Asher, sipping his beer, "journalists in groups are even less pleasant than journalists in individual-bite sizes. You look very much the part tonight, Reese. Where did you get those khakis?"

"My mother," said Reese. "Now look. I'm afraid I have some bad news. That fellow you put me on to at the World Bank. Well, the office said the piece was fine but lacked attribution, so I called the guy up and we had a talk, not much of one, but we had a talk. I mean I identified myself as a journalist and we had a conversation, and so you see, I'm naming him."

"You fucker," said Asher. "You're going to get the guy fired."

"Hey, what can I say? He talked to me, okay?"

"What did he say?"

"Well, like I said, not much."

"But you're going to quote him anyway. I'm sure he assumed it was an off-the-record conversation."

"Like I said," said Reese, "I announced myself as a journalist, so I'm sorry. The office had to verify that the document was actually from the World Bank. They said a letterhead wasn't enough. Here, let me buy you a drink. The man won't be fired, don't worry. It was a good leak. Besides, this is my going-away party. My little sister's getting married and I've got to give a talk at my alma mater. You got anything you want mailed back to the States? I've been given the chore of temporarily replacing the Cambodian snail mail. Fucking Remy gave me a love letter addressed for Paris, said it would take a month from Phnom Penh. They gave me three weeks' vacation. I can't wait."

"When are you leaving?" asked Asher.

"Day after tomorrow, early."

"I got this script," said Asher. "You know you were wondering what I've been doing since the UN pullout? Well, I've been writing. It's grown into something of a monster. The manuscript is like five hundred pages, right, pretty heavy too, and there's this guy who's interested in New York, see. He wants to go in on halves with me."

"Yeah," said Reese. "I always did wonder what you did besides tennis on Thursday, but you never seemed to offer so I didn't ask. What's it about?"

"What?" asked Asher.

"Your script that you've been working on. What's it about?"

Suddenly Asher was stuck. He needed some time.

"Let's go out to the balcony," he said. "It's too crowded here."

Boat lights cast dim jewels onto the Tonle Sap River, and the air smelled faintly of diesel. Across the way was a small abandoned island where Buddhists had taken up celebrating an obscure holiday. There was one light on the island and a series of saffron-colored flags could just be seen flapping gently in the wind. Directly below on the street the cyclo and *moto* drivers waited and churned.

"I always wanted to write," said Reese.

"What do you mean?" said Asher, suddenly inspired to flatter his carrier. "You do. You fucking write. You're the wire, man. You're the nocturnal express train, a high-speed corridor of information. You cast beams that land on little old ladies' porches in Sydney. Shit, your stuff gets sent out from this hellhole to the planet, man. God knows how many papers all over the joint pick up your copy. They read you in Lahore. They read you in Bangkok. You write."

"No, I mean write write. Like what you're doing. So what's it about?"

"What's what about?"

"Your script, Asher. If I'm going to be carrying your cargo, I want to know what it's about."

"Oh."

There was a pause. The din of the journos behind him was paralyzing his short-term imagination.

"It's about a, well, it's about a drug deal."

He couldn't believe he said it. It was the journos; they were driving him to partial truths.

"Yeah, where's it set?"

"Uh, Burma . . . yeah, Burma. See, this guy goes up to Burma. Ever been there? It's a fabulous country, minus SLORK, of course, but this guy has no choice but to get in with SLORK."

"Excellent," said Reese, sipping his drink. "Go on. So the guy's in Burma. He's in Burma and . . . but I thought that Khun Sa, the drug lord in the north, is the one you have to deal with when it comes to the, you know, the narcotics trade."

"Exactly," said Asher, turning toward the river. "Exactly."

"So why's the guy dealing with SLORK? Khun Sa's boys have been fighting SLORK for years. Shouldn't he be in with Khun Sa?"

"Well, see, in order to infiltrate Khun Sa's operations he's got to establish some contacts with SLORK. You can't just walk straight into Khun Sa's neighborhood, and believe me, there are some strange allies up in the north of the country. I've been there," Asher lied. "See, this hero of mine is a fake double agent."

"Fine, so there's this fake double agent and where does he get the drugs? Who does he sell them to?"

"You know what," said Asher. "I'd rather not talk about it right now. I'm a superstitious writer. You're the first guy I've even laid out the basic plot line to."

"That's fine," said Reese, slapping Asher on the back. "Don't use it up on chatter. Don't waste it. Hemingway used to say that every word he yakked about his work was one word not written. And hey, Asher, I'm sorry about naming your friend."

"Hey, where are you going to stay in New York?" asked Asher.

"The Gramercy Park Hotel," said Reese. "I'm going to unwind there before I have to deal with my mom."

"I've stayed there once," said Asher. "Good location."

"Yeah," said Reese. "I can't wait."

"You owe me," said Asher. "You owe me big time, and don't expect me to throw you a bone anytime soon because I won't. That was utterly uncool. If my pal gets sacked, it'll be on your head."

"Come by the office tomorrow," said Reese. "With your script. Who is this guy who you're going halves with?"

"It's actually not a guy. It's this old girlfriend of mine who knows this guy at Miramax. She works at Miramax with this guy."

"Miramax," said Reese. "They're a pretty good outfit, right?"

"Yeah, man, they're tops."

"And this old girlfriend of yours, she pretty good-looking?"

"We lived together in L.A. a few years ago, before I came out here. I don't know what she looks like now."

"I bet she was a looker."

"You could say that," said Asher.

"Well, I got to get back to the boys. You take care, bud. I'll see you tomorrow. If I'm not in the office, leave it on my desk or give it to Pin, all right?"

"Cool," said Asher. "I'll come by tomorrow."

Asher smiled to himself. He'd been sitting on his supply for four days now wondering what to do with it. He'd considered just mailing it straight, but a package from Cambodia would definitely be sniffed at customs. He'd e-mailed Julie with the idea. Glen, her boss, hadn't gone for it. Julie had e-mailed back. The boss was waiting. Then the server had crashed and all communication had stopped. Now this Reese had fallen out of thin air. Asher leaned his back against the balustrade of the FCC and watched his carrier join his colleagues. Khakis, worn Top-Siders, blue button-down shirt, glasses, cropped haircut. The guy would slide right through customs. Asher imagined Reese arriving in Kennedy. He'd probably be in a navy-blue blazer sporting an air of professional diligence. The man was the wire. He might already be in the system as clean. He finished his drink and continued to study Reese. There certainly were no prior convictions there. Still, there was the downside to consider. What would happen if Reese was so straight that he answered the nifty new questions they'd just started asking at airports like "Did you pack your own bags?" and "Has someone given you anything to carry?" That bullshit. What would happen if he played citizen on that one?

Reese was throwing back what looked to be a vodka tonic with Gerald Coats, the editor of the *Phnom Penh Post*. Coats was a juicer and known opium smoker. Asher decided that Reese was a citizen, all right, but not stupid, not intolerably straight. You'd have to be fucking out of your mind to declare at Kennedy customs that you were carrying parcels from third parties, and that the parcels had originated in Cambodia. No, Reese wasn't that moronic. He probably enjoyed carrying Remy's love letter. Come to think of it, he was perfect. That was what had drawn Asher to Reese to begin with. He sensed in the man a solidity he himself lacked, and since his bags would be checked at Pochentong all the way through to Kennedy, he probably wouldn't get asked the security questions to begin with. Pochentong wasn't that kind of airport. Now his only task was to find a proper envelope. He needed a good one, something close to a legal redweld. The *Phnom Penh Post*. That was it. They bought their stationery in Bangkok. Once, a photographer friend had delivered him an astonishingly large amount of cheap Cambodian grass in a *Phnom Penh Post* envelope. He'd go over and have a visit with Katherine. He'd go over there now, as a matter of fact. It had been a long time since he'd visited the *Post*'s office, and a specific errand was always good. Specificity of need—experienced journos like Katherine could relate to that. Plus, it would be pleasant to see her again. It had been a while.

He descended the stairs of the FCC and into the onslaught of *moto* drivers. A few called out his name and waved their arms in his face. It was worse than usual and in the confused thicket of faces and arms, he couldn't find Smiley. Then he felt a tug on his sleeve.

"Ah, Smiley," said Asher. "You character. Shall we ride?"

The night air was soft and forgiving, a perfect reception to Asher's high. There was a night watchman at the gate who said that Katherine Coats was still in the building. Asher climbed the steps of the white concrete building and entered the front office. Once past the formidable bank of computers, it was a tremendously sexy place. Ceiling fans slowly rotated above rattan chairs cushioned with pillows upholstered with fabric from the Russian market stalls. In the back of the room was a long couch that stretched the length of a wall. There in the middle of the couch sat Katherine smoking a joint.

"Asher, how splendidly perfect. I've just closed the issue fifteen minutes ago. Come sit and smoke with me."

Asher had a seat in a chair across from her. About a year ago he and Katherine had slept together. It had been wonderful, entrancing. It had helped him forget Julie. But it had been poorly timed. She'd been going through her divorce and though Asher had called her up for more, she'd steadfastly turned him down. He'd felt used and peevishly stung. For about eight months he never spoke to her, not at the FCC nor the Heart, nowhere their paths occasionally crossed. Then there was the long period where if he went out at all, he refused to go to where the journos went, and so it had been a long while since they'd spoken or even laid eyes on each other. Asher thought she looked wonderful. Moonlight was coming in off a side terrace and the trees outside blew in the wind, splashing strange silver onto her dark hair and heavenly breasts. She was five or six years his senior, in her early forties, his first older woman. Asher sat in front of her, now silently accepting her resinous joint, and then exhaled toward the bank of computers, which were the only source of light in the room besides the moon.

"You got a drink?" he asked.

"Scotch or vodka?" she said. "I'm sorry, but we're a bit short on mixers. The staff pilfers."

"Vodka, but just tell me where it is, Katherine. You're looking wonderfully stationary there."

"This couch *is* rather difficult to get out of once sat upon. You know, I do rather think we're going to have another civil war soon."

"Really," said Asher. "Where's the vodka?"

"In Gerald's office off to your left there. You'll see a little fridge in the corner."

Gerald was Katherine's ex-husband. They'd founded the *Phnom Penh Post* a year before Asher had arrived. He'd never been in Gerald's office before. Now poking about in the dark he felt the thrill of trespassing. There was a large wooden desk cluttered with minicassettes, notepads, and issues of the competition, the *Cambodia Daily.* Gerald's office. He wondered how he and Katherine still worked together, how they could run the paper in a state of divorce or was it annulment? Gerald was a Stoli man like himself. He came out of the office with the bottle and sat down. There was a bamboo table between them with teacups on it. Asher picked one up and filled it.

"Would you like one?" he asked.

"Just a spot."

"Just a spot," he said, mocking her British accent. "That was very Kensington High Street–sounding of you."

"Have you ever," replied Katherine, "*been* to Kensington High Street?"

"No," replied Asher. "But I see it as a state of mind."

Katherine didn't take his bait. She was too stoned to be made fun of. She was gazing out at the terrace, staring at the moon between the trees.

"So," said Asher. "You were saying, civil war. But why? Almost all the Khmer Rouge have come over to the government."

"No, no, not that kind of civil war. I'm talking about the CPP and FUNCINPEC. *In*side the government, darling. Bugger the Khmer Rouge. We've been getting reports that the supposed united armed forces of Cambodia have been at each other's throats up in Samlot."

"Samlot," said Asher. "I think I was there once a long time ago."

"You've lost some weight, darling."

"Does it suit me?"

"Yes, I suppose it does, but I hope it's not from powdering your nose."

"Who, me?" said Asher. "Never."

"Do you have some with you? I'm at my wits' end. This issue just went on and on and on, and now the printers are threatening to strike."

Asher reached into his shirt pocket and took out a folded half page of an old *New Yorker* his mother had sent him months ago.

"Oh, wonderful," said Katherine. "I'll run and get the tray."

"Hey, Katherine," said Asher. "Before we slip away, I was wondering if you could do me a favor?"

Katherine turned. She was wearing a spaghetti-strapped dress, a local copy of something probably picked up at Harvey Nichols. The bottom hem whirled with her turn. She looked at him now hungrily.

"What is it?"

"I need the largest envelope you've got in the office."

"Right away, darling."

He wished he didn't, but he loved being called *darling*. He drained his tea glass, refilled it, and drained it again. Katherine came back with a bronze tray, which she laid upside down on the table, and a large manila envelope with the nifty emblem of her publication. The words *Phnom Penh Post* were underlined by two mythical Khmer snakes known as Nagas, their tails joined at the middle.

"I like your Nagas," he said.

"My knockers—why, thank you."

"Those too."

He spilled the entire contents of *The New Yorker* onto the top of the tray and then rolled up a red five-hundred-riel note. With a business card Katherine huddled over the pile, forming four lines.

"Just a wee one for me, please. This stuff is not to be fucked with," said Asher. "In fact, I highly advise temperance and caution."

"How fabulous," she said. "This does look a cut above what the Armenians are dealing."

Asher had never scored from the Armenians. He'd heard about them but never actually seen one. They were said to deal out of a shop down the street from the Heart, a big journo watering hole. Katherine rolled her long dark hair up in a temporary bun, seized the rolled bill, and snorted up a line.

"Oh my," she said. "Definitely not Armenian."

"No," said Asher. "Try the Ministry of Interior."

"Ah," said Katherine. "Straight from the heart of the beast. How did you manage that?"

"Through contacts and connivance."

"You really are an enterprising young man, aren't you? What *have* you been doing with yourself?"

"I've been playing a lot of tennis and avoiding the company of dilettantes," said Asher, leaning down over the tray. "It's been good for the circulation."

"Well, why haven't you invited me? I adore tennis."

"I play with Reese. He's got a very steady backhand and is a citizen of my native land. You would be a distraction."

"Oh my," said Katherine quickly, rising from the couch. "Oh my."

She disappeared into the bathroom. When she came out, her hair was wet, spindly, and partially hung down over her face. Her mouth was moist and she'd broken out into a sweat. Then she leaned back into the couch, closed her eyes, and said, "Come here, come here, darling, and make love to me if you can."

He came at her, lifted her dress, and slowly took her down to the floor. She was supple and lubriciously pliant, wonderfully British in her utterances.

Afterward Smiley took them to the river, where Asher paid the *moto* driver well for his time, patience, and loyalty.

"Why don't you," said Katherine, breaking a long silence, "go home."

The river was still now, still and flat and running against the moon.

"Home," considered Asher, "is filled with raccoons. At night you go to take out the garbage and all you see are their eyes flashing light back at you."

"I see."

"No," said Asher. "I don't think you do."

"Exactly," she replied. "I meant that in the British sense, which is to say I don't see at all."

"Oh."

"You see, I've never been to America."

"I don't suppose," said Asher, "you'd fancy it."

She lit a cigarette with a Zippo lighter and clanked the top back in place.

"I adore Zippos," she said. "And *they* are very American."

"As American as they come, sturdy," said Asher. "And structurally sound."

"But I don't suppose the Americans you see out here are your typical cross-section of the country at large."

"On the whole that is a structurally sound observation but not entirely correct."

He put his arm around her waist but was rebuffed.

"Not here," she said, then asked, "Where do you come from in America?"

They were passing the FCC. The third floor shone with conviviality, and a few backlit figures could be seen leaning on the balustrade. Asher could feel her tense up. No, it wouldn't do to be seen with him, would it? Where was he from? The question annoyed him but he said nothing.

"The last place I called home in the States was the City of Angels, a metropolis of lights and motor vehicles. I came there by way of Chicago. You see, I am from Chicago. We are hearty people, meat eaters, traders of the highest order. Currently I'm on a Merchant Prince kick."

"You want to, as they say, make a bundle."

"That is correct."

"I didn't know that was part of the Asher plan. The Asher I knew was a restoration man, a UNESCO team player, a great mender of ancient Khmer culture."

"I have never been, but for basketball and doubles tennis, a team player," he said. "You see, darling, I am a rugged individualist and Merchant Prince of the land."

"And how about this country and its complicated wranglings and goings-on?"

"I've been here long enough to understand that I know very little about Cambodia. It's a lovely country but its political and military machinations are beyond me. That being said, I am, like most *barangs,* Royalist-leaning in my politics. But the Royalists are weak and no match for the one-eyed Hun Sen and his Cambodian People's Party."

They were suddenly joined by a team of ragged street youths who began tugging on Katherine's skirt and holding out their hands for money. The couple ignored the children.

"I have a theory," said Katherine, "as to why we Westerners are drawn to and disgusted by the Royalists, by Prince Ranariddh and all his half-assed half-brothers in their half-baked political party, FUNCINPEC. Want to hear it?"

"Let me guess," said Asher. "We see in their faults, our faults.

They are guilty of nepotism. They own apartments in Paris and wear Hermès ties."

"In the Hermès tie . . . Get away from me, you little pests. Go home. It's too late to be begging," said Katherine, fixing her skirt. "In the Hermès tie lies the downfall of FUNCINPEC."

"Take the photographs you run in the *Post,* all those shots of Ranariddh and Hun Sen speaking as supposed equals in one another's ear," said Asher. "If you look closely, you'll see the prince wearing a fucking Hermès tie. Can you imagine Hun Sen wearing an Hermès tie?"

"And don't forget the South of France," replied Katherine. "Who is going to call the shots at the Ministry of Interior, he who spends one out of every four months in Antibes, Arles, or wherever it is King Sihanouk's progeny sun themselves, or he who hunkers down in the Tiger's Lair clutching the keys to all the tanks of the kingdom? I kid you not. Hun Sen, when he travels abroad, takes with him all the keys to the tanks in his briefcase. He's got them all on one great chain. The man's paranoia is only matched in ferocity by his power yen."

"And we distrust an overly developed power yen, don't we? It's not what the international community threw the most expensive election in history to foster."

Still quite high, Asher was becoming overwhelmed by Katherine's musings. Could it simply be that a fucked-up country attracted fucked-up foreigners? Could it be that Cambodia rounded out the sadness that lingered in the hearts of the strangers who chose to make this strange place their home? Suddenly Asher felt a presence on the river. It was a massive freighter stacked with containers, ominous and silent, passing them by in the night.

There was something about the scale of the ship that was disconcerting. A single floodlight lit its way, bouncing the night fisherman's boat in its wake.

"We should return to the great era of the God King," Asher announced. "Bring him on, fuck democracy."

"We're both stoned," said Katherine. "And I'm sick of politics."

They had passed the FCC now and she put her arm around his waist. It was nice to be high and have a woman moving by his side, touching him gently, their hips vaguely in synch.

"Let's go down there," said Asher. "I've never been to that place down there before."

It was a new restaurant on the river, and from a distance it looked quite merry. Multicolored lights arching from pole to pole flickered in the night.

"I heard this place was owned by Hang Boonma," said Katherine. "It's one of his many launderettes for drug money. Still, it does look cheery."

There was a planked walkway leading down to the floating restaurant. It was a thatched wood and bamboo structure secured by four pylons sunk deep in the river. As soon as they entered they knew it had been a mistake.

At three different tables sat about a dozen uniformed men of the Royal Cambodian Armed Forces. They'd been drinking heavily. Bottles of Hennessy brandy, Angkor beer, and Johnnie Walker littered the tables amid buckets of ice and the detritus of a Cambodian gorgefest. Spines of fish and heads of snakes were strewn on the floor, where two cats scampered about. Asher had seen the setup before, two or three high-ranking generals hanging out with their trusted bodyguards. The bodyguards were in olive-green camouflage, and they'd left their M-16s and rocket launchers in a pile on the floor. The generals kept their hats on the table. Katherine and Asher took a table a safe distance away. A waitress arrived, a blue sash advertising Tiger beer slung diagonally across an outfit of white taffeta not unlike a cut-rate wedding dress. Her hair was sprayed in place and her elongated black eyelashes blinked beneath the house lights. Tiger beer had clearly not been the choice of the generals and their boys. They'd stuck with Angkor. The waitress looked forlorn. The purple-sashed Hennessy waitress and the red-sashed Angkor waitress were milling about the military tables filling glasses with ice and pouring liquor and beer. Katherine and Asher ordered two Tigers and leaned back in their chairs, but it was difficult to relax. The initial military ribaldry precipitously dropped off into hushed whispers. A fat specimen of Cambodian high brass with a horizontal grease stain below his lower lip glared at Asher, who recognized him from his UNESCO days in Siem Reap. Back then the man was rumored to be linked to a group of smugglers of Khmer lintels and Apsara figures headed for Thailand.

"We shouldn't have come," said Asher. "The armed forces of this country sense in me a denial of their values. They are raccoons, especially that one who is staring at me. He used to be in the smuggling of art biz. You know the wonderful pieces of pink carved sandstone you find marked up for sale in various boutiques in Bangkok and New York? Well, that guy is the beginning of the food chain."

"He looks rather high up on the food chain to me," said Katherine.

"They're all Hun Sen lackeys, Cambodian People's Party monsters."

"Yes, I know," said Katherine. "And they've been plotting

something. Those bodyguards aren't just bodyguards. They're Hun Sen's secret service, a bunch of murderous bastards on the take."

She leaned back and sipped her beer.

"They should be shot at dawn," said Asher.

"Here, here," said Katherine. "Shot at dawn."

"At dawn," said Asher. "I like that. Let's get out of here."

They paid and left. Halfway up the planks Asher realized that he'd forgotten his *Phnom Penh Post* envelope and he had to rush back to retrieve it.

"What do you need the envelope for?" asked Katherine as they walked toward her apartment.

"It's part and parcel of my Merchant Prince kick."

"Really?"

"Yes, really. But I'd rather not talk business with a lady."

Katherine lived above a restaurant called the Rendezvous and across a courtyard from a coffin maker. It had been nearly two years since Asher had been to her place. Gerald hadn't quite moved out then, and Asher remembered the apartment as a whirlwind of their bitter split, empty vodka bottles rolling on the floor, half-packed bags in the hallway, spilled pills, and broken picture frames. Now the place was all Katherine. There was an oval-shaped couch fitted with pregnant pillows below a print of Klimt's "The Kiss." There were Buddha heads on stands and a large octagonal mirror. There was a teak bookshelf stuffed with hardcovers and well-thumbed black Vintage classics. Asher was impressed. In the center of the living room was a coffee table with an ashtray the size of a discus. Most apartments in Phnom Penh were slapdash, a futon on the floor, a small desk, a cheap bamboo bookshelf, maybe a poster or two, but Katherine, no, Katherine was here to stay.

Asher had a theory about Katherine. The theory was that she was a Brit, a well-educated, upper-class or upper-middle-class Brit who had bumped up against the peculiar behavioral codes of her native island kingdom. Asher's theory was that these peculiar British rules, like the one about marrying within one's own accent, that sort of shit, hadn't settled with her. Before Gerald he saw a string of pasty London men and their peculiar bedside manners. There was probably a powerful but peculiar daddy in there somewhere, henpecked by his own stuffy second wife, and this daddy served to reinforce the absolute necessity of observing these peculiar obligations as to how to live one's life to a British T. Asher's theory went that Katherine had absorbed all this peculiarity and, as they say, chucked it.

Now she was making tea.

"You can take the Brit out of Britain," said Asher, falling into the couch, "but you can't take the tea out of a tea bag."

"Stop talking rot," she replied with her back turned to him. "And line me up some more of your smack, darling."

And so they stayed up all night drinking tea and snorting heroin and playing backgammon and falling asleep and waking up and lighting candles and playing music and telling soft tales of their lives outside Cambodia and massaging each other and telling tales of their lives inside Cambodia until the sun began to come up and Katherine fell into a deeply drugged sleep.

Asher climbed out of bed. In his boxers he went into the living room and smoked down the last third of a joint left in the ashtray. Then he took a shower among Katherine's cleansers. They were wonderfully packaged items, exotic reminders of feminine civilization and foreign capitals. He shaved for the first time in three days with an old Bic razor, perhaps a Gerald leftover. His hands were steady but the razor dull. He nicked himself near the Adam's apple. When he'd pulled on his pants and stuffed his button-down shirt inside his waistband, he felt what a terrible shave it had been. His face felt tight and abused.

Out on the street it was late dawn. Though he hadn't really slept, he felt strangely rested. It was a light, ephemeral feeling, a by-product of the drug. A yawning waiter with a hose was washing down the sidewalk. Ah yes, the drug; in a while its synthetic reverence would wear off and it would be a fight *not* to seek its relief again. Asher had kicked once before. He did not want to do it again, but now he would have to watch out. The sooner you move it the better, he said to himself.

He took an outdoor table at the Rendezvous and ordered coffee and a bowl of morning noodle soup. He bought a *Cambodia Daily* from a street kid and found out that it was Easter Sunday.

"Well, how about that," he said.

Holidays. He thought about his mother for the first time in months. She'd always liked Easter. Perhaps she'd call. It was not yet seven in the morning and already the sun was beginning to blister. He paid for his breakfast and strolled down the riverfront road considering the weather. It was always around this time that he began to need the rains to cool things off. The rains, the rains—if they would only come to deliver him from this terrible heat. But then when the rains finally did come, things would begin to be a drag. The roads would flood and melancholia settle in on the soaked town. Only the cyclo drivers liked the rains because they could peddle through the flooded streets, while the *moto* drivers ruined their spark plugs. The rains. Already he was sweating through his shirt. He could use the relief.

The path along the river was fairly wide and composed of pale red sand he called Jupiter crimson. Up ahead came two Mormon missionaries biking to work. They were sporting identical black aerodynamic bicycle helmets, black shorts, and white button-down shirts over black jackets. Insane, thought Asher. Mormons in AC/DC outfits.

"Happy Easter," hailed Asher as they passed. "And God bless the Great Salt Lake and the deep powder skiing of your native state."

The Mormons did not reply. They were like termites, these missionaries, termites slowly eating their way into the fabric of the country. And it wasn't only the Mormons. There was the Assembly of God, rumored to be the largest nongovernment organization, or NGO, in the country, the Seventh-Day Adventists, Catholics of various stripes—the whole holy hodgepodge. Most did not waste their time in the capital. They fanned out into the provinces preaching crop rotation and the Word of the Lord.

Asher turned inland at the FCC and was passing the Samart mobile-telephone outlet, when he noticed activity on his periphery. He turned. Down the street a throng of people were marching toward the National Assembly building. It was a demonstration of some sort. Banners attached to bamboo poles fluttered against the sky. There were a few Buddhists in saffron but, by and large, it looked to be a secular crowd. Asher wondered if anyone in the crowd knew it was Easter. He approached. Ah, it was Sam Rainsy's people, the opposition, vocal government critics with little real power. One could always tell Rainsy's people by the large numbers of women. Most of them were textile-factory workers in simple wraparound dresses and flip-flops with *kramas* about their heads to ward off the sun. The crowd was large but relatively quiet. At the front of the procession was their leader, Sam Rainsy. The press had tagged him as "outspoken," but Asher had always found him a gentle man, not one for amassing troops and guns. Rainsy was a great hater of Hun Sen. After the UN election, he'd been forced out of Prince Ranariddh's FUNCINPEC party, which had then been forced into a power-sharing arrangement with Hun Sen's Cambodian People's Party. But the CPP had never given up power, and as FUNCINPEC finance minister, Rainsy had never stood a chance of keeping his job for long. He was an intellectual, relatively clean, and was said to own a sizable property in Paris. Rainsy. The man had style, but he was swimming upstream. His support was Phnom Penh based; they didn't know him in the provinces.

Now the crowd began to circle and chant in front of the National Assembly building. What they were protesting, Asher could not make out. His Khmer was poor and many of the banners were in Cyrillic. He wondered where the journos were; obviously in bed. Rainsy had picked a poor time to march, coveragewise. Every single foreign journo was sleeping it off. Still, a march by Rainsy's people—there wasn't much news there, not for the wires at least, not for the foreign *barang* press. Probably there were some Khmer reporters from the local sheets. Now the crowd was beginning to attract collateral attention. A woman rolled a sugarcane stall to the shaded side of the street and began to do business.

Asher headed past the Royal Palace and took a left onto his street. His apartment depressed him. He turned on his fan and walked into his bedroom. From beneath his bed he pulled out Mao's bamboo pole and then came back into his living room. The fan was on rotation mode. Obviously that would not do. Asher pointed the fan to the ceiling and went into his kitchen for a knife. He cut open one end of the bamboo pole and, standing at his desk, watched as the powder descended onto the table. The sight of the drug drove him to a rumination that was not unlike a prayer. He was doing this to get back on his feet, right? To land back in the world. Three and a half years was a long time to be away from home, and still the powder descended in circular clumps, flattening slightly as it landed on the table. Home, Chicago, it was an abstraction. Even his mother had stopped calling at Easter. The last two years they'd only spoken at Christmas. Without his fan he began to sweat on the drug. Home was a ship getting farther and farther out to sea or an industrial-strength rubber band stretching itself out from his fingers. If he didn't get home soon, Asher considered, the thing could snap. And as for supply and demand, well, he hadn't created the cold calculus of that one, and he wasn't in any position to alter it either.

"That would be arrogance," he said out loud.

In the distance he could just hear the soft din of the Rainsy demonstration. From the sound of it, the crowd had arrived outside the National Assembly. No, he could do nothing about demand. Faced with an American world, there were just too many taxpayers who demanded to get high. If not he, someone else would satisfy. Still, it was a cop-out and, baseline, he knew it. He took his L.A. gym card out and began to scoop the powder into the envelope. He considered Katherine. Now *there* was an expatriate, but her expatriatism had a grounding. She was a Brit who hated Britain. Asher was an American who had no strong feelings about his country except that it was home. It was home, yes, home. That was a very strong word. It was important not to forget home. For years now he'd been listening to the seductive calls of the Asian Sirens. They'd lulled him, the Sirens and the Lotus Eaters. Now he had awakened to the necessity of reengagement with home. A man needed a home that was not this apartment in this dusty, witchy little city of which he had tired. But a home in the context of America meant money. America equaled money and, right now, he didn't have enough money to even buy a ticket home. He continued to shovel the drug. His thumb and forefinger were dusted with white and he took a tiny sniffle.

No, he would return to America as a Merchant Prince. He would not return to America penniless. That would be very un-American. As he shoveled powder into the envelope he remembered tossing his mother's cat, Allistair. Asher hated Allistair but for the way she landed on her feet. Once Allistair had been crawling all over an old, old girlfriend, sniffing at her privates as they lay on the couch, and generally being a nuisance. Asher had taken to throwing Allistair high up in the air. No matter how many times he flipped, Allistair landed, still Allistair, on the ground. He went over to the turntable and put on "Year of the Cat." No, America certainly equaled money, and money equaled supply and demand. What he was shoveling now was the only substance in Cambodia where supply vastly outstripped demand, and wasn't that the key to money? Sell high, buy low, the law of supply and demand. They were irrefutable American concepts, iconic canons of economic life. If he fell on the battlefield of this deal, another soldier would fill the gap. If he could, he told himself, he would, but he could do nothing about demand in his native land. It was not his mission to interrupt the market of need. A three-thousand-dollar investment minus whatever he'd end up owing Mr. Hawk turned into eighty to a hundred grand. The whole transaction had to it the power of exponents. Amazing. How many hot dogs would one have to sell in New York for that kind of money?

He could land safely back home. It would buy him time.

Katherine had been right when she'd said by the river that he should go home. He'd get the money wired from Julie's boss and send Julie her cut once he'd landed safely home. He'd go back home to Chicago and rest. Asher shoveled and rationalized. This deal was all about landing back on his feet. That was all. Landing on his feet. If he could only . . .

An explosion hit. Was it thunder? No, this was the dry season. It had come from the direction of the Rainsy demonstration. Percussion grenades, no doubt about it. The sound roared in his ear. Asher ran downstairs and jumped on his Dream. His landlord was standing on the sidewalk.

"What the fuck!" screamed Asher. "What the fuck."

His landlord looked at him blankly, one side of his face twitching with disorder. The old ghosts, thought Asher, the twitch, the death thing. He roared past the palace and shortly was on the scene. About one hundred yards away lay the dead and the soon to be dead. In the grass before him sat a leg blown off at the knee. He watched as the plastic sandal on the foot turned red against the grass. There was a silence. A woman with a shrapnel wound walked slowly toward him, expressionless, bleeding from the shoulder. As Asher ran to help her, he noticed a man in a black T-shirt running toward the crowd with his arm cocked to throw something. Against the blue sky Asher saw two grenades arch through the air.

"Get down!" he screamed, tackling the wounded woman. A glint of light penetrated his closed eyes and then came the horrible sound. It was biblical. The ground shook beneath him. Asher stood up. The grenade thrower was standing near the edge of the park admiring his work.

Asher ran after him. In the bright light he sprinted across the grass, feeling nothing, feeling not his legs nor any sense of anything whatsoever. He ran at a diagonal toward the man with the intent of tackling. The grenade thrower did not see him coming. He was staring straight in front of him. A whistle sounded, and suddenly the man in the black T-shirt's head twitched toward him. He turned his back to Asher and began to run in a diagonal. For a moment Asher was still gaining on him. Then they were crossing a street at the back of the park and had entered the grounds of the Botum pagoda. There were no monks to be seen, only Garudas standing guard beneath an ornamented gateway, the lintel of which Asher had always admired and through which the soldier was now running. Once through the gateway he found himself in a section of Botum with which he was unfamiliar. They were running down a narrow path with walls on either side. Now the soldier was gaining ground on him.

"Hey!" screamed Asher. "Hey!"

The alleyway gave out onto a small square with a yellow pagoda building. There were other soldiers here, all armed with M-16s, and as they saw Asher coming, they closed in on him. Asher stopped and raised his hands. The grenade thrower ran up the stairs of the pagoda and disappeared. The chase had come to an end. Three soldiers dressed in olive and black camouflage, all of them of the Hun Sen variety he'd seen the previous night, had their guns pointed directly at him and were saying heated things in Khmer. One of them withdrew a pistol from his holster and approached Asher. So here it came, death time. Strange that this was how it was going to end, a bullet in the head on the grounds of the Buddha on the day Christ Rose From the Grave. The man with the pistol was of higher rank than the others. He didn't wear a helmet, and was sweating beneath a red beret. He took Asher's hands in his and pressed the palms together in formation of Buddhist prayer or greeting. Then he took his gun and pointed it at Asher's forehead.

"No!" screamed Asher.

He closed his eyes, his hands still in prayer. Suddenly he felt a great stinging pain against his knuckles. He opened his eyes. The commander was pistol-whipping his hand. Asher took another hit to the hand. No sooner had he knelt to the ground than the commander grabbed him beneath the arm and started moving him toward the alleyway. Asher stood up and turned to face the scene one more time. A soldier fired half a dozen rounds at his feet.

"I'm leaving now," said Asher.

As he ran down the alleyway, he saw a figure sprinting in his direction. From the gray outfit and lack of armaments it looked to be one of Rainsy's bodyguards. He had cropped dark hair and a compact build. His eyes were blown wide open with adrenaline and he was running right at Asher.

"Don't go in there," said Asher. "They'll fucking blow you away."

Asher tried to stop the man. He tried to short-arm him, but Rainsy's bodyguard cut Asher's forearm away with a short, chopping martial arts move. Asher watched as the man entered the square. He could hear a tearful shout from the man, a high-pitched insult. There was something about a brother in there. Shots rang out. Asher did not wait to see if the man would return. He ran down the alleyway, back to the front entrance of the pagoda, crossed the street, and stood panting against a tree at the perimeter of the park.

"Call a fucking ambulance," he screamed at the scene. The walking wounded were trancing out. He saw a man standing in the park alone, just standing there, a solitary figure bleeding from the head. Then he fell to the ground. Okay, said Asher, catching his breath. The time has come to assume the mantle of the rational man. Running after a killer into the lion's den, he realized, was not the mantra of a rational man. Suddenly Asher felt a calm. In the distance he saw two men load a mangled body into the back of a pickup truck. The sun was hot, beaming down on scores of other bodies flopping in the street, moaning in the grass.

A phone. He needed a phone. He needed a Western journo who habitually carried a mobile phone, but he did not see any of them. Asher took off his T-shirt and cursed the journos. They were missing a story and he could use one of their phones to call Calmette Hospital. It was a T-shirt he'd bought years ago on a visit to the set of *The Young and the Restless*. It was a white T-shirt and on the back were autographs of the various soap opera stars. With his teeth, he made an incision and began to tear *The Young and the Restless* into shreds. Then he ran across the field. The sugarcane lady's stall had been blown to bits. She was lying inside her cart with her lower intestines, big bubbling worms, crawling out of her stomach. Near her stood a crowd, many of whom were slightly injured. Asher broke through them. They were huddled about a terrible scene. It was the clothing that got to Asher. Why were the clothes still so goddamned everyday? Why had the clothes simply changed color while the people inside them had . . . Asher put his hand to his mouth. A tourniquet would not be needed here. He ran across the street to a phone booth. They were newly installed European imports that required phone cards. Furiously he looked for his phone card but shortly found that he did not have his wallet. He saw a policeman wandering about the scene doing nothing. The man had a walkie-talkie.

Asher ran up to him.

"What the fuck are you doing, man!" he screamed. "Taking a Sunday walk in the park? Calmette, call fucking Calmette! The hospital, call Calmette Hospital and all the other ones too. Get on that thing and get some help."

The policeman turned from him and walked down the street. Asher closed his eyes and took a deep breath. Okay, the rational man. You are fucking Thomas Hobbes. Before us is the Hobbesian view. Man as monster, man driven by self-interest. Breathe. When he opened his eyes he saw that the first journo had arrived. It was a Welshman, a Reuters photographer named Richard Davies. Asher walked up to Davies, who was sweating and cleaning off his lens with the end of a *krama*.

Asher went with Dylan Thomas.

"This must be better than all the cats in Wales," said Asher. "Standing on a line in a row."

"Bugger off, Asher," said Davies, who had begun to unload his roll into the scene. "Bugger off, you're in my light."

"Hey, Davies, man. You got a phone? Give me your fucking phone. We've got to call Calmette."

Without taking his eye off his viewfinder, Davies threw Asher his phone.

"Do you know the number?" asked Asher.

"No, I don't know the bleeding number. Call . . . Call Reese at the AFP office. Pin has the hospital numbers on the wall. It's 015-830-910."

Asher dialed the number. He got a recording that the cellular customer had turned off his phone or was out of range.

"No one is picking up."

"Fuck," said Davies. "Give me that."

Furiously he dialed a number.

"Here," he said, handing Asher a spare camera. "Go nuts."

Asher looked at the scene through the viewfinder. It was much better behind this, much better.

"Katherine, Katherine, for fuck's sake, love, get up!" Davies yelled. "Get out of bed, love. There's been a massive explosion in the park across from the National Assembly. Call Calmette and the others, darling. Call them! Tell them to send every bleeding ambulance in the city here at once. . . . What? No, the park outside the National Assembly, darling. Wake yourself up and call all the hospitals you can. There are at least a dozen casualties."

Asher took a photograph of Davies talking to Katherine on the phone. It made sense. He worked for Reuters but on the side shot for the *Phnom Penh Post*. He'd been fucking Katherine. Oh Lord, how selfish are men, considered Asher. Even out here among the limbs he was stung by the revelation.

Suddenly Reese was by his side.

"Ah, fuck," he said. "Ah, fuck. Jesus fucking Christ. This is sick. What the fuck happened here?"

"I saw a guy," said Asher. "I saw one of Hun Sen's boys throw a grenade into the crowd. It was a Rainsy demonstration."

"You what?" said Reese, taking out his notepad. "Hun Sen's boys. What did they look like?"

"Mesh on their helmets, olive-green camouflage."

"Sounds like them. Fuck. What am I supposed to do—interview these people?"

"Here," said Asher, handing him two strips of *The Young and the Restless*. "Make some tourniquets."

They waded into the crowd together.

"Hey," screamed Davies. "Give me that camera back."

chapter three

T HE DEAL WENT DOWN this way. It was a standard Thursday night at the Stopless. Julie took the train into work. She
wore a black skirt and a white T-shirt. On her face she'd applied
base makeup so as to protect herself from the environment, the
smell of the industrial-strength rug cleaners, the mentholated cigarettes, the breath of the drinkers, the cherry-scented air freshen-
ers. The Stopless was a rank little hole. Glen, the owner, met her
at the cash register.

"I just fired that cunt Courtney," he said. "She couldn't keep
up with the clock if it were shoved up her pussy."

"That was stupid," said Julie.

"Yeah?" asked Glen, who secretly deferred to Julie's judgment.

"It was," replied Julie. "She's got a lot of loyal customers."

"I don't give a shit," replied Glen. "If she's on the big board,
she's on the big board. That means she's got to show up and dance,
and she never does. She's fucking with the rotation and has been
for forever."

"She's trying to be a musician. Why don't you give her a
break?"

"She's lost way too much weight," replied Glen.

"And why do you suppose that is, Glen? Let me guess, could it possibly be drug use? No, that would be too sinister, not drug use."

Glen took out his notepad and checked the register. Then he went into the back office and came out with a bucket of ice. When behind the bar, Glen liked to rub up against Julie's ass. This had been going on for months. Julie had said nothing. She internalized it. It helped her build rage. She liked hating Glen. It was one of the things she lived for. Since she'd begun work at the Stopless, her hatred of Glen had grown exponentially. At first she thought he was just stupid. Then to her horror she found out he wasn't stupid, only sleazy, and that the intelligence he did possess was channeled into cheating on his taxes and achieving the highest probability of successfully receiving blow jobs from his employees. He wasn't hot on health insurance either. Julie suspected him of stealing from her tip jar. He was practically a midget. He lived on Long Island.

From nine to about eleven-thirty Julie worked hard and made good money. She moved effortlessly from glass to ice, to bottle, to napkin, to straw, to "gun," as she called her soda hose, to ice, to cash register, and back, a great loop, a rhythmic circle. Occasionally she came out from behind the bar to serve the leering patrons sitting near the stage. As a rule she didn't know these men. They came exclusively for the dancers, and the dancers, as a rule, Julie found ugly and depressing. The Stopless was not Stringfellows or some corporate chain in Texas. There were no busty cornbread prairie girls just off the bus. Several of the dancers had kids, others habits to feed, some even had habits and children to feed.

At the bar that night sat two insurance adjusters from the

Travelers Group whom Julie called the Dow Components; a Con Edison meter man, Frank or Fred or Francis; Rick from AT&T; and Tommy from Mars, who liked the fanciest drink in the house, a Sex on the Beach. Then at the far end of the bar sat Weatherly, a recently divorced Upper East Sider whom she quite liked. He was a change-up pitch, blond, thin, button-down shirt, the exterior of respectability. There was humor in Weatherly's misery. He could hold up his end of a conversation with a stripper without sounding stupid. He and Julie both shared a great hatred for the music played at the Stopless. Julie liked to eavesdrop on Weatherly's conversations. He was funny. He tipped well and twice he'd asked her out on a date. Once, she'd very nearly accepted. For you see, Julie was just as good-looking as and vastly smarter than any woman in the bar. She never danced.

At about a quarter to ten she grew hungry. There was a lull in business. The postwork crowd had all shuffled off home to their wives and the latecomers had not yet arrived. Julie went downstairs to order some food. Usually she made Dwayne, the stoned bouncer, get her food since he did nothing all night but sit in a chair next to the door and be stoned. But Dwayne had called in sick and she didn't like his replacement, a criminally cracked-out black guy who talked a lot of shit and scared her.

Julie went downstairs into the changing room, where she found Sapphire smoking a small water pipe. The smell of crack and smack commingled in the air. On the wall was a house phone wired for calls only within the 212 and 718 area codes. It had been installed the previous day. The dancers had been making a stink about phone access for months and Glen had finally caved in. Julie picked up the phone and immediately put her hand over the receiver. Glen was on the other line. NYNEX had fucked up the wiring. The line down here was picking up on one of the three business lines in the office.

"I want to tell you something, okay? I want to tell you something about supply," came Glen's voice. "And demand. Right now Airport John just hasn't been coming through. He fears wiretaps. He doesn't like this neighborhood. He's been pussy whipped by some spic model who's trying to make him change his ways. Airport John is really fucking pissing me off. That California asshole. We have demand, but our supply is fucked. Right now it's called a seller's market but pretty soon we're not going to have anything to sell."

"Fucking Airport John," came a voice Julie had never heard before.

"Fuckin' A," said Glen. "We should have the guy capped."

"Cap yourself, you fool. Keep your eye on the ball, okay, Glen? That's what I'm telling you. You know, I appreciate that little lesson in economics you just wasted my time with, but now I'm telling you something. Ready? Here it is. Keep your eye on the ball and get some supply and make it the downtown shit, not uptown."

"Got ya," said Glen.

"Good."

They hung up. Julie put her hand to her mouth. Of course, Glen was dealing.

She looked up. Sapphire was still sucking on her water pipe. Demand, thought Julie, shaking her head, there it was, the tyranny of demand. Now if that wasn't a lesson—if Sapphire wasn't a lesson in what one didn't want to become, Julie didn't know what was. Glen dealing, wow. The guy on the other line certainly did not sound like Rico. Rico dealt to the dancers. He didn't seem like

Rico's scene at all. Perhaps he was Rico's boss or maybe this was bigger than Rico's boss. Julie had always wondered where Rico got his supply. This is where I get in, she said to herself. She passed by Sapphire without a word and returned to work, where a very drunk writer bought her a drink she very much needed.

Glen came behind the bar and brushed up against her ass again. That was it.

"Hey, Glen, I want to tell you something. Ready? You touch my ass with any part of your filthy body again and I'm going to have you capped. Supply and demand, you fucking criminal, but I'll tell you what. First thing, you get that downstairs phone line rewired; second, if you're looking for supply, you come to me. See, I know a boy. I know this boy at the source."

Glen squinted at her.

"Later," he hissed. "We'll talk later, after closing, and you better have something to say or else you're fired."

"Oh, now Glen," she said. "Why would you want to do that? I thought you said I had so much class."

On her day off Glen called Julie at home. He told her that they needed to discuss business matters of the previous week before the Stopless opened. This annoyed her greatly. She had to call off a coffee date with a boy she wanted to bed. The L train took forever. Now she and Glen were in the changing room at quarter to noon. It was a bright windowless bunker, and as soon as Glen got her downstairs he clicked open a switchblade. Julie knew the sound. Since she'd moved to New York, she'd been mugged twice and very nearly raped. All had involved knives. Turning, she saw Glen approach her. Julie backed up against the wall and threw her hands up. He was standing about two feet away from her and his nicotine breath was like a slap. The blade—she could see or feel nothing but the blade.

"So before I wire your connection what he's due, I want to know *when* his carrier pigeon is arriving. That was how you described this individual, a carrier pigeon who doesn't know what he had up his ass, right?"

"That is correct, Glen," she replied. "He has instructions to mail you the goods."

"What flight is he on?"

"What?" asked Julie.

The tip of the blade was transfixing her with horror. It was catching light off the makeup mirrors.

"This delivery boy of yours," asked Glen. "Where's he staying and when is he getting in?"

"Put the knife away, Glen, please," she begged. "Just put it down."

Glen approached. Now it was inches from her neck. Julie tried not to think about it.

"Where's he staying?"

"The Gramercy."

"Good," he said. "Now we're getting somewhere."

He retreated a few feet and dangled the knife by his side.

"How do you know he's staying at the Gramercy?"

"Because I know."

"How?"

"The guy I know over there, our connection, told me. There was a going-away party in Cambodia."

"When is he getting in?"

Julie breathed out. In the oval makeup mirror she caught the reflection of her face and the back of this awful man's head. Her fear abated somewhat and she was able to think. The time of truth had come on this deal, and she was now going to deliver a big fat lie. To avoid the tranced-out fear of Glen's knife, she looked at her watch. This was going to take some quick calculation. As she looked at her watch, she had a moment. Since Glen would probably rip her off anyway, she was now going to take control of this deal herself. She was going to be the daddy of this mother. After she took Glen for a ride, she'd quit the Stopless and move out of New York. The flash came in one package.

"Well, what time is he getting *in?*" asked Glen.

"Hold on a second, Glen," she said. "I'm calculating, just hold on."

She was thinking of Asher's e-mail. He'd been quite specific. Reese was landing at Kennedy around six tonight.

"He just got in the air a few hours ago," said Julie. "I'd say twelve to fourteen hours depending on layovers."

"What time is it now?" asked Glen.

"Almost noon."

He clicked in his switchblade and squinted. A speck of sour cream from a bagel was sticking to his ghastly mustache. His eyes were red little slits of horizontal distress, eating at her. Now the cousin to fear, anger, rose in her.

"Look, the guy is straight; that's why my guy chose him, you stupid motherfucker. You know how slow the mail is over there. If we moved it by mail, it would take forever and they've got drug-addicted dogs who'd sniff a Phnom Penh package in a second. Our carrier, this guy just thinks he's doing a favor for his buddy, mailing a screenplay. His name is Reese."

Immediately she wished she hadn't said his actual name.

"He's carrying damaged cameras, a postcard, and fucking love letters."

"And our package?"

"And our package, yes," said Julie. "He'll be a pushover, don't worry. He thinks he's doing everyone a mail favor, okay? They call it 'snail mail' over there. If you're so uptight about him not putting it in the mailbox, then get him at the Gramercy in thirteen hours."

"What's he look like?"

"I don't have a photograph of the guy, okay? I know his name and where he's staying his first few nights. He wants to see friends in New York before he has to deal with his family in Connecticut or something. He'll look like a straight journalist. My guy says he's got dark hair and likes navy-blue blazers. He told me that: Name is Reese. He usually travels in a navy-blue blazer. My guy's seen him leave for the airport before."

"Where the fuck is the Gramercy again?"

"Right on Gramercy Square Park," she said. "The uptown side on Lex."

To her surprise Glen put the knife away and actually took out a pen. Then he drew a business card from his wallet and wrote the address down on the back.

"How many hours did you say?"

"What am I, an air traffic control tower? Just ask for a guy named Reese thirteen to fifteen hours from now. Then you won't have to wait around. He'll be jet-lagged and in his room."

"Running this hole is fucking exhausting," said Glen. "I know where you live, but there won't be a phone call. Got me? Everything you own, including yourself, will go up in flames. I'm down with some guys in Astoria who make it their business to know a lot about butane and kerosene."

"Those are the facts, Glen," replied Julie. "Act on them, and everything is going to be cool."

"Get the fuck out of here," he said. "You'll get your cut in two days if this number pans out. Get out. I'm sick of seeing your face every single fucking night in this shit hole."

Julie ran up the stairs, grabbed her purse from behind the bar, and flagged a cab. A feeling of immense relief came over her. She would never see, smell, nor taste the Stopless again. It was a wonderful spring day, and she had five hours. Now all she would have to do is go back to Brooklyn, doll herself up, and get to the Gramercy before Reese checked in.

"It's all you, baby," she said out loud. "All you."

chapter four

REESE STOOD in the blue line. He was clean. He knew he was clean but for his bloodstream, but as he approached the immigration officer he felt increasingly unlawful. He hadn't recalled Kennedy's immigration lanes being so orderly and hygienic. A color photograph of the president hovered over the bright linoleum floors. He was in a sea of passengers, mostly foreigners, and for a moment he was comforted to be a white American. For one thing, his line moved more quickly.

Reese gave his passport and immigration form over to a black man in a white short-sleeved shirt. During his two and a half years in Asia, Reese had come into contact with only two black people, a Cuban rice dealer in Saigon and a U.S. Army MIA investigator in Phnom Penh. This was a man of a different stripe. He was elderly and strangely paternal. Patches of gray spotted his Afro. Slowly the man fingered the pages of Reese's American passport, and then scanned the first page through a computing device. After a while, the immigrations officer looked up at him. He wore clean rimless glasses, and he took his time staring into Reese's eyes.

"You've been gone for quite some time," said the man.

"Yes," replied Reese. "I have."

"Welcome home, son," said the man, coming down hard with the stamp.

Reese's eyes flooded with tears. It had been a long, anxious period. A friend and two acquaintances were dead. The Cambodian lies and the deadlines had exhausted and aged him. And yet these two and a half years that felt like five were all he now possessed. What had come before it, his former life, was an abstraction, a dream. Now he had three weeks to see what that dream had been all about.

For customs' sake he carried a pink *Financial Times* under one arm of his blazer. It was a trick he'd picked up years ago. A man, Reese's reasoning ran, who read the pink *Financial Times* didn't carry on his person meats. The paper was a subliminal sign of law-abiding international capitalism. He was waved through customs immediately.

Reese took a taxi into the city. All around him came the sounds of hostility and aggression. Shortly he fell into a light sleep. He dreamt briefly of a roadblock. A Cambodian soldier was banging on his window demanding to take a look through Reese's binoculars. The soldier didn't want money, proof that his was in fact a dream. He just wanted to see how far he could see with Reese's binoculars. When he woke up, the cab was speeding down what looked to be lower Lexington Avenue.

Reese checked into the Gramercy Park Hotel. He'd faxed them his credit card information from the AFP office in Phnom Penh and was surprised to see his reservation actually confirmed. There was a woman standing at the desk. She was leaning on a section of the fake marble a few feet down from him, pivoting her upper body sideways. Reese enjoyed catching her staring at him.

He smiled at her. Well, that was nice. She was prettier than rain in Queens.

He had a porter help him with his bags. In the elevator they spoke of the Rangers and the weather.

In his room he dropped his bags and withdrew a bottle of Johnnie Walker Red he'd purchased in the Bangkok duty-free store. Scotch; Asia had forced him to acquire its taste. It was what the generals drank. He found a plastic glass in the bathroom and then left his room in search of an ice machine. An ice machine; now that was a magnificent concept. He floated down the hallway adrift with jet lag and the American novelty of his errand. In Cambodia, clean ice was always a fight and a worry. Nestled between a ventilating shaft and an emergency exit door stood a great humming box, a never-ending source of safe ice. Outstanding. Reese pressed the button and watched with glee as the machine gurgled out uniform cubes into his plastic bucket. Back in his room, he threw open the window and toasted the ice machine.

"To the land of the free," he said to the street. "And to the defeat of tropical illness."

The ice in Cambodia had fucked him. He'd gotten cocky in Battambang and come down with an intestinal infection and fever. There had followed a week of shaky misery, vomiting and nausea, a lesson in ice. Reese took off his pants and proceeded to get drunk to the evening news. Peter Jennings, Reese decided, had not aged an iota. The Canadian was as suave as ever. There was little foreign news, and no news whatsoever out of Asia. Reese drank copiously from his bottle and once Peter had signed off, he stood up and dialed Weatherly's number. Weatherly was not home. That was fine. He would have plenty of Weatherly tomorrow.

Reese left a message with his friend telling him where to find him in the morning. Then he lay back down on the bed.

"Johnnie Walker Black is the whack," he said. "Johnnie Walker Red will make you dead."

It was an old jingle from a long-forgotten grade-school friend he'd seen featured in a razor blade advertisement during his layover in the Bangkok airport hotel. Cushman had been featured with shaving cream on one side of his face, staring handsomely into a mirror. In that moment, as the meaningless Thai voice-over sounded off, Reese had understood the trajectory of his friend's career. The segment had probably been cut in Japan, which meant Cushman hadn't made it in L.A. Too bad. He'd taken his first drink with Cushman, pilfered from a liquor cabinet in an Upper East Side apartment. Scotch, as a matter of fact.

He unzipped his duffel bag and was taking out film and stacks of notepads when he was hit by the smell. It was at least a month of filthy clothing. Knowing he was coming to New York, Reese had neglected his laundry. It was the smell of the central market, street curries, sweat, and cigarettes. He dug deep into his bag and made a great ball of dirty clothing.

"Guilty by association," he said, throwing it all in the corner.

Then he got into the shower, washed himself, and was toweling off when he noticed the mail. He'd completely forgotten about the mail, and now he was glad of it. Reese spread the mail out on his bed, wondering what a handwriting expert would make of all these little labors of love. It had been a fine going-away party, and taking responsibility for delivering this cross-section of Phnom Penh's expat community's mail had made him feel useful and needed. There were three letters and two packages. The addresses were all handwritten but for Asher's, which was neatly typed to an address in Long Island City and was fairly hefty. Remy's envelope was well worn and already marked PAR AVION. The Frenchman had also written URGENT. Oh well, he'd deal with the mail later.

Let's see; he had to look at his *Financial Times.* Tomorrow was . . . tomorrow was Thursday. He'd go to the post office in the morning before Weatherly picked him up. The idea was to get some rest, get this lecture out of the way, collect his money for it, and come back and do two more nights at the Gramercy in order to acclimatize himself before moving over to his mother's apartment. But so far he wasn't acclimatizing at all. Perhaps it was the plane. You couldn't just get on a plane and expect everything to be different. Reese decided that his mind was a lot slower than an airplane and that New York was freaking him out. In his boxers he squatted on his haunches against the hotel wall, Cambodian style. He hadn't said a word of consequence to anyone of any importance in how many hours? He did not know; a long time. Economy class all the way, and in the rush to pack after filing the grenade attack story, he'd forgotten to bring any Valium. Stupid. In Phnom Penh he'd often fantasized about these days in New York. He'd do what he wanted. He'd go to McDonald's. He'd see a real movie, a first-run high-budget thriller. He'd sleep with a woman, a white one. He'd eat food from around the world, with a weighting toward Europe. He'd see his sister, take her out to Raoul's. He'd sit in the steam room of the Racquet Club. He'd see friends. He'd live. But now drunk and in the Asian crouch in the corner, he was turning dangerously inward. He was terrified to go outside.

He took the elevator down to the bar. In the lounge, cocktail candles cast a dim, conspiratorial light onto the crouched drinkers, and in a near corner a pianist he could not see was tinkling out voiceless music. Reese passed by the tables and into the next room, where he took a seat at the far end of the L-shaped bar. At his back was a slab of dark cherry-wood paneling. It was a good position from which to observe the room. He leaned forward as the bartender placed a napkin in his downward glance. So far everyone was making the right moves, and Reese felt in lubricious synchronization with the room. He ordered a Maker's Mark and sat back on his stool. Nothing much, really. He was pleased to see that the Gramercy bar had continued in its state of reliable dissipation without him. In his mid- and late-twenties he had drunk heavily here with friends. The clientele had reinforced their collective feeling of relative youth. Now Reese wasn't so sure. He cast about the bar for the hard-drinking geriatrics that had lent the place its bygone sense of tragic flair. He didn't quite see it so unequivocally now. There were two couples, men in their early forties drinking with much younger women, two secretaries in sneakers, and men of indeterminant middle age. It was a divorce bar.

Then the woman he'd spotted at the lobby walked in and sat down on a stool next to him. She had pale white skin and hair pulled back into an efficient bun held up by what looked to be a broken knitting needle. Reese tried not to stare, but as she ordered her drink, he ventured a longer look. She had thin arms and bracelets that clanked against one another. It was a homecoming jingle for Reese. He'd had a girlfriend years ago with a similar sense of pouty urban disdain coupled with an experienced sex drive. When her gimlet arrived, she pulled out the knitting needle and let her long hair fall over one shoulder. Oh God, thought Reese, what a move. It was not good to gawk, but since it was precisely this kind of woman that was in such short order in Cambodia, he couldn't help himself. She began to dig into her large black bag for something. Reese had not seen a woman dig through a handbag for quite some time. Women did not go about with expensive handbags in Phnom Penh. She moved the candle closer to the operation and in time took out a pack of mangled Marlboros and placed them on the bar.

"Cigarette?" she said suddenly to Reese. "I'll trade you a cigarette for a light. These deli matches are finished, and I don't like to light my cigarettes on candles. Someone told me it was bad for you."

Patting himself down, he found a pack of matches from the Foreign Correspondents Club in Phnom Penh.

Reese slid them down the bar.

"Thanks," she said, lighting up. "Where you from?"

"The East Side."

"The East Side, huh?" she said, exhaling his way.

"Yeah."

"What do you do on the East Side?"

"I'm a reporter."

"A reporter," she said. "Sounds cool. What do you report on?"

"A very fucked-up country."

"Yeah, the Lower East Side is a mess, man."

Reese saw in her past pounds of marijuana use and assorted venereal diseases. She wore a black skirt and a silver top with a circular zipper pull. The top had a shiny rubberized quality that Reese normally associated with wet suits.

"I've been out of the fashion loop for quite some time," he said. "That's a really nice top you have on."

"Thank you."

"What do you do?" he asked.

"Oh," she said. "A lot of different things. I'm supposed to meet my partner here, but I have a feeling he might not show. What's your name?"

Reese told her.

"How about Roman numerals? You a second or third, anything fancy like that? Because, I don't know, I'm seeing a Roman numeral."

"Sorry, no numbers," said Reese.

"That's okay. In college I used to go out with a fifth, very inbred family. I called him Rudy Five, nice guy. His father was a beer bottle."

"A what?"

"A beer bottle. He was shaped like a beer bottle. On a sunny day you could see right through him."

"Foreign or domestic?"

"Definitely domestic."

"Yeah? What did he taste like?"

"Thank God I never found out. He tried once, though. His current wife is my age."

"So what happened to the son of this beer bottle?"

Gently she took the stem of her gimlet and moved to make a toast.

"We broke up," she said, touching her glass to Reese's.

"Where I've been," said Reese, "in this fucked-up country I've been trying to report out of, in all the time I've been there, I haven't seen one decent-looking Western woman who wasn't married, a tourist, or taken."

"Wow, that sucks. Where were you, Africa?"

"No, Cambodia."

"Yeah, and what kind of nasty diseases did you pick up?"

"I'm clean," said Reese. "I had a very troubling case of fever, but that was from the ice and it was a while ago. Dr. Jeremy, my resident physician and an accused pedophile, said the blood tests looked good. No hep A or anything else."

"And you trust this man who rams little boys?"

"I believe he is a trustworthy physician and that he was set up by missionaries and their allies in nongovernment organizations. CARE people, to be specific. But the Mormons are my favorite. They bike around town in black shorts wearing those snazzy bicycle helmets."

Reese didn't know where to go from here. Perhaps he'd overwhelm her mentally and take her to bed. He was ready for that. Subtle war stories, followed by dinner, where he'd illustrate the drama of judging peril's way in the interests of news. Crazy, that was a factor. He didn't want to come off as a crazy. She probably hated the press. Bourbon ice slammed against his teeth, sealing a personal promise not to come off as crazy. He'd have to watch out for that. New Yorkers were good at spotting crazies.

"Have you ever talked to a stranger on a chairlift?" she asked.

"That's a yes-or-no question," said Reese. "It's not a very good way to garner information. I'd go with 'What's the worst conversation you've ever had on a chairlift?' "

"Yes, but how do I know you've ridden a chairlift before?"

"Assume a hunch. I do it all the time at work."

"Assume a hunch." She lingered on the concept. "That doesn't sound very healthy."

"It isn't," said Reese. "Assuming a hunch wasn't designed that way. It was designed to verify something you suspect to be true."

"Wow," she said.

"Healthy," said Reese, "has nothing to do with it."

Reese was visited by an expansive feeling of wonder, luck, and lust. This sordid conversation, this wonderful girl, the jet lag and bourbon, they all coalesced into a dreamy concoction he hoped would not curdle.

"So do you think this guy's going to come, your partner?" he asked.

"What time is it?"

"I really couldn't tell you."

"But you've got a watch."

"I know, but I stopped looking at it a long time ago."

"Oh."

"Hey, you want to hear the best thing I ever heard on a chairlift or not?" he asked.

"Sure."

"Well, it wasn't really a chairlift. My sister and I were in a lift line waiting for the chair. This was in the great Scott boot era of late-1970s western skiing, you know, Rocky Mountain High, the whole thing. This ski bunny goes, 'Single,' and this cowboy goes, 'Single.' My sister and I listened in on their conversation. He had really short pump skis. Anyway, it turns out that this cowboy and this ski bunny, they're practically neighbors back down the canyon, right? So then out of nowhere the cowboy goes, 'So, you want to hump?' "

"That simple, huh? What did she say?"

"I can't really remember. I know she laughed."

"Will you buy me a drink?" she asked.

"Surely," said Reese.

"The cowboy and the bunny," she said. "Which one do you want to play with me?"

The elevator took forever. When it finally arrived at the lobby floor, they were joined by a pair of gay German tourists who, on the way up, spoke roughly to each other in their native tongue.

"Do you want a tour of my hallway?" asked Reese when his floor arrived.

"Sure," she replied. "I'd love it."

"That's the problem with hotels, hallways. The tour is obligatory."

She laughed out loud.

"Also I've got a minibar. It's not unlike a Korean deli, an enemy of promise, and too close to my bed."

Before the door could close he had her up against the wall. For a blissfully small moment her face and hair were lit by the hallway light and then extinguished.

"I don't do this every day, you know," she said.

He was unzipping her top.

"So what if you did," replied Reese.

"No, seriously, I don't want you to get the wrong impression. I'm not a hooker or anything. I'm just going through a weird period."

Reese cupped one breast in his hand.

"I really don't care," he said. "It's just it's been so long since . . . so long since I've been with . . . you know, a white woman."

"Just take it easy, okay, honey?" she said. "Don't blow your top."

She could feel him panting. His chest rose and fell against hers as she massaged the back of his neck. It was a shame. She hadn't expected it, but she enjoyed Reese. He was a boy, really. She'd expected a man. Actually she'd expected a bloated middle-aged pervert, a Bangkok massage parlor aficionado who'd weasel all over her. For that eventuality she'd brought two Rohypnols, the date-rape sedative of unconditional blackouts. Now she found herself in urgent, not altogether unskilled hands, and though she tried not to give into it, his vitality was contagious. Her hair splayed back on the bed as she kicked off her heels. Then she waited as he nervously fumbled with a condom. The condom application, it was annoying as a skipping record, but she was glad she didn't have to ask him to put it on. She tried to change mind-sets. After all, she had friends in Williamsburg who would pay for this, a straight-up normal lay. To be fucked by a citizen; where Julie came from there was novelty there. Since graduating she had been in the process of marginalizing herself. It was a lifestyle, marginalization. It was cheap and considered cool. And yet it was exhausting her. They fucked solidly, stranger to stranger, for a respectable amount of time. When she felt he was about to come, Julie slipped out from beneath him.

"Not yet," she hissed.

Julie threw off her top. She was moist and running now, ready for it. For a moment they lay side by side in silence. Then she vaulted on top of him, pressing his chest down against the mattress with her hand. She had to suppress the urge to tell him. She had to consciously hold back the telling and this got in the way of her orgasm. What would happen if she simply mentioned Asher? If she said, "Asher," what might he do? But she didn't. She shut her mouth, closed her eyes, and concentrated on herself. She got off.

In the bathroom, she gulped water from the spigot and crushed a Rohypnol into a glass of water and stirred it with her finger. Returning bedside, a thin column of platinum moonlight filtered through the nearly closed curtains. Vaguely Reese could see her now. She had thin hips and stringy hair, wet with sex. Moon-light on a woman wearing nothing, a wonderful sight. Reese yanked off the moist condom and threw it against the wall, where for a moment it stuck.

"The spaghetti is ready," said Julie.

They both laughed nervously.

"Thank you," he said. "That was . . . that was, I don't know, good for me."

"You're a sweetheart," she said.

Reese drank hungrily from her glass. Then they lay side by side, gazing up at the invisible ceiling, saying nothing. It was an awkward moment in the dark. Julie waited. Thank God for the drug, she thought. It was nearly tasteless. This guy reminded Julie of some of the Eliot House boys with whom she'd recklessly slept her freshman year. Straight, determined young men, they'd lacked any sense of sexual malfeasance. She'd tired of them quickly. But that had been years ago. Now she found Reese a welcome college reunion. In the dark she waited. The moonlight fell in a slant across the carpet, illuminating Reese's cassette recorders and re-porter's notepads lying in shambles on the floor. She couldn't be-lieve her life had come to this, and yet, at the same time, she was thrilled. She'd held a lot of jobs, worked for assholes, all of them, asshole New York City males. She'd been an assistant to a fashion photographer. She'd fact-checked. She'd modeled shoes. She'd worked as a night paralegal. Miserable drudgery and male egos, a nightmare, an equation for drug use.

Reese rolled over on his side, facing her. Julie ventured a glance. A good-looking guy. She wasn't sure about the haircut, but so what? At least there was a conspicuous absence of a ponytail or jewelry. All the men who'd hit on her recently seemed to have one or the other. He was a natural, good-looking guy, this Reese. He had dark short hair, normal hair, and a solid, almost square jaw that lent his dark stubble a handsome gravity. He did, he looked like a real journalist, and now, she noticed, he was fast asleep and drooling.

On her back she slowly counted to fifty. Then she got up and went to the bathroom to piss. With the door closed the bathroom light came off the white tiles, shocking her into lurid self-awareness. Her nudity in the full-length mirror cut her with shame. She drank more water and then sat on the toilet with her head in her hands. Then she stood up and approached the full-length mirror.

"Treachery," she whispered at her eyes. "Treachery and treason."

With her old lover Asher's large manila envelope addressed to her boss secured beneath her raincoat, Julie walked to Union Square and got on the L. The ride was an agony. She cursed each stop that had no bearing on her final destination. They were useless stops. It was late and unwanted attention was paid her. It baffled her the way Hispanic men felt they had the right to stare so directly, to linger on her in such unadulterated lechery. At Bedford she hurried down the street until she came to Mugs. The bar window was lit with a conviviality utterly unaligned with her mood. David Star, still holding a bourbon glass, came out of Mugs to talk.

"Julie, hey, Julie, what's up, girl?" said David. "Come on in. We're having a roast for Jordan. She has now been hired and fired from every publication in the city that has *New York* in the title."

David Star was a musician who should have gotten out of the business years ago. The arc of his career was a neighborhood cliché. He was thirty-three and still putting up flyers at night. His band had come close but never been signed. Lately, the turnout at his gigs had slackened and he'd gone about guilting his friends, playing head games with who was on or off the guest list. He did not have a ponytail, but he had an earring. Julie had never slept with him, but in all probability it was he who had given her roommate genital warts. She had no time for David tonight.

"Sorry, but I've got to get home."

David followed her down the street.

"Come on, Julie, what's your problem? It's a party for Jordan. A lot of your friends are in there."

Julie turned.

"You know what, David? You're wearing me out, man. Just let me go home, okay? I've had a weird night."

"Well, fuck you," said David. "I was only trying to be friendly."

"That's fine. I'm just not ready for Jordan's shit. Not tonight."

"Fine," said David and walked away.

Her hands were trembling as she fit her key into the door.

"Karen," she said as she walked through the door. "Karen, are you home?"

There was no answer. Julie heaved with relief. It was just past one in the morning. If Karen wasn't home, that meant she would be sleeping with her boyfriend in Manhattan. The apartment was wonderfully empty. Julie flipped on a light switch and headed for the kitchen. She pulled the package from her raincoat and laid it on the butcher block.

"The naive carrier," she said. "What a concept."

She had to hand it to Asher, this Reese was perfect. She'd spotted him right away from Asher's e-mail description as he'd checked in at the Gramercy. Definitely a journalist, definitely bedraggled, but certainly as Asher had promised, certainly a citizen. Julie wondered if they were friends, this Reese and Asher.

When she'd worked as a paralegal, she'd seen envelopes similar to this one. It was well sealed and traditionally reserved for sending sets of hefty legal documents. She wondered how Asher had gotten his hands on something so professional-looking. From a kitchen drawer she drew a steak knife and cut the seal. BLOODY SUNDAY was the first thing she saw, a headline. The thing was wrapped in pages of a newspaper called the *Phnom Penh Post*. Julie threw the envelope on the floor. There was a color photograph of a woman with no legs crying out for help. Then she noticed that this woman's legs from the knee down were on the street beside her. With the knife she quickly cut the newspaper away. Her hand rose to her mouth. Inside a zip-locked bag sat an unfathomably large amount of heroin. Julie turned away. She couldn't look at it. She went to the ice box. From the freezer she poured herself a measure of syrupy vodka and drained it. Then she poured more vodka into a stainless-steel shaker and added lime juice and ice. She shook her shaker, poured out the drink, and gazed down on the madness. She hadn't counted on being this scared. One of the reasons she contrived this deal was for the aesthetics and morals of it all. It would be aesthetically pleasant to get back into Asher's twisted life. Enough time and dreadful, twitchy men had separated her from Asher that she'd felt compelled to get back in touch with him. It wasn't love necessarily, but a feeling, a desire to see a favorite painting of one's adolescence. That was the aesthetics part. But then she remembered that last night, in the parking lot of the Brig on Abbot Kinney, with that evil L.A. sundown coloring the contortions of his swollen face, she standing there with car problems, inside the sphere of insults received. His jealousy, considering his laziness, his lassitude was outsized, bloated, insanely passionate. And she'd truly loved and hated him for it. He was a negativist, Asher. That was what had drawn her to him to begin with. He was splendidly, drunkenly, vehemently down on the world. They'd lived together in a Venice shack. Even the bikers complained about their yard. Asher was the beginning of her marginalization. He was a man who only got around to displaying love by showing his violent disapproval of it being taken away from him. But that had been a while ago, how long ago she could not really tell, a distant powerful blur, a far-flung feeling, an aesthetic.

She wasn't going to rip Asher off, but with Glen, on the other hand, there was an immediate moral obligation to work vigilantly against his interests. The aesthetics of love, the morals of business.

She walked over to the drugs and unsealed the zip-locked bag. She took her wallet out of her purse and dipped into the pile with her driver's license. On the butcher block she cut out a small line and then paused. It wasn't just the golden rule of drug dealing—never dive into one's own supply—that gave her pause, it was the tyranny of need she'd witnessed at the Stopless. She was going to do this line for confirmation and for pleasure, and then she was going to put the drug away. She would reseal the package with her own electrical tape and put it under the couch. For the road of excess, she'd learned, most definitely did not lead to the palace of wisdom. The drug had spread like pink eye to the bars of her neighborhood, to the Stopless, and out over the wide American landscape of need. Friends of friends had been found dead in their bed. Julie got out a bill, rolled, and snorted it up. Shortly she was kneeling on her couch, staring without registering the view from her window. The aesthetics of love, the morals of business, she said to herself as she lay down on the couch, and, oh Lord, there *was* such pleasure here. It was a lethal, lethal thing, perhaps the most ruinous of all delights. But inside the drug's snug cocoon it was difficult to imagine the consequences. She forced herself to go to a separate place in her brain, the place that fears and respects bills and the alarm clock. She imagined the sound of her alarm clock. Then Julie headed to the closet for her electrical tape.

chapter five

REESE RAN ACROSS the Circle. In the moonlight the chapel stained his periphery. His destination was a Richardsonian building the color of Harvard, a university to which he had not been accepted. Still he ran. He ran to sober up in time for his lecture. The flight to Bangkok, seventeen hours to Kennedy with a ghastly layover in Osaka, one incredibly disorienting evening in New York, and after all that, he was still left feeling guilty for crossing this soggy field, this Circle. It was a sacred Grove School rule, do not cut across the Circle, go around it. That's what this place did to you, he thought; it planted guilt in your heart forever.

Reese entered the schoolhouse by the side door and effortlessly climbed the back stairs. The upstairs hallway had narrowed. The floor was no longer wood. What once had been a bathroom was now a storage closet. He walked the length of the hallway opening doors at random. At Ramsdale's English classroom he found a timed light and turned it clockwise. In intervals the overhead fluorescent flickered on. Clearly this was Ramsdale's class no longer. It was a science room. On the raised shelves sat Bunsen burners and beakers with red measuring-cup lines. Reese was visited by a selfish, conservative impulse. From the outside the school appeared unchanged. They'd just done a job on the inside. It was not helping his jet lag. He considered the school. It was a beautiful school, but like New York, it was no longer his. Wave after wave of students had passed through it, and with each graduation his own triumphs and those of his class had been pushed farther into the archival reaches of the school's memory. With every year that passed, Grove had become more promiscuous. Time had sullied her, and besides, who knew what the students were like these days? Who knew what sort of alchemy had taken place since he'd graduated? Reese closed Ramsdale's old classroom door and moved on.

"Fucking science," he said.

He marched down the hallway opening doors until he came to a handicapped bathroom. His hair was matted and his eyes a mess. Dirt caked the gutters of his corduroy jacket sleeves, and his lower palms and wrists were raw and scratched. He took off his jacket and splashed water on his face. Then he moved closer to the mirror and found himself swaying before the reflection of his pupils.

A moment of meditative prayer, that was what was required here, a quiet moment to collect his thoughts. Reese closed his eyes but it was not very meditative.

"Oh God," he said. "I'm drunk."

He washed his face beneath the faucet and decided that the stinging pain was helping him focus. He took off his jacket and surveyed his shirt. He was wearing his dead father's button-down. It was white with pale pink stripes. The cotton had torn through at the right elbow. Reese rolled the shirtsleeve up and dabbed at his chest with a moist paper towel, removing spots of dirt. Then he noticed his pants. His knee was coming through a small tear.

Below him now he could feel the rumbling of the student body entering the schoolhouse. Dinner was over. He checked his watch. It was five minutes to game time. At the end of the hallway he found a supply cabinet. A mop handle struck him in the head and rolls of toilet paper fell from a rack. He took off his pants, turned the torn leg inside out, and was applying a strip of electric tape when he sensed someone at the top of the stairs.

"What are you doing, Harry?"

No one called Reese Harry anymore. It was Ramsdale, his old crew coach and English teacher. A red exit sign outlined his black figure.

"'Worcester,'" said Ramsdale, "'get thee gone, for I do see danger and disobedience in thine eyes.'"

Henry IV, Part One. Ramsdale had been good with that one. Prince shall one day become king and inherit the earth and its responsibilities. It was a "put away childish things" play, very Grove. It was also a sign that Ramsdale was drunk and in a high Shakespearean mood.

"Your classroom," said Reese, getting into his pants with a ridiculous hop. "I see they've turned your classroom into a fetal pig laboratory."

"Yes, I suppose they have, haven't they?" said Ramsdale. "And they tell me you've become a newspaper man."

Feeling way too crazy to be terrified, but terrified nonetheless, Reese came out of the closet and shook his mentor's hand. Engage, thought Reese, engage and confuse.

"Did you know, Arthur," said Reese, "did you know that it only takes one one-thousandth of a second to take a good photograph? Sometimes I wish I'd become a photographer instead."

"I see," said Arthur Ramsdale, "that you've been drinking."

"Yes, Arthur," he replied. "Yes, I have, and I suppose you have too."

There followed a silence. Reese had never called Ramsdale on his drinking. The man had always had the hypocritical upper hand on that one. Ramsdale, though a drunk, hated himself for drinking and expected his rowers to do as he said, not as he did.

"Well, at any rate they're waiting for you downstairs," said Ramsdale. "Weatherly told me I might find you up here."

"Did he tell you that we were stoned?" said Reese. "Stoned by Fairfield students?"

"He did not," replied Ramsdale. "Now why don't you come along."

They'd stopped off at a package store and finished off a pint of vodka on empty stomachs. Then Weatherly had proceeded to let himself be goaded into folly by the townies at the Grove House of Pizza. They'd had to run from hostile adolescents who'd thrown stones at them. Secretly Reese had been proud of his friend for finding the capacity to mix it up in such a youthful, sordid setting. The man's wife of three years had just left him and he was filled with a silent, creeping rage that had finally found a deeply juvenile expression.

Now Ramsdale positioned himself behind Reese as they descended the stairs. Reese could feel him up there pressing him down with disappointment. Below, the auditorium hummed with the distracted yammering of youth. He reached into his inside pocket. His cue cards. Fuck, if he'd lost his cue cards? The cue cards were there. Now he was at the bottom of the stairs. In the hallway Weatherly was talking to the headmaster and the dean of students. Dean Weirhman had never been an ally of Reese's and seeing the man's completely bald head (a wonderful work in progress), a bolt of sixteen-year-old fear took him. But for his head, Dean Weirhman had not aged a bit. He was wearing a baby-blue sweater vest as befitted a golfer. Headmaster Humphrey saw Reese coming and seemed to genuinely light up.

"Well, there he is," said Headmaster Humphrey. "The next David Halberstam, with photographs, I hope, as good as Robert Capa's."

Insane, thought Reese, really fucking crazy.

"Well, hello, Mr. Humphrey," said Reese, reaching for maximum ingratiating charm and bonhomie. "I tell you, it's really . . . it's really . . ."

He could not decide what it really was to be back, and so he stood there stammering, shaking the headmaster's hand.

". . . It's really, uh . . . Robert Capa stepped on a mine in 1954. He was a great photographer but now very dead. Don't worry, though, I'm going to give you all one hell of a dog and pony show, don't you worry."

All faces fell.

"Say," said Headmaster Humphrey. "You look a little . . . how should I say . . . you look a little peaked."

"My plans changed at the last moment. I had to cover a grenade attack. Killed sixteen people. Then the flights got all funny and it came down to the difference of nearly two thousand dollars. My point is . . . You see, I've been on a plane for as long as I can remember."

"Oh my Lord," said the headmaster. "All the way from Phnom Penh."

"I'm proud to be here," said Reese. "But I'm afraid to say that I've received very little sleep."

The headmaster clapped him on the back.

"Well, I'm proud of you, nonetheless."

"I wouldn't," replied Reese, "have missed it for the world."

"Jake," said Dean Weirhman to Headmaster Humphrey. "We'd better get going."

The headmaster checked his watch.

"Susan Rivers is going to introduce you, Harris," said Dean Weirhman, not offering him his hand. "She's our new librarian."

Reese and the dean walked down the hall together. Emotionally Reese was oscillating within an ever-widening trading range. The present, light on the wings of vodka, felt dangerously ephemeral. He decided to focus on the dean's head. The man had the same steely control, the same clear blue eyes that in baldness seemed sinisterly ramped up. Tonight, Reese decided, Dean Weirhman's eyes are flying saucers, invaders of his night, the enemy.

"Here," said a figure, leaping up beside him. It was Weatherly, drunk, blond, and smiling. He handed Reese a plastic cup. "Take this. It's properly chased, and good luck. Oh, and don't forget, 'Nisi Parat Imperat'—unless it obeys, it commands, baby. I expect you to sing for your supper out there."

"Oh, thank you," said Reese. "Thanks for the Latin lesson."

Dean Weirhman introduced Reese to Susan Rivers, then thankfully left them alone. Behind the heavy curtain, a single stage light beamed down upon the librarian. Suddenly Reese remembered her. The milky-white skin, the famous breasts, the great object of lust and locker room conjecture. At the time she'd been two years older than Reese and thoroughly out of his league. Now he had caught up to her. The tables had turned. In her return to Grove there was a latent sense of defeat, possibly an early divorce, an abdication of some sort. Susan Rivers gazed directly into his eyes. Yes, it had happened. Someone had broken her heart. She had wonderful Black Irish looks. With her dark hair pulled sharply back, her forehead appeared enameled in the direct light. She wore a blue paisley blouse, and her breasts heaved with excitement upon shaking his hand. For the first time in his life, Reese felt famous.

"I've been following your work. They even let me do a very expensive LEXIS/NEXUS search. I didn't realize how many newspapers pick up the wires," she said breathlessly. "It's all penetrated my subconscious. Did that grenade attack *really* happen on Easter Sunday, because in my dream I'm going to church and suddenly there's this explosion?"

"It's a Buddhist country," said Reese. "The irony of Easter was lost on them."

"Oh," said Susan Rivers.

She'd expected a brief moment of geopolitical discussion, but instead Reese stared down at her breasts, savoring the withholding of conversation. She had a low center of gravity. Reese badly wanted to take her to bed. She stood facing him with her feet turned out in a balletic position. Then she handed him a remote-controlled slide changer and explained to him its machinations. Their upper arms touched.

"Okay," said Susan Rivers. "Now I'm going to introduce you. What should I say is the title of your talk?"

Reese hadn't really thought of a title, but now looking into Susan Rivers's wonderful blue eyes, he felt supremely confident.

"I don't know," he said. "Why don't you call it, 'Leap Before You Look: How Journalism Can Fuck Your Life in Five Parts.'"

Susan Rivers's famous breasts shook with laughter. Reese took a long sip of Weatherly's concoction and shivered. The bastard had made it insanely strong. He was trying to undermine him.

"Well," she said, "I can work off that. Good luck."

"Hey . . . ," said Reese, who'd wanted to invite her for a drink in town after the lecture, but she was gone.

From the bawdy applause, he could tell that Susan Rivers was a hit with the students. There were catcalls from boys in distant rows and licentious whistles. Her introduction was detailed and informative. He'd forgotten about his stint at the *Vietnam Investment Review*. It had been a terrible job. He'd been a flack for the joint ventures, the great Vietnamese money grab of the early '90s. Perhaps he would work it into his talk. From his breast pocket he withdrew his cue cards and quickly reviewed his talking points. His hands were red and bloated with blood. They quivered beneath the stage lights. When it was time, he bumped into Susan exiting the side of the stage and splashed some of Weatherly's drink onto her blouse.

"Oh," she exclaimed, looking up at him expectantly. "Good luck."

"Thank you," said Reese. "I'll need some."

Earlier that day Weatherly double-parked and walked into the Gramercy Park Hotel to pick up his high school friend. He'd banged and banged at Reese's door. Finally he heard a little whimper, and Reese had opened up. He was in a towel and looked terrible. He'd already begun to go gray before the move to Phnom

Penh. Now his hair was salt and pepper. Still more pepper than salt, but aged nonetheless. The man didn't have his glasses on and now Weatherly found himself squinted at.

"You," said Weatherly, shaking his friend's hand, "should take a shower."

A half hour later they were driving up the FDR in silence listening to the radio, a dull awkwardness sitting between them. Perhaps everything there was to say had already been said. They were two friends in motion, two men driving backward toward the school of their youth. Through the jumble of blue Exxon stations and red McDonald's signs, in the slipstream of the passing trucks and the withering monotony of municipal green exit signs, they pushed through neutral Connecticut toward the Massachusetts border. The "classic rock" stations had changed format, Reese noticed, so as to include bands that had sold the Seattle sound down the river. Reese was disappointed. It was his first negative cultural omen.

"I remember these lectures," offered Weatherly. "What were they called again? They hauled you in after dinner, right?"

"I don't know why I'm doing this," said Reese. "Some very strange shit went down last night. I think I got laid."

"Because they asked you to is why. Come on, you should be proud, and what do you mean you *think* you got laid? What the fuck does that mean?"

"Proud of what? They needed to fill a slot."

"To come back not as some schmuck like me, but as someone who's done something with himself. I mean, look at me. I'm tagging along. A tagalong. That's what I am on this trip. My fucking wife left me. You arrive in town and on your first night are complaining about getting laid, and I'm smoking and drinking again, and you . . . you . . . your copy even gets picked up in the paper of record from time to time. What do you have to complain about, for Christ's sake?"

"You never should have gotten married to begin with."

Weatherly didn't say anything to that. The curt bitterness, the indicting accuracy of his friend's statement filled him with rage. The clutter of 95 passed by, building his anger and self-loathing.

"Way to lead with the news, Reese," he said, tears coming to his eyes. "Your timing, as usual, is immaculate. Tell you what, you want to drive?"

Reese registered the quivering in his friend's voice. He was in no mood to defer to self-pity. The insanity of this trip, the scheduling fuckups, the full flights, the ugliness of America all conspired to create a bluntness in him, a paranoid cruelty that was, come to think of it, a Cambodia thing. The country had made him paranoid and cruel. As for his old friend, well, the guy had lost his grit. The Weatherly of their rowing life together was gone, and in his place there was only the emptiness, the ambiguity of adult life and a divorce. The Weatherly of the seven seat coming down on the last five hundred meters of a tight race, the Weatherly who whispered in his ear, who knew better than he, in the stroke seat, when to jack up the rating, that Weatherly, the superior athlete, the svelte rower at Reese's back, where was that wonderful boy now? Gone. Their speed and excellence had been usurped by the cruelty of time. Rowing together at Grove had given them a clarity of purpose the adult world could never offer. And now look at us, thought Reese, the old stroke bearing down to deliver his first-ever lecture in this unfathomable country he was supposed to call home, sitting next to his former seven seat, the two of them speeding backward in time to pay homage to the only place in their lives that had given them any real sense of victory. And they both knew it. They knew there was nothing they could do together now, as grown men, that could match the grace of their lives as rowers. There just wasn't anything that could approximate that exalted feeling of speed. And so they were left with their infantile memories. They had been good, as rowers, but never the best. They'd lost some close ones both in America and in England, and those losses, especially the last one, the tight one at Henley, still haunted Reese. So they did not talk about rowing. If they did, it would have been to admit its power over them. But in the tedium of the drive Reese wondered if Weatherly relived the big races in his mind's eye as he so often did, in bed, on airplanes, anywhere where mediocrity and boredom reigned: Reese returned to the water, to the shell running out from beneath him, sliding beyond the puddles of the previous stroke and coming up onto the next. Often he dreamt of the speed.

"She held you hostage, Kay did," said Reese. "It was a gun-to-the-head wedding, and you were both, especially you, way, way too young. And now you have a kid. How's your kid?"

"Her name is Penny, and she's fine."

"Good," replied Reese. "And look, don't feel that you're tagging along because you're not. I mean, you are, but that being said, I'm not sure I could do this one alone."

"Sure you could."

"Perhaps, but it would be deeply uncomfortable," said Reese. "Yesterday I woke up in this fascinatingly lethal country and now I'm on I-95."

In Phnom Penh the thought of being paid five hundred dollars to lecture Grove students had filled him with a lucrative felicity. Returning to the grounds of his adolescent malfeasance as a success story, oh, there were so many sunny ironies to savor there. The teachers who had meant something to him, who'd helped him along in life, to them he'd be excited to show off his minor celebrity. As to all the rest, all those at Grove he disliked, Reese couldn't wait to snub them. But all these feelings of vindication had occurred months ago when Headmaster Humphrey had first e-mailed him. Now he was car sick, nervous, and hungover. He'd prepared a slide show borrowing a few shots from Davies and Krantz but couldn't match up the images in Cambodia with the sunny faces of the well-heeled students of Grove School. They were incompatible extremes of his life that when forced to commingle increased his confusion and jet lag. He lit a cigarette and cracked open the window. The sky had clouded over to a heavy metallic cast. It was becoming a New England sky.

"I saw on the Weather Channel that it was supposed to snow," said Weatherly.

"What are you doing watching the Weather Channel?"

A few miles from the Grove School, Reese got out of the car to piss. His back ached. His eyeballs ached. It had been a more difficult drive than he had anticipated and his throat was dry and his bladder full. Spring was a soggy drag, and in the light rainfall he felt a broken promise. Massachusetts as an honorable way of life; it hadn't happened. Reese was wearing a green corduroy jacket and black jeans. When he'd first put on this outfit, he'd been pleased. Now he was ashamed. A corduroy jacket, the uniform of the secular humanist, the liberal. It marked him. He wished he had worn something more neutral. He pissed just off the curb of the road at the perimeter of an apple orchard. Dusk had quickly given way to a starless twilight. In the distance he scanned for armed apple-orchard workers but saw no one. One spring, many years ago, he'd been stung with a salt gun while making out beneath an apple tree with a girl whose name currently escaped him. The migrant apple pickers enjoyed taking potshots at Grove students. Reese looked at his watch. He had two hours to kill before his lecture. He was fidgety and nervous. The proximity of his old school was undermining him. Perhaps it was the New England night. It had arrived too quickly.

"Let's go into town," he said.

"A package store," said Weatherly. "Isn't that what they call them here?"

"Yes!" exclaimed Reese. "A packy."

In town was a lesser school than Grove. It was called Fairfield, and Reese was glad to see the fashion of the student body hadn't changed since his day. The boys still wore flannels and tan work boots. The girls smoked. Reese and Weatherly passed by the hangout, the Grove House of Pizza, feeling the old animosities.

"I wonder if Hollins is still headmaster?" offered Weatherly.

Hollins—now that was a name Reese was glad to forget. He had been a severe disciplinarian, an overbearing mathematician who, upon sensing a lack of upward mobility at Grove, had become headmaster at nearby Fairfield. In his first year in power, Hollins was said to have thrown out scores of students, purging Fairfield of the metal heads and pot smokers. During a hockey game, Reese had been blindsided into the boards, decked by a Fairfield winger who upon impact had muttered in his ear, "That's for giving us Hollins."

Reese now felt sorry for Fairfield. Hollins was the type to hang on to power, and it was not at all inconceivable that for the last sixteen years the Fairfield townies had had to put up with his bitter New England zealotry.

Weatherly came out of the package store with a pint of Popov vodka and cigarettes. Popov; it was a time trip.

"I didn't even drink that rotgut in college," said Reese.

"I know," said Weatherly, breaking the seal. "But since this is a sentimental journey, I thought we'd make it a sentimental journey."

Weatherly took a swig and passed the bagged bottle to Reese. In the lights of the connected storefront windows Reese opened up his throat. Vodka streamed into his empty stomach, and tears welled up in his eyes. He had to meditate away a puking reflex.

"Chaser," said Reese. "We need chaser."

They walked into the Grove House of Pizza for chaser. Fairfield students glanced up from their video games and grinders in leering disrespect. Even the video games bleeped an electronic dismay at their arrival. Suddenly Reese was happy to have Weatherly along. He sensed a joyful belligerence build in his divorced friend. He was enjoying the hostility from three Fairfield boys lounging at a nearby table. Two sported attempts at mustaches; all had advanced cases of acne.

"We'll have two Cokes and a steak and cheese grinder," said Weatherly at the counter. "Or is it hoagie? I can't remember what you're supposed to call anything up here anymore."

The Grove House of Pizza, in Reese's day, was run by a family of Greeks from Pylos. He'd had a crush on one of the daughters, a fine brunette. Now he saw no sign of the former owners. Perhaps they had already made their fortune and moved on.

"You hear that, Mikey," said one of the Fairfield students. "The preppy doesn't know what the fuck you call your sub."

"Sub," said Weatherly, turning to face down the trio. "Yeah, a sub. I guess that's another option. How much for the sub and two Cokes?"

"Preppy fucks," came a voice. "What are you guys, substitute teachers?"

"We," replied Weatherly, "control the means of production."

Reese was horrified. At the cash register was a blond woman with winged hair. Her greasy young face barely reached up over the cash register.

"Shut your trap, Johnny," she said to the table and rang up the order.

"Shut your trap, Johnny," mocked Johnny.

"You too, Phipps," she said.

"Johnny and Phipps," said Weatherly, taking a swig from the bottle. "I like that."

"Shut it," said Reese in Weatherly's ear and then slammed a ten onto the counter. The Grove House of Pizza was silent as she made change.

"Could we have the Cokes now?" said Weatherly. "My friend is thirsty."

"You can't drink that in here," said the girl with the winged hair, pointing to the bottle.

"Fine," said Weatherly. "We'll be outside with our Cokes."

"Good," she said. "I'll call you when your order is up."

"Did anyone ever tell you," said Weatherly, "that you're a dead ringer for Debbie Gibson?"

"I said I'd call you when your order's up."

Reese took Weatherly by the sleeve and guided him out of the Grove House of Pizza. They walked around back to a small parking lot. Reese had forgotten about this protected nook. Ventilators from the connected storefront businesses blew exhaust in the direction of a BFI dumpster. Then there was a litter-infested wooded area that led down to an abandoned set of train tracks. This was where skateboarders, Fairfield students, and the town youth gathered to smoke pot and avoid the police. Reese had always been slightly scared of this hidden back lot. It was not Grove turf.

"Look," said Reese. "I hate to say this but I have a lecture to give."

He took the bottle from Weatherly's hand and chased a shot. This one went much more smoothly.

"I've got to do something with myself," said Weatherly. "I can't remember the last time I did something constructive with my life."

"Harassing Fairfield students isn't what I'd call constructive."

"I know, I know," interrupted Weatherly. "It doesn't come under the rubric of constructive engagement."

"I'm ashamed to see Ramsdale," said Weatherly.

Everyone who rowed under Ramsdale had been marked by the man. Ramsdale's cosmos was filled with moral relativists and weaklings unfit for the trials of rowing.

Reese was touched by his friend's fear of Ramsdale. In adult life, he too had been haunted by the old coach's voice. Even out of college Reese bumped up against Ramsdale's guilt-inspiring worldview. But as the years went by, Reese had eventually come to realize that life was not rowing, and rowing not life. Over time he'd arrived at a vision of Ramsdale that was not far from the truth: the man was a broken-down New England zealot, driven by his own bitter isolation and addiction to whiskey.

Weatherly, Reese discovered, was suffering from an inability to put Ramsdale and the cult of rowing in perspective. He took another swig from the pint and put his arms around his friend's shoulder.

"Look," he said. "Ramsdale is a sour New England psycho."

"I know, I know," said Weatherly. "But I still feel like I've failed him. My whole life, I feel as if I failed him."

There came a clamoring of voices from the top of the parking lot. Reese turned. Someone was carrying a hockey stick. He saw the blade of the stick rise like a scythe and fall to the pavement.

"We've got your grinder," came a voice. "Come and get it."

In the partial light it was difficult to see how many of them there were. But it did not matter. Suddenly they were coming.

"The train tracks," whispered Weatherly.

Running down the small hill, Reese tripped and fell. This was absurd. He was rolling in dirt. Getting up, he was hit in the back by a rock. He ran. Another rock stung him in the back of the head. An unarticulated panic and rage filled him, but he did not look back. He was sprinting, but his legs felt spongy and weak. His mind was clear but sorely unable to channel fear and energy down to his legs, which were noodling. When his foot struck a wooden rail bed, he just saved himself from falling again. That was it. He scampered sideways off into the woods and lay down on his stomach. His lungs burned in his chest. In the distance, the Fairfield students' laughter and townie jive contorted the night.

"Fuckin' A, Johnny . . ."

"Ya preppy fahts . . ."

And then various things about mothers.

The applause for Reese was polite to tepid. There was a gold-plated eagle on top of a well-shellacked lectern. As he placed

Weatherly's drink in a well holder, he looked out at the crowd and breathed out. He'd lost his glasses at the train tracks. Now he found himself squinting myopically at his notes.

"Well," he said. "Thank you all, thank you, and it's great to be back at Grove."

Feedback filled the hall. In the lights his audience was a watery abstraction. He took a sip of his drink and coughed. He caught a glimpse of Susan Rivers darting to one side of the room.

"And I'd like to especially thank Headmaster Humphrey for having me back to the scene of so many adolescent crimes."

There was no laughter. The feedback continued.

"Don't talk so close to the mike," hissed a voice.

Reese pulled back. His stomach dropped. The vodka was strengthening the gastrointestinal collision between East and West. He had gas, and if he wasn't vigilant he would shortly shit his pants.

"And I'd like to thank Susan Rivers for that wonderful introduction. I didn't . . . I didn't know I had worked for that many news organizations until she spelled it all out for us tonight. Like people, some news organizations are better than others. I'd like to thank Richard Weatherly, Grove class of 1982, for coming back with me and babysitting."

Still no laughter. What was up with these kids? In the middle distance Reese could hear paper shuffling. Maybe they were doing their homework.

"There are some people in this world who have a very negative view of journalists. Much of this negativity may have some grounding, some of it may simply be neurotic speculation. For instance, and I kinda hate to do this, but Janet Malcolm, the notorious critic of psychoanalysis and author of *The Journalist and the*

Murderer, once wrote, 'Every journalist who is not too stupid or too full of himself to notice what is going on knows that what he does is morally indefensible. He is a kind of confidence man, preying on people's vanity, ignorance, or loneliness, gaining their trust and betraying them without remorse.'

"I am here today to say that this does not have to be the case. In Cambodia, enough people are physically preying upon one another that as a journalist, I feel a moral obligation to be as accurate and fair as possible. I do not feel and never have felt the need to prey upon anyone. Yes, as a journalist it is important to gain confidence in one's sources, and I suppose I have more than once betrayed that confidence, but it has always served a . . . I won't use the word noble . . . a worthwhile end; accurate, important information delivered to my readers."

Here Reese paused and drank from his cup.

"I'm very excited about Grove's new dark rooms and though I'm not a news photographer myself, I've spent some quality time with them, so tonight I'm just going to try to give you some sense of what covering the news in Cambodia entails and show you some pictures, okay, but first I'm going to give a small talk about something called news hole."

Reese did his number. He talked about news hole and its shrinkage in American newspapers. He spoke briefly and bitterly of the Gannett chain and the focus-group-driven nature of American media. Then he made his pitch for overseas. He spoke of the *Cambodia Daily,* where he'd worked for a year and a half before leaping over to the wires. He gave the *Daily* a nice little stump speech. If any of these kids was going to go into journalism, the *Daily* might be a good place to start after college. He spoke about the difficulty of establishing body counts in a war-torn country.

Worried about slurring, he watched out for words beginning with *sh*.

"First slide, please," he said.

A silence came over the crowd. Susan Rivers suddenly appeared in the front row and pointed at the left-hand side of the lectern. He'd forgotten that the slide machine control unit was in his hand. He tossed it to Susan, who thankfully and quite smoothly caught it.

"Susan's going to be running the show tonight."

"All right!" screamed some punk in the back row. Reese laughed, but increasingly he found he needed the lectern to stand. Things were shifting. He was moving vaguely outside himself. He seemed to be taking small snapshots of things in his peripheral vision.

"The good news about photography and one of the reasons I often envy my colleagues in that field is the following: it only takes one one-thousandth of a second to take a good photograph. The only problem is having the guts to get there, to get in the right position from which to take the important news photograph."

Reese liked that bit. It was tough talk, very Hemingway. He doubted if any of the Grove students had what it took to get there.

"As the immortal war photographer Robert Capa once said, 'If your pictures aren't good enough, you're not close enough.' But what does close enough really mean? After all, Robert Capa died getting too close."

The first slide was upside down and woefully out of focus. A chuckle rippled through the room. Thank God Susan was on the ball. She quickly sharpened the image.

"You can keep it upside down, Susan," he said.

It was one of Reese's favorites. Davies, a Reuters photographer, was standing next to a badly mangled white car with the word NEWS printed on the white hood in red. The top of the windshield was cracked at the spot where Davies had struck his head. Reese had taken the shot with Davies's camera.

"I call this," said Reese, "the great Cambodian insurance shot. I took this photograph after a nasty car accident. You see, there was this Scandinavian stringer, and she made the rather stupid decision that our driver had been driving for too long. She insisted on taking over the wheel after a very long day in a hostile environment. This was the result. She sideswiped an ox cart and then slammed into a tree. The car's axle was broken and this photograph was submitted as the official Reuters news agency's insurance shot. The Khmer Rouge, who had staked a position in the mountains on the left, later stripped the car. We were lucky to get back to Phnom Penh."

That was a bit of vain bravado, but what the fuck, he thought.

In the back well of the auditorium stood a lone man not associated with Grove. He wore a full-length black leather overcoat, and inside the pocket of Glen's overcoat was a Motorola walkie-talkie. The other handset was in the possession of a man named Dwayne. Dwayne was very stoned. He was stoned and sitting in his sedan outside the schoolhouse listening to music. Dwayne and his boss did not share musical tastes, and so now with the boss inside this building, he was trying to soak up Snoop Doggy Dogg's *Doggy Style,* but he was having a difficult time getting with Snoop tonight. No one was watching his back and he nervously looked into the rearview mirror. The moonlight on the circular field scared him, as did the alien architecture. Nestled beneath

Dwayne's right leg was a nine-millimeter. "The Fine Nine" is what he called it. Dwayne was under instructions to sit. He was quite good at that. He did a lot of sitting at the Stopless. He was incredibly fat and he did what he was told. That being said, this was the first time he had been out of New York with his boss, Glen. All the way from the Gramercy Park Hotel they'd tailed Weatherly and Reese. Dwayne did not know why. Stoned, he did what he was told. He drove. Now his instructions were to sit. His instructions were to sit and see if either Weatherly or Reese came out of the building. If that occasion were to come about, he was to notify his boss on the walkie-talkie. Dwayne was getting paid time and a half. In some ways it was a welcome change from the Stopless. He was taking a hit off his joint when the interior of his sedan was suddenly flooded with light. Dwayne quickly stabbed the joint out in the ashtray and reached for his walkie-talkie. A man was getting out of a green truck not unlike something from the city's Parks Department. A Parks Department cop, thought Dwayne, no problem. Dwayne snapped off the music and spoke into his walkie-talkie, "Got company."

"Come back," came Glen's voice.

"Some cracker, I got company."

"Get rid of him, but don't fucking shoot him."

"Check."

Dwayne put the sedan in reverse and angled it so that his beams lit the oncoming figure. It was not in uniform. In Dwayne's headlights was an elderly white man. This elderly white man tried to shade his eyes. Dwayne flipped on the high beams. He was wearing green pants and a thick flannel jacket. The man was short and bowlegged and now he was tapping on the tinted window of Dwayne's black Lincoln. Dwayne did nothing. The man continued to rap on the window. With every knock, Dwayne grew more agitated. He didn't like the sound of this bum-fuck country cracker knocking his vehicle. He opened the window a slit.

"What you want?"

"I'm fairly familiar with all the vehicles on school grounds, sir, . . . but I've never seen this car so I was kinda wondering . . . I was kinda, well, you know . . ."

"Wondering what a nigger's doing in a place like this, right? Well, I tell you something, it's none of your business, so why don't you get your sorry ass out of my face, Mr. Massachusetts. I don't dig your state."

The man stepped back from the window. It turned out he too had a walkie-talkie. Dwayne could just hear the crackle of communication. After a moment, the man returned to the window.

"Sir, this is private property you're trespassing on. It is a private school, private grounds. I've just radioed the town police, who will be here in," he looked down at his watch, "in approximately seven minutes. You can leave now or deal with them later."

Dwayne rolled up the window.

"Glen, hey, Glen, come in."

Glen had a stiletto in his pocket, and the long drive north had put him in a cutting mood. This wasn't how the day was supposed to have panned out. If things had gone as planned, he would have simply followed this Reese to the post office to make sure his package was in the mail. Instead, Reese had gotten into a car with this other guy he actually recognized from the Stopless. He was a regular. This coincidence he found suspicious.

At first Glen thought Weatherly and Reese were heading for

Boston, perhaps to make a drop instead of mailing the package to him. Then they'd arrived here, and he'd made it for a small-town deal. Everywhere he sensed betrayal. It was his nature. He had made a living out of chiseling and cheating everyone from the city of New York to his own employees. Still, he was badly in debt. That was why this package was so central to his well-being. He had little doubt that someone was trying to rip him off and so the idea was to stay vigilant. Now he wished he had wired Julie's old boyfriend at least a third of the money as downpayment on the drugs. Then it would be clear that people were down to him. But as it stood, the only leverage he had was on the sale side. Now, the only thing he was certain of was that he was dealing with amateurs and about this he was equally hopeful and bitter. Glen had moved around drugs long enough to know that one never knew. All would be settled soon, he told himself. If only Clark Kent at the pedestal would finish his fucking speech and make his move. Then he and Dwayne would bear down on whomever Clark Kent and his blond butt-boy were dealing with and get both the money and the goods. The weird part was, he'd seen the butt-boy before. A few months ago they'd spoken of Wayne Gretzky's trade to the New York Rangers. He and the butt-boy, they'd spoken of the Great One. Glen didn't think the Great One had it left in him. The butt-boy had disagreed. Now Glen kept an eye on him. Maybe he was the key to all this. Maybe it was the butt-boy who was holding. Glen's overcoat pockets were filled with Yellow Jackets. They were tablets of low-grade speed, and with the lights out he swallowed another one dry. Suddenly the butt-boy was getting up. Glen's heart fluttered in anticipation. The blond guy was leaving the auditorium in the middle of his partner's speech.

"Glen," came Dwayne's voice. Glen turned the volume down

and exited the back of the auditorium. "Glen, man, we got to ride. They just called the cops on me."

Glen hissed into his handset.

"They what?"

"This fuck just radioed the cops. The cops, they're coming."

"You fucking stupid-ass nigger," said Glen. "They'll get a description of the car. I'll be out in two minutes."

Glen followed Weatherly down a long corridor. Along the walls were framed photographs and letters from presidents.

"He's in the bathroom," said Glen into the walkie-talkie. "I'm going to flush his shit."

"Check," said Dwayne. "But make it quick, though, like real quick."

At an adjacent urinal Glen took up position and listened to his prey piss. All day and for much of the night he'd been waiting for this moment to arrive. The sound of the butt-boy's piss pleased him. He couldn't decide if he should jump him in midstream or catch him zipping up his fly. It was almost too easy.

"When you got to go, you got to go," said Glen. "Looks like you got to go bad."

Weatherly's head turned sideways and Glen watched as his features contorted in recognition.

"Why, you're that guy . . . from the . . . from the . . . What are you doing here?"

Glen shoved Weatherly's shoulder. Piss splattered upon his black leather jacket. Then he caught Weatherly in the balls with his steel-tipped boot.

"I'm only going to ask you this once," he said. "So look at me, motherfucker."

Weatherly was hunched over, gasping for air.

"Look at me!"

Weatherly's watery blue eyes turned upward. Glen grabbed his cheek in one hand and with the other clicked open his stiletto and placed the flat side of the blade beneath Weatherly's chin.

"Where," said Glen, "might I find my package?"

"Your what?"

Glen crushed the bridge of Weatherly's nose with the handle of the knife. Weatherly fell to his knees. It had been years since someone had done anything remotely violent to his soft body, and now numb, helpless oblivion crept over him. Then Glen reached inside Weatherly's waistband, grabbed his boxer underwear, and pulled.

"It's wedgy time," said Glen. "How does that feel, huh? Sort of like a homecoming, right? Underwear riding up your butt crack, isn't it, butt-boy? And the weird part is you're sort of liking it."

"What do you want from me?" moaned Weatherly.

"Your partner, he was supposed to have sent me a very important package. The contents of this package have a great deal to do with my financial health."

Glen went over to the toilet bowl and pissed in it. Then he dragged Weatherly by his underwear into the stall.

"You pissed all over my coat, asshole."

"Oh, fuck, please, mister, don't . . . Please stop. I'm telling you, mister, I don't know what the fuck you're talking about. If I did, I swear to God it's not like I'm with the French Resistance. I mean, if I knew what you wanted, I swear I'd tell you. I swear to God I would. I'd tell you but he hasn't mentioned anything about . . . about . . ."

Glen grabbed Weatherly by the hair and dunked his head in the toilet bowl.

"Tell your partner I'm watching him, and that when he doesn't go to the post office or deliver the goods directly to my place of residence and then skips town, it pisses me off. You got that? Tell him I'm expecting a delivery."

Glen ran out of the building and leapt into the sedan. Dwayne stepped on it, fishtailed, and began a loop around the circle. Then they were out the gates, and on some country back road.

"Is that gun registered?" asked Glen.

"What the fuck you think?"

"Get rid of it."

"Glen, daddy, this is my Fine Nine."

"Dwayne, if you want to stay in my employ, get rid of that unregistered weapon. In the woods there, toss it. And for fuck's sake open your window. This car reeks."

"No," said Dwayne. "This is my Fine Nine."

Glen breathed out. They were bumping along a road that was a long way from New York City. There were cows here.

"Fuck it," said Glen. "This sucks, the whole trip, goddamn it. I don't know what I was thinking. We should have jumped them in the city."

"We could go back and find 'em," said Dwayne.

"We could go back and find 'em," mocked Glen. "With the cops and the ambulance there to take care of butt-boy. That would be great, Dwayne. A return to the scene of a crime. I tell you what happens now. Get us back to the city, motherfucker. Take some back roads for an hour or so and then find a sign for 95. You got that?"

"I got it," said Dwayne. "But I ain't losing my Fine Nine."

"Fine," said Glen. "This isn't my car. But let me tell you something, Dwayne. Right now the Massachusetts police have your license plate number in their computer. They're going to be running a check on you, brother. Carrying an unlicensed weapon last time I looked is a major-league parole violation."

"Man," said Dwayne. "Man, you got to understand. This is my Fine Nine."

chapter six

WEATHERLY SAT in the front seat, moaning. Already both his eyes were clouding up. His hand was wrapped in ice and paper towels were strewn about the cabin of Susan River's car. Susan Rivers and her famous breasts drove in silent awe. Occasionally she'd come out of her thoughts, shake her head, and say, "It's just so strange." Then she'd collapse back into herself and come up with "I feel so—God, I don't know—so invaded. . . ." Reese remembered their route from the buses driving to and from away games and from holidays. It was strange being so low to the ground. When they got to the hospital, Susan Rivers got out of the car and rushed to the emergency entrance. Weatherly turned to Reese. It was the first time they'd been alone.

"He was after *you*," he said.

His nose was black and so bloated that his eyes squinted at him.

"What?" he replied. "They weren't Fairfield townies?"

"Not at all," said Weatherly. "I actually know where the guy works. He says you have a package for him. He wants some package delivered."

"What?" replied Reese. "What the fuck are you talking about? Oh, shit, the mail. I forgot to mail the mail."

"Look," said Weatherly. "My nose no longer exists. It's, like, spread all over my face. If I were you I'd go home. Go to your mom's place. They won't know about your mom. I'll call you at your mom's."

"Who the fuck are 'they'?"

"Whoever," said Weatherly, sucking spittle in for breath, "fucked my face up is who. They'll do worse to you."

Susan Rivers came out of the hospital with an actual doctor in a white lab coat. Nashoba was a semirural hospital. During Reese's day at Grove, the majority of Nashoba's cases had come from the nearby army base, which had recently been downsized. Weatherly slowly got out of the car.

"Okay," said the doctor, placing his arm behind Weatherly's back. "Tilt your head back."

"Dr. Harrington, this is Mr. Weatherly," said Susan Rivers.

"I remember you," said Weatherly. "You're still here? You set my arm after a hockey game my sixth-form year."

Susan Rivers drove Reese to the Littleton train station. She had a schedule in her car. He'd get into Penn Station at two in the morning, she informed him, but that was the best she could do. A few passengers stood at lonely intervals illuminated by the platform lights. Susan Rivers parked her car and lit a cigarette. A cigarette; so much had happened that he forgot he smoked. He patted himself down for cigarettes but couldn't find one. Silently she handed him her pack and exhaled. A newer, tougher Susan Rivers was emerging.

"Weatherly has spilled his blood on your shirt," said Reese.

She didn't answer him.

"You know," she said, "I wish I could get on the train with you. Sometimes I really do."

"It'll be okay," said Reese, taking a lock of her splendid dark hair in his hand and moving it behind her shoulder. "You'll find someone again."

"Last month," she said, exhaling against the window. "Last month, Coach Weirhman made a pass at me. I literally vomited. I got back to my apartment and vomited."

"He's a careerist," said Reese. "A Grove School careerist. You don't want to be that, do you?"

"Of course not."

"Well, then, leave."

"I don't," said Susan Rivers, tears coming to her eyes, "know where to go anymore."

A train whistle sounded deep in the depths of the night. Reese ached for her. He turned her shoulder gently toward him and they kissed. Now he had his hand on a famous breast. Her hair splayed out onto the side of his face as she flung herself sideways into him. Her tongue was thick and skilled. Then she suddenly pulled away.

"Go," she said. "Go get your train."

"How do I get in touch with you?" he asked through the window.

"At the library," she said. "Call me at the library."

"I'll do that," said Reese.

"I'll send you your slides," she said. "But you've got to call me."

"I'll do that."

"Your speech," she said. "It wasn't that bad. I mean, it was a disaster, but at least it was an interesting disaster. *I learned some-thing.*"

"That's all that counts," said Reese and he ran for the train.

At South Station he bought a pint of Maker's Mark and nursed it as he waited for his connection to Penn Station. He'd been lucky. The hour for Massachusetts liquor stores had long passed but he'd seen a Chinese man in the back of his store taking inventory and had pressed a twenty against the window. The Chinese man had looked down at his inventory sheet, looked back up at Reese, squinted at him, and then opened his door a crack. The Chinese and their secrets, thought Reese. They were a godsend. Reese was glad to be wearing his corduroy jacket now, and with a pint of bourbon in his hand, he toasted the uniform of the secular humanist and waited for the train. When it arrived, he took a seat and was shortly awakened by a conductor.

"We've reached Penn Station, sir."

Now he sat on the bed smelling his laundry. Each shirt was spotless and crisp. His pants were creased. It was incredible, even more miraculous than boundless amounts of clean ice. But standing up again, the room whirled dangerously. He stumbled toward the door and turned off the overhead light. He went into the bathroom and drank water. Then he called his mother.

"Yes?" came a tired voice.

It was Reese's mother's new boyfriend. They had never met.

"Let me speak to my mother."

"Peggy," came the voice. "It's your son."

There was a long silence.

"My what?" came a voice in the muffled distance.

"Your son."

"Oh."

"Mother," said Reese when she was on the line. "Mother, I'm in Phnom Penh. I'm at the airport on the VIP line so I don't have much time. Sorry to call so late but I've been really busy. I'm coming home, though. I should be home this time, this time tomorrow. Yeah, tomorrow."

"Harry?"

"Mother, I'll be home tomorrow."

"Harry, darling?"

Reese hung up the phone.

He turned on the bedside lamp. At the far side of the bed the mail sat in a tidy pile. He reached for the top letter and was about to tear it open when he thought of his mother's red kettle. He'd get to the bottom of this tomorrow with the red kettle. He'd steam the mail open. Then with the lights still on he went to sleep. He dreamt of the bitter fruit. He was lost in the grounds of a pagoda. His notepad was drenched with water and he kept flipping the pages in order to come up with a dry sheet. Buddhist statues whirled about his head. It was a dream strangely intertwined with remembrance. The day after the grenade attack, he had visited the pagoda into which eyewitnesses had claimed the grenade throwers had run. The pagoda, it evolved, fronted an army compound reserved for Hun Sen's elite guard. There he'd interviewed a few of Hun Sen's troops standing about in the heat. They'd been eating a green fruit in the shape of a grenade. His translator said it was called "the bitter fruit." It was a detail one could never print, but it had stuck with him and confirmed his suspicion that Hun Sen was behind the attack. The guards had smiled and laughed at his questions. Did he want a bite? No, they had not been on duty during the attack. It was too hot to talk. He had better move along. No, they did not know who had been on duty the previous day. Then they had laughed at him and broken off a bit of the fruit for him to taste. Then they'd pointed their guns at his chest and told him to move along.

The geography had been creepy. Only once one was inside the grounds of the pagoda did the interconnections become apparent: Hun Sen's military compound, the American embassy, the pagoda. They all backed onto one another but publicly fronted different streets. In the dream he was wandering through pathways imbued with secret connections, conspiracies, and dark allegiances, wandering with his wet notepad until he came to a bright square. There a cluster of troops dressed in dark green camouflage were throwing bitter fruit at his feet with the unspoken understanding that one was the real thing, a live grenade. One of the troops kicked his legs out from underneath him and he was on all fours scrambling to find the grenade. But he could not find the grenade. Everywhere he went he was squeezing the outer shell of this awful green fruit. Finally he felt something hard bounce off his back. He turned. It was the grenade, pin pulled, ready to blow. As he lunged for it, a soldier's boot sent the grenade bouncing end over end across the square. Now he was running for it, now he had it in his hand, now an epic energy was filling his soul for the great throw but it was all moving in this dreadfully deliberate slow motion. Instead of the quick release, his right arm stretched back and back until there came a great flash and he woke up in his bed.

chapter seven

REESE WALKED INTO the Racquet Club and was handed his roll of athletic gear as if he had never been away. He stretched out in the newly renovated weight room, and noticed that George Plimpton was on one of the new Concept II ergometers. Plimpton looked to be rowing at a pleasant twenty-four strokes per minute. Well, good for George, thought Reese, a man his age still on the erg. Reese got up and sat down on the erg next to George Plimpton. He grabbed the handle, adjusted the flywheel, and took off. It had been a long time since he'd been on an erg. The machine was well oiled and hummed pleasantly, giving digital readouts at every stroke. In high school and college he'd hated these machines. They were made to torture and, though brutal in their honesty, they did not necessarily translate into speed on the water. Nevertheless, it was a kick to be rowing next to Plimpton. Shortly, he found himself getting in synch with the man. Reese was getting through the stroke a beat faster than the older man, but this only left him more time to drift up to the next stroke. For ten minutes Reese and the famous writer rowed at a comfortable twenty-five strokes per minute. Then Plimpton began to jack up the rating to twenty-six, then twenty-eight.

Reese followed. It was a Plimpton sprint at the end of his piece. The man was losing ratio but what the fuck. Reese was impressed. Plimpton got up off the machine after twenty minutes. Reese, who had been on twelve, was already exhausted. In the mirror he watched as Plimpton put a towel around his neck. He would have to keep rowing for at least another eight minutes, eight minutes or until Plimpton left the room. Shortly he began to feel the old, numbing exhaustion. After three more minutes, Plimpton left the room. Reese rowed on. He couldn't just stop right as Plimpton exited. How would that look to all the other men who'd no doubt taken notice of their erging? Reese's legs burned. In the mirror he noticed he'd turned beet red. Finally he stopped and crawled over to the stretching mat, lay on his back, and breathed.

"What in the world is my problem?" he whispered.

Weatherly came into the room dressed in whites and carrying two court-tennis racquets and with a huge bandage over his nose. He had two swollen black eyes.

"Get over here," he said. "I have much to tell you."

"You look like you're wearing mascara," said Reese.

"I know, isn't it something? I've been going quite insane."

They bound up another flight of steps and went through a door that gave onto a narrow corridor with photographs of great court-tennis players of the past. Many of them had mustaches or Ironside sideburns. They turned a corner. This room had green carpeting and couches. Through one window Reese could see the sloping net of the court.

"This is it," said Weatherly. "Welcome to our assigned cathedral."

It was not unlike a church, thought Reese. There was a set of observation pews behind a twine net that ran horizontally against a section of a back wall. Now they were standing in a large atrium with sunlight sprinkling down from the windowed roof. The sounds echoed. Reese found himself inordinately breathless.

"How can you play with that nose?"

"It's set," said Weatherly. "I'm a mouth breather anyway and I need the exercise."

Reese's heart was fibrillating and his knees felt weak.

"I have a feeling," said Weatherly, serving a ball along a raised shelf, "that your problems have to do with a strip joint."

Weatherly's return rolled gently along the raised shelf, forcing Reese into a cramped corner. His racquet kissed the back wall, disrupting the timing necessary to make contact with the little blurry white thing. Nearly bounceless, the ball touched the floor and rolled toward Reese's cornered feet. They played on. There was a nice long rally that ended in Reese smashing a winner into the horizontal net at Weatherly's back.

"Swish," said Reese. "I love that spot."

These were the first peaceful moments Reese had enjoyed since coming home. His worries dropped off the shelf of his mind. He focused on the ball, and he moved. It was a game of anticipation and movement. What Weatherly had to say about a strip joint was of little consequence. He enjoyed watching the ball run along the slate mantel above his head, gauging where it would fall and getting there to return it. In that sense it was not unlike roofball. You chased down the angles. For a moment he saw himself as a third-former at Grove tossing the tennis ball and crying out some other boy's name. Happier times for sure. He loved slate. It was a rare thing these days. What had happened to slate? Even blackboards weren't made of slate anymore.

After the game they walked downstairs and sat in the steam room. Reese began to cough.

"All that commie air you've been breathing," said Weatherly. "It ain't good for you, chief."

"No," agreed Reese. "It isn't. The air is filled with dust and deprivation."

"Dust and deprivation," said Weatherly, "that doesn't sound so healthy."

It was incredibly hot in the steam room and Reese was suddenly visited by claustrophobia. Once he'd seen a movie where the bad guy locked the hero in the steam room, left the guy there to steam. How the hero got out, Reese couldn't remember, but wouldn't it be nasty, he thought through the mist, wouldn't it be fucking ghastly to be locked in here? The tiles shimmered in dangerous abstractions. Weatherly was a pink blob across the way. He couldn't see his friend's face. Imagine being locked in the steam room. You'd slowly roast. Reese considered it. First there would be the compounded heat and then every ounce of water in your body would drip away until you passed out and were found a prune on the scalding tiles.

"I'm going to get out of here," he said.

"Come on," said Weatherly. "We just got in."

The fact that Weatherly was enjoying himself made his inability to take the steam room even more frustrating. His heart began to race.

"A strip joint, huh?" asked Reese.

"Yes," said Weatherly. "A place called the Stopless. I didn't tell you earlier, but the guy who took my nose out works at the Stopless. I've, uh . . . been frequenting the Stopless because there's this bartendress . . . this bartendress who . . ."

"Who what?"

"Who I like a lot."

"I'm sure," said Reese, "that she rises well above her circumstances."

"Fuck off," said Weatherly. "She'll know what's up. But what the fuck are you doing carrying people's mail?"

"Everyone does it," said Reese. "It's a kind of ritual over there. The mail takes months, so if you know someone who is leaving, you give him something to mail. I just didn't know this guy Asher was going to . . . you know . . . screw me over."

"Who is this Asher?"

"Asher is a friend of mine, a source. We play tennis together."

"A friend of yours, huh? Well, with friends like that, who needs an asshole. I suggest you call this Asher."

"I don't know his number."

Reese left the steam room, turned a corner, and ran right into Tom Chandler. For a moment Chandler didn't register Reese, who'd been friends with his older brother in grade school. Chandler had a towel over his shoulder, the beginnings of a premature receding hairline, and the same baby-smooth face. Reese had never seen Chandler except at the Racquet Club, where they'd played backgammon half a dozen times.

"Hey," said Chandler. "It's . . . it's, yeah, Reese, how you doing, old man?"

Old man, Reese thought, what an asshole. Chandler was wearing jeans, a light blue button-down shirt under a double-breasted navy blazer. A head of a fox was embroidered in gold upon the dark velvet tops of his slippers, which he wore sockless. Reese found it difficult to take his eyes from the foxes. Chandler was four years his junior and there he was with gold foxes.

"I'm doing fine, Tom," said Reese. "How you coming along?"

"Want to roll some later?" he asked.

"Sure," said Reese. "Sure, I'll roll some with you, Tom."

"Good," said Chandler, giving Reese a Racquet Club wink. "I'll see you down there in half an hour."

Reese sat hunched over in the locker room waiting for his body to stop sweating. Then he walked over to the scale and weighed himself. Jesus Christ, he was down. Healthy for Reese was 170, maybe 175. Now, if he wasn't in such revolting shape, he could almost make a lightweight crew team. He was down to 160. Then he took a long, extremely pleasurable shower. The spigot was right above his head and it rained down strong, healthy water upon his body. New York water and court tennis: so far they were the only things that had given his vacation a modicum of comfort.

Weatherly walked into the shower room.

"I could nearly make the lightweights," said Reese.

"Sure, yeah, right, the lightweights with the way you smoke, yeah, sure, the lightweights, right. But keep saying that to yourself."

"Hey, I think George Plimpton out-erged me: bet you've never had that pleasure."

"Plimpton, huh?" said Weatherly. "Well, good for him."

"I just ran into Chandler. He wants to play backgammon at the bar. I'll see you down there."

"He'll take your money," said Weatherly. "The man does nothing else. It is the center of his universe."

The Racquet Club's changing room was one of Reese's favorite places in New York. As he walked to his cubicle he noticed a napping old man stretched out on a leather couch with a green towel half wrapped about him and a *Wall Street Journal* splayed at his feet. Reese's changing cubicle reminded him of his old cubicle at Grove. As he changed, he studied the opposing wall, where wooden placards sported names of the victorious men of various racquet sports. Many of them, no doubt, were dead now. The dead champs. Reese wondered how many of them had been with the CIA. Well, he thought, we all have our little day in the sun.

He walked down the main staircase, past the cigarette and cigar stand, and entered the bar. Chandler was sitting at the far end of the room, having already secured a table. To deal with Chandler would require a drink. He approached the bar and ordered a pint but when it arrived, he realized he'd forgotten his membership number.

"I'm sorry," he said to the bartender. "My number has escaped me. I've been away for too long."

"We'll settle it somehow, sir," said the bartender. "Just print your name at the bottom."

"Thank you," said Reese and approached Chandler with his pint.

Reese lost the first game but came back with a very satisfying back-game victory in the second. Then Chandler began to chat, perhaps to throw off Reese's concentration. He wanted to know about Cambodia and Reese did not want to tell him. Currently Chandler was working as an analyst for a financial concern which, in his absence from the city, had been taken over by another company. Weatherly arrived and took a seat next to Reese. His friend began to hurt his luck and when Chandler doubled the cue early, he conceded.

"That was smart," said Chandler. "I got a lot of points early. So, I hear your sister is getting married, but none of us have ever heard of him."

"How do you mean, none of *us*?" asked Reese, sensing that his sister had had something going on with Chandler while he'd been in Cambodia.

"Well, you know, people," said Chandler. "People who are generally . . . I don't know, generally known."

"I understand she met him on a golf course in Boca Raton. It all happened terribly quickly."

Chandler laughed at that.

"Old Sallie met her boy in Boca. I hear he's nearly twice her age."

"To tell you the truth," said Reese, "I can't tell how old anyone is anymore."

Like the numbers on the doubling die, his hatred for Chandler was increasing exponentially. Real hatred for an opponent was not good when it came to backgammon. After hitting one of Reese's open men, Chandler doubled the cue. Reese took it. Chandler smiled. For a long, maddening time Reese couldn't roll a five to come in. Then Chandler doubled up on the five spot and, as they say, closed the door. Now all Reese could do was sit and wait to lose to the younger brother of an old friend. Reese leaned back and watched Chandler move his chips around the table, angry that he'd let his personal feeling for Chandler get in the way of his own judgment.

"We'll start a tab, old man," said Chandler after the game.

"Sure," said Reese. "A tab will be fine."

Outside it was a windy, clear day. All the Park Avenue banners were flying. It was nearly three and already Park Avenue was jammed with cars and cabs.

"Oh my God," said Weatherly. "Run! It's the guy from the Stopless!"

Weatherly took off across Park Avenue, weaving through the traffic. Reese turned. There was a short man wearing baggy New York Mets blue shorts running directly at him. Reese followed his friend across the street.

"FAO Schwarz," said Weatherly.

They ran uptown. At one point Reese heard the dwarf scream, "Someone stop those guys. They stole my wallet!"

Pedestrians turned their heads but no one was buying it. At Fifty-eighth they whirled through the revolving doors of the famous toy store.

The toys, the animals, the games—they were everywhere, monstrously gaudy, a miasmic whirl of horrific colors flashing by. Reese's elbow hit something and he heard boxes crash to the ground behind him. A security guard darted their way but he was too late. They were already past the huge Nutcracker and then into another revolving door that gave out onto Fifth.

"Change of plan," said Weatherly. "Grand Central."

"Perfect."

Down the block Reese ventured a look behind him. The dwarf's face was pressed against the Plexiglas of the revolving door. He'd barged his way in with a father and child.

"Fuck, he's still with us," said Reese. "Let's jump that cab."

A woman was getting out of a taxi which had a green light. Already cars were honking as Reese and Weatherly jumped in and locked their doors.

"Grand Central, any entrance," said Weatherly.

"He must have been waiting outside for us," said Reese. "How could he know about the Racquet Club?"

Weatherly squinted. The cab took off. In the days leading up to his divorce, he'd diverted his business mail to the club. There had followed those difficult nights when, not wanting to go home, he'd carried his mail all over Manhattan. Twice in the last three months he'd left a pile of bills and junk mail at his final destination, the Stopless. Then there had been the phone call. As he'd been stretching out in the weight room, a club attendant had called him to the house phone. The person on the other line had hung up. The dwarf had gone through his mail. Weatherly kept silent. Explaining all this to Reese would be humiliating and time consuming. Weatherly looked out the window, scanning other vehicles for the dwarf. The city was a jumble of cabs, women in afterwork sneakers, sirens, and hot dog umbrellas. There was no dwarf to be seen.

Now they were headed downtown on Park, had a green light, but crosstown traffic was stalled in the intersection.

"Don't block the box," screamed Weatherly. "They're blocking the fucking box. Driver, get around this, please."

The driver gazed suspiciously at them and then darted behind a delivery van.

At a light on Vanderbilt, Reese paid and then jumped out of the cab and began running toward Grand Central. At the entrance the two friends paused and looked back. A block and a half away, a yellow door flew open. The dwarf emerged.

"Should we slow down or speed up?" asked Weatherly as they hit the rush-hour crowd.

"Between," said Reese. "Let's march."

As they descended the stairs Reese looked back. The dwarf was just coming through the door.

"Fuck," said Reese. "He saw us come in."

"All right," said Weatherly. "*French Connection* time."

His nose bandage had come undone and was flapping up and down against his cheek. As if late to catch a train, they moved through the crowds, Weatherly leading. The escalator down to the subway was filled and so they ran the stairs. Reese was impressed with how deftly his friend jumped the turnstile. The old Weatherly. He was in good form. Reese did the same and turned. There were no policemen to be seen. On one track he saw a 6 express pulling into the station. The dwarf was a few paces behind them now. Reese and Weatherly ran down the platform against the direction of the train, Weatherly slightly ahead. When the doors hissed open, they got on. Through the window Reese could see the dwarf was getting on an adjacent car. Then as the doors were about to close, Weatherly grabbed Reese's hand and they slithered out. It was a fabulously timed move. The train began to pull away from the station. The two friends watched as the dwarf's enraged red face pressed itself against the glass and then he was gone.

They stood on the crowded platform, breathing.

"Thank God for *The French Connection*," said Weatherly. "I've always loved the train scene."

"Yes," said Reese. "Or it would have been third-rail time."

"To the Oyster Bar," said Weatherly. "That guy doesn't look like an Oyster Bar kind of guy. To the Oyster Bar and then a cab. He'll think we've taken the next train."

"Yeah?" questioned Reese. "But what happens if he's the kind of guy who knows we're the kind of guys who are the Oyster Bar kind of guys?"

"My bet is that *that* guy doesn't even know what the Oyster Bar is."

"You're right," said Reese. "From us, he will expect flight, so let us not give it to him."

"Exactly."

They were shown to the back smoking room.

"Never, I mean rarely ever, never," said Weatherly, "never have I ever needed a drink more than I do right now."

They had martinis and New England clam chowder.

"So let me get this straight," said Weatherly at the bottom of his first martini. "You were given this package to mail. The package disappears after you spend a night with this woman who comes on to you at the Gramercy Park. So we've got a situation where this femme fatale has put us in a fucking fatal position because whatever was in that package, that asshole who broke my nose thinks you've sold it or double-crossed him or done something ugly to his self-interests."

"Those are the facts, that's right."

"And you're sure the package wasn't in your hotel room when you got back from Grove."

"Positive."

They ordered more martinis.

"What we're needing here is a little objective thinking, you know what I'm saying, some journalistic empirical thought. I thought that was your department."

"My department," said Reese, "was supposed to be vacation. I came to the land of the free in order to relax and see my little sister wed."

"I know that, but you fucked up. This guy Asher, what did he say he was mailing?"

"A script, a script for some movie he's doing with an old girl-friend."

"Was the package addressed to the old girlfriend?"

"I don't remember."

"Fuck," said Weatherly, slamming his hand on the table. "I bet Julie will know."

An elderly couple at an adjacent table looked up at them.

"You boys want to keep it down?" said a man with a southern drawl. "We come a long way for this meal, and we plan to enjoy it."

"Sure," said Weatherly.

"Sorry, sir," said Reese.

"Okay, okay, okay," hissed Weatherly. "Let's think. We haven't had time to think. We got to think."

"I didn't come home to think. I came home to relax."

Weatherly disregarded his friend's statement.

"Let's do it this way. Let's go for the reverse interview."

"You mean you play the journalist."

"Exactly."

"Fine," said Reese. "Shoot. Make it on the record. I don't give a fuck."

"This Asher guy. Tell me where he's from."

"He worked for UNESCO and then who knows what, maybe a stint at the World Health Organization, known as WHO. We play tennis."

"Is he American?"

"Yes."

"From where?"

"Once I think he mentioned California."

"Where in California?"

"L.A.," said Reese. "But we were both drunk. He had a very

destructive relationship with a woman whom he claims has since moved to New York."

"Bingo," said Weatherly. "The girl that picked you off at the Gramercy is very cunning. She probably heard where you were coming with a package and picked you off before you could mail it to the dwarf or the dwarf's associate."

"How do you know?"

"Reese, buddy, I'm not saying you're not Cary Grant, but a girl just coming on to you at that weird bar . . . Doesn't that sound out of line to you? I mean, she wasn't a hooker, right?"

"Not a hooker, no. But if this girl is connected to Asher, then why didn't Asher just put her address on the package?"

"That I don't know," said Weatherly.

Suddenly Reese remembered the label on the Phnom Penh package. It had been to somewhere in Long Island City.

"Long Island City," he said. "The package. I'm pretty sure it was going to Long Island City, which, come to think of it, *is* weird because Asher said the script had something to do with Miramax."

"What did this girl look like, the one who took you off?"

"Good-looking, a little hard. You know some miles under the hood for her age. She was a brunette."

"It's Jasmine," said Weatherly. "I have her number."

"Who is Jasmine?"

"Jasmine's real name is Julie. She works at the Stopless. I've been trying to get her into bed for months. Did this girl mention Harvard? Because she's sort of into slumming. She went to Harvard."

"We didn't get into higher education, but she was articulate. I'm not sure what Harvard material is like anymore, but she had about her a kind of postgraduate Adams House barroom manner.

It looked to me as if she'd spent a long time at a bar. She had wonderfully pale skin."

"Sounds like Julie. I bet you got taken by Julie because the guy that broke my nose has Long Island City written all over him, and one thing I know from spending *way* too much time at that strip bar is that Julie *hates* her boss, hates that guy with everything she has."

"Julie took her boss off," said Reese, leaning back. "Julie took her boss off before I could mail the package to him. It's a definite possibility."

"Better than fifty-fifty," said Weatherly, "it's a definite maybe."

"Wow," said Reese. His first martini was well into his belly. Now he could feel it begin to spread about his body.

"So this Asher," said Weatherly, slurping his clam chowder. "He said he was giving you a script, right? Did you ask him about it? I mean, did you, like, read it on the plane?"

"I got drunk on the plane."

"Script, my ass," said Weatherly. "It must have been drugs, coke or something."

"They do not grow coke in Cambodia," said Reese. "They are, however, known to—"

Reese pulled up short in recognition.

"Heroin," he said. "The place is a major transshipment point for heroin."

"Wow," said Weatherly. "This really is turning into *The French Connection*."

"Perhaps," said Reese, "we should pay a visit to this Stopless?"

"No," said Weatherly. "We'll go back to my place and give the Stopless and Julie a call. I'll settle this one."

chapter eight

W ITH HIS FINE NINE tucked between his leg and the front seat of his Lincoln, Dwayne and Julie drove up the Henry Hudson Parkway.

"I thought we were going to Brooklyn," she said.

"How it is, before these gentlemen used to operate out of the Greenpoint area, see," said Dwayne. "But then one of 'em got, you know, got busted, so they moved to a different hood in Harlem. You got the stuff? 'Cause they know we're coming and if you don't got the stuff—"

"I got the stuff."

Internally she was chanting, *the aesthetics of love, the morality of business*, over and over again. It had become her mantra. It helped calm her. She was wearing a pair of green hospital orderly pants with a pull tie, an oldie from a guy even before Asher, and a black T-shirt that said CAT POWER. Between her legs was the largest handbag she could find on sale at Bloomingdale's. It held five kilos of heroin.

"How much you step on it? I hope you didn't step on it *too* much 'cause these gentlemen are the ones who do the stepping, you know what I'm saying."

"It'll be worth their while," she said.

The math had been very simple. She'd gone to a stupid head shop in Soho and bought a scale. Then she'd taken Asher's three kilos and turned it into five with cornstarch. Her deal with Dwayne was 10 percent and silence. With the lights of the George Washington Bridge in sight, they turned off the highway and found themselves heading east on 157th Street. Marks of weariness, marks of woe, thought Julie. Blake. Now there was a man who understood the hallucinatory horrors of a city. Lonely black men with bagged bottles wandered the streets. The sun had set and dusk was quickly handing itself over to the night.

"So, how is this going to go down, Dwayne?"

"Very simple. I go in with the stuff. They check it out. We get the money. We leave."

"No, that is not how it will go down. If that were to be the scenario, *you'd* leave and I'm left with your criminal car while you fly to Cabo."

"What the fuck is Cabo?"

"Cabo San Lucas. You know, where O.J. Simpson used to hang out. You know O.J., right?"

Dwayne didn't say anything. He was wondering how the Haitians would take to a white lady. He looked over at her.

"So you want to come in."

"No, I don't *want* to come in. I will come. See, I'm the principal in this deal."

"Baby, you're white as milk and these gentlemen are Haitians. Like, they don't *know* you."

"Where do they live?"

"Off St. Nicholas."

St. Nicholas. Julie decided not to linger on the irony. She was too scared.

"Yeah, few years back, the area got busted so many times the cops, they forgot about it now. The place is old school."

"Great. We're going to hang out with a bunch of Baby Doc Duvaliers at St. Nicholas. They better have the money."

When she first moved to New York, she'd had an affair with a Haitian. It hadn't lasted long but he'd been a wonderful man, a bag handler for Aristide when Aristide was in New York, a great cook. She'd admired his oscillations between maudlin introspection and brutal passion. Haitians, they turned on a dime.

"Look," she said. "Wouldn't it be better if there were two of us? You could, you know, cover me, watch my back, so to speak."

"Okay, baby," said Dwayne, backing into a parking space on 158th Street. "But you better be cool."

They got out of the car. St. Nicholas Place was a small, V-shaped concrete construct. They walked south on it for two blocks.

"Okay," said Dwayne. "Here it is."

Julie breathed out and looked up at the sky. The stars were out. The stars of Harlem. Please, she said to herself, please, stars, please behave yourself tonight. They walked up a tenement stoop and Dwayne pressed an intercom button.

"It's D," said Dwayne.

The buzzer rang.

The stairwell was not unlike many others she'd seen in the city, not unlike that of a building she'd lived in in the East Village. It was just a ratty municipal stairwell, narrow with sharp turns at each landing. As they climbed, the bag began to feel heavy and

Julie light-headed. She hadn't eaten anything all day. On the fifth floor a door was cracked open and a man with dreadlocks was sticking his head out at them.

"Who is the lady, D?"

"The lady is who it is, she cool."

"Lady, you a cop?"

"No," said Julie. "Not at all. Law enforcement has never been my bag."

"Then what is your bag?"

"Weight."

"I like that," said the man with dreadlocks. He had terrifying whites to his eyes. "Step on in. We been waiting on you."

The place reeked of grass, which at once comforted and terrified her. The Hassassini; she'd once been fascinated with that particular cult of men. Eventually the *H* for *hashish* had been dropped. They were Middle Eastern assassins imported to Venice and elsewhere. They killed on hash. They smoked and killed in alleyways and the occasional oasis. These guys looked to be some atavistic mutation of the Assassini. There was a shotgun on a table next to what used to be referred to as a Q-P, or quarter pound of pot. There were two other men sitting on a couch, their backs to a window with the shade drawn. Julie couldn't quite make them out. The only light was coming sideways from what looked to be a kitchen. She dropped her bag between her legs and rested her hands on the edge of the table. There was the distinct possibility she might faint.

"Brother D," said a man from the couch. He didn't sound Haitian. "Brother D, how you making it? That's a fine piece of ass you got riding with you. Who are you, lady? This here is my place of residence and I ain't never seen you before."

Definitely not a Haitian, she thought, more like hard-core Harlem.

"I've got five K's of smack here. It came by way of Cambodia. It's serious shit."

Hard-core Harlem began to laugh. The Haitian who'd opened the door squeezed her ass as he passed by and disappeared into the kitchen.

"A white lady with five K's, now ain't that something?" said Hard-core Harlem.

The man next to him on the couch had dreadlocks and was silent. In the little light she could make out a scar running diagonally across one cheek.

"Believe me," said Julie. "It's something."

"She's for real," said Dwayne. "She got contacts."

"Yeah, like who?"

"A friend of mine," said Julie, "he knows a lot of people in Cambodia."

"Cambodia," said Hard-core Harlem. "They got the fine shit, those gooks, right?"

"It moves through Cambodia," said Julie. "They don't grow it there."

"Yeah, well, money don't grow on my knob, neither," he continued. "So, D, why don't you grab that scale over there and let's see what we're fucking with."

"She won't burn you on weight," said the Haitian with the scar. "She'll cut it on you."

"You could step on this shit ten times over," said Julie, "and every junkie on the corner would OD."

"Hey, D, where did you find this chick, this Miss Cat Power? I like her. She got a fine set of titties and she talks real tough."

Julie heaved the bag onto the table, unzipped one of the five zip-locked bags, and spilled about a gram onto the table.

"Here," she said. "Have a taste."

The Haitian with the scar got up and came over to the table. He had a claw for a pinkie. Julie stood back. He was terrifying. The Claw took a hit off his pinkie and stood looking straight at her. Julie closed her eyes. Her compulsion to get out of the room was rampaging. It was keeping her from fainting. The Claw with the scar sniffled, and then went back and sat down on the couch. Shortly his head kicked back. Good, thought Julie, a good sign. Then the Claw whispered something into Hard-core Harlem's ear.

"My associate is impressed. Let's see the rest of it."

Julie took another zip-locked bag out of her purse.

"Hey," said Dwayne. "Like I don't mean to be speedy, but where's the money?"

"At the store, daddy. At the store," said Hard-core Harlem.

"Well, why don't you send someone to the store."

"I'll send someone to the store when we've verified that everything is cool."

Hard-core Harlem got up and flipped a wall switch. An overhead light shone down onto the table. He wore tan pants and a purple rayon shirt unbuttoned so as to display his chest jewelry. Now all five bags were on the table. He opened one and worked his index finger down to the bottom, came back up, and took a hit. Then he got a scale out and began to place the bags on it.

"Okay, D, let's you, me, and Miss Cat Power go down to the store. But I'm only going to give you eighty 'cause that's all I got. That fine with you, lady?"

"The deal was a hundred and ten," said Julie.

"Like I said, eighty is all I got."

"I'll say it again," said Julie. "The deal was a hundred and ten. Now I'm hearing bullshit."

She couldn't believe it had come out of her mouth. She was role-playing an argument, the lines of which had been handed her from cinematic moments of years past.

Hard-core Harlem straightened up. A knife was dangling at his side. Now he was facing her from across the table.

"I like you," he said. "You got some fine titties. Later on we can party. Right now it's eighty. My mother still bakes with cornstarch."

"I guess," said Julie, "I'll take it."

"Tell you what," said Hard-core Harlem, taking out a box of Kools and emptying the cigarettes on the table. "I'll make up the difference to you."

He dipped the empty cigarette box into one of the bags and filled it with powder.

"I hope you're cutting back to less than a pack a day," he said.

Everyone in the room laughed. Then he handed the pack to Julie.

"Now," he said. "Let's make it down to the store."

chapter nine

LATER THAT NIGHT as she was packing her things and wondering where to spend the night, the phone rang. She let the machine take it.

"Julie, this is your friend Weatherly from the Stopless. If you're there, pick up. My friend who you met at the Gramercy bar, we've been getting hassled by the dwarf. I wish you'd come over to my place and—"

Julie picked up the phone.

"Where do you live?" she said. "I've got to get out of here before the dwarf puts any of this together."

Weatherly told her.

"I'll be there as soon as I can."

"Don't be late," said Weatherly.

The dwarf knew where she lived. She had $72,000 in a shoe box beneath her bed. Eight had gone to Dwayne. She would pack a bag. She would pack her money. She would pack her drugs and she would flee. The phone rang again.

"Fuck," said Julie. Again, she let the machine take it.

"Julie, sweetheart, if you're there, please, baby, please, pick up

the fucking phone. I just called my Indo-Suez account and nothing, I mean nothing, has hit my account. Please, sweetheart, if
you're there, please—"

She picked up the phone.

"Hi, honey," she said.

It was the old voice. She was at once surprised, ashamed, and
comforted by its easy return. It had effortlessly swum up through
the swampy depths of a strange lake of love, broken the surface
and was breathing again.

"What time is it there?" he asked.

"A long time."

"Are you drunk?"

"I'm everything, honey."

"Same here, and all the time," said Asher. "Now look. I need
your boss's money. I need money now or I'm going to die."

"You're not going to die. You always think you're going to die,
but the only person who's going to kill you is yourself."

"Would you stop it with that drivel? Why hasn't your boss
wired me the money and why?" said Asher, now breaking into
sobs, "why have you been screening my calls?"

"I'm sorry, honey," she said. "I'm sorry. I've fucked things up
again."

"Well, you're not alone. Two of my three grand got stolen by
the police on my way to score. I have very little actual money and
more and more debts to this loan shark. The loan shark employs
kickboxers trained in Thailand. I need to come home. If I don't get
home soon, I'm not going to get home at all. Believe me, if it had
something to do with me and my L.A. death wish, I'd tell you, but
it's not about me anymore. It's about compounded debt. They pile

it up out here and there's no debtors' prison. If there was a debtors' prison or hospital, that would be nice—a debtors' hospital, I would definitely check in—but they don't have them. Not here."

A car alarm cut through the night. At the window she could just make out two figures backlit by street lamps running down the block.

"I need to leave this city," she said. "I think I'll come to you."

"What?"

"Who flies to Phnom Penh?"

"Sweetheart, I love you. Wire the money."

"I don't have a bank account because of all that credit unworthiness in L.A. However, I'm in a sea of cash. I'm coming to you. Are you in Phnom Penh?"

"Can't you Western Union it?"

"No," she replied. "I'm coming to you. Where are you?"

"Siem Reap, where the monuments are."

"Oh, I've always wanted to see those. Are you still cleaning bat shit off them?"

"That job ended years ago."

"Honey," she said, "I have about seventy-two grand plus a ton of tips and, as of tonight, a former employer with associates who are not pleased with me. See, I took Glen off. I'll see you in Phnom Penh fifty-two hours from now. Who flies there?"

"Take Thai Air through Bangkok. Go to the Foreign Correspondents Club. It's on the river. The taxis will know it. I'll leave you a message."

"The Foreign Correspondents Club, fifty-two hours, maybe less. I've got to look into the flights."

"Julie, is this another one of your put-ons? I mean, you're high.

Are you putting me on again, because if you are, just tell me now because I need to know."

"I'm not putting you on. It is imperative that I leave this city. I'm going to be traveling east, right into the sun. I'm going to save you."

"We can go somewhere nice," he replied. "With that kind of money, we can do a lot. You really have all that money in cash?"

"I'm looking at it right now," she said. "I'm counting it. I took Glen off and moved it myself. I'm taking it out of the shoe box as we speak, and I'm counting it. Do I need a visa for Cambodia?"

"You buy one at Pochentong airport. Bring a passport photo. We can forget L.A.," he said. "I'll talk to Tommy Travel. He's very good with visas. Maybe he can book us a junket to Burma. In the north there is a massive lake. No one will find us but each other, for centuries. No one."

The police had arrived at the car alarm. Reds and blues splashed against her window.

"A lake," whispered Julie. "Not a loud lake but a quiet one; oh, honey, that would be really great. I need a lake right now."

"I love you," he said. "But you've got to promise me that you're not putting me on. I want you to promise me that you won't wake up tomorrow and a, have forgotten this conversation, or b, feel ashamed by it."

"I'll be there," she said and hung up the phone.

The police had gone. The car alarm was finally silenced. "But as for shame, as for shame . . ."

And yet she was thrilled. She went into her kitchen, found her favorite wineglass, and smashed it on the floor. It was a beautiful sound.

Weatherly was making gimlets in a silver shaker, a registered wedding gift his wife had purposefully left behind. Over the years he'd come to dominate it. Reese was seated on a leather ottoman by the window cleaning off his glasses. There was something equally reassuring and absurd about Weatherly's well-appointed apartment. There was a ceiling-high bookshelf complete with a slender ladder that rolled laterally on wheels. Many of the books were leather-bound and unread. Weatherly walked into his library, handed Reese his drink, and from a small wood-paneled closet withdrew a canister of Zippo lighter fluid.

"Let's light this fire," said Weatherly.

Weatherly lit a pack of deli matches and threw it on the fire.

"Other day I did my first tour of duty with the parental patrol. Want to hear the threat?"

"Surely."

"The girls of St. Fermin," said Weatherly. "We're supposed to be proactive and keep an eye out for undesirables. Problem is, the weirdos in the raincoats, the flashers and streakers have all disappeared."

"Maybe," said Reese, "they've gone underground."

Reese got up from the ottoman and stood next to his friend by the hearth. As the fire caught he sensed in Weatherly a surging transformation. He looked over at his pale face glowing orange in the sinister, rising light. Something was being burned clean but what it was he couldn't exactly tell. Weatherly's eyes were fixed on the flame as he sipped his drink. Perhaps it was the staleness, the sedentary ruminations of an early divorce that was going up in flames. The broken nose, the chase through midtown, all the imported troubles which had nothing to do with the guy's sorry life save one weird coincidence, could they have been a godsend, a call to action and change?

"A chemically wrapped log set ablaze by lighter fluid on a room-temperature night," said Weatherly. "A fire laid by the maid, an abomination."

"An abomination," agreed Reese.

The buzzer rang.

"Here she comes," said Reese. "The lady of the night. If I were you, I'd hide my valuables. She's a thief."

"She is not a thief," replied Weatherly. "She is a lapsed Harvard graduate. Lapsed but nevertheless filled with *veritas*."

In the hallway Julie stood before Weatherly in all her glory. She wore a pink tank top with black shoulder straps and black jeans. Her blond hair was greasy and matted, her skin wonderfully smooth and fair. In each hand she gripped a plump piece of luggage. Weatherly was impressed with her arms. They were the arms, he decided, of the modern woman. The triceps bulged and within the sinuous forearms ran blue veins.

"Here," said Weatherly. "Let me help you with those."

"Thank you," said Julie, still standing in the doorway.

"Please," said Weatherly. "Come on in. Come in."

Now she was standing in the doorway doing a terra incognita routine, looking all about her in a haze of wonder and suspicion. Weatherly watched her profile, watched her jaw muscles flex and neck tendons tighten and stretch. He left the bags in the hallway and took her by the elbow.

"This way, Julie," he said. "Here we go up these stairs."

"Did I hear someone say *veritas*?" she said finally, climbing the stairs.

"You did," said Reese.

She was standing at the edge of the library landing looking at Reese, who had retired back to the ottoman.

"Weatherly here seems to think you're just filled with truths. I told him he was mistaken. I told him you were a thief."

"For what it's worth," said Julie, "I don't have to be here. I could be at a friend's apartment but I thought I'd come to explain myself. All parties had it coming, all but you. I'm sorry. You weren't part of my calculations. I mean, you were. I intentionally stole from you, but it wasn't really you I was stealing from. . . . May I have a drink, please? Seriously, though, Reese, I'm sorry this has been such a menacing hassle for you. Asher's an old friend of mine."

"We're making gimlets," said Weatherly. "Would you like a gimlet?"

Reese stood up and opened a pair of French doors that gave out onto a wrought-iron fire escape. Outside it was a clear night with a cool wind blowing in off the reservoir. He was between Park and Madison on Ninety-third Street. It was Woody Allen residential, a quiet side street that ran downhill between the avenues toward the park. For a moment Reese took comfort in the safety of the Upper East Side. With its private schools and museums, its reliable grid and lack of nighttime activity, it seemed unlikely the boys of the Stopless would bother to come up here. Still, there was a possibility she had been followed; if that were indeed the case, it would be necessary to watch the street. At the top of the hill sat a red-brick Greek Orthodox ministry abutted by a row of town houses with sunken street entrances. On the corner of Madison, lights from a deli lit the uptown traffic. Reese tapped out a cigarette and sipped his gimlet. His sister's wedding was scheduled for tomorrow. It would be necessary for him to give a toast. That was unfortunate. He tried to feel his extended family but could not grasp it. He tried to visualize just his mother and sister but he could not see them either. He tried to embrace the spirit of his college and high school friends, but he could not touch it. A black Lincoln with tinted windows turned off Park and came rattling to a stop below him. Reese watched as a black guy got out of the car and came around to open the passenger-side door. The dwarf stepped out.

"They're here!" he shouted. "Turn off all the fucking lights, now! Hit the main switch, man. They're here."

Weatherly leaped up from the couch and ran downstairs. Julie could hear a dead bolt thrown and then all the lights went out but for the fire. Julie crawled toward what looked to be a bathroom. She locked the door behind her and turned off the light switch. She dug into her purse and with the help of a lighter began looking for a place to hide the money. The lighter fell to the floor and then she was on all fours with her handbag with the shoe box in it. When she opened the bathroom cabinet below the sink, she came face-to-face with Mr. Clean. He was staring her in the face, his arms crossed in disdain for her actions. Julie hid the shoe box behind Mr. Clean and considered the situation. She'd seen Weatherly pay with a credit card. Of course, he did not arrive at the Stopless intending to pay with a credit card, but few who patronized the establishment did. Dancers not on stage migrated to Weatherly, seeing in him an easy touch for a six-dollar drink, thus creating a bar tab that, by the time Weatherly finally decided to go home, far exceeded the cash he had on hand. The dwarf had simply checked the old credit card slips, pinned down his given and Christian name, and called Information. It had been stupid to come here, but she'd come on a whim because it was the Upper East Side and Weatherly liked her and was rich.

"Call the cops," said Reese.

"I don't want to call the cops," said Weatherly.

"Why not?"

"I don't like cops."

"You don't like cops," mimicked Reese. "You don't like cops. What the fuck are you talking about? You're a fucking home owner. Put your fucking property taxes to work and call the cops or I will. God, I thought I was paranoid. There's a black guy and his accomplice, both of whom no doubt are armed, breaking into your home on the Upper East Side, and you don't want to call the police."

"That's right," said Weatherly. "They sense in me a denial of their values, the police. They'll start asking questions about Julie here."

"Julie here," hissed Reese. "Julie here almost got us killed."

Weatherly's apartment had three stories. There was the bedroom on the top floor, a library and bar in the middle, and below was the front door and foyer, which led back into the kitchen and Penny's room.

"Do you think they saw the lights go out?" asked Weatherly.

"I don't know," said Reese. "I'd say it's fifty-fifty. They parked across the street."

Weatherly was standing in the middle of the library with moonlight coming in over one shoulder. He was taking slugs from a bottle of tequila and chewing on a section of lime.

"So," he announced to the room. "Are we ready to make some

radical home improvements? Huh? How about it, folks? No cops, just a better than fifty-fifty chance that we have the element of surprise on our side. We know the nature of the enemy, we know the terrain, and we have the light on our side. Remember that, folks. The light is on our side."

"I'm ready," said Julie, coming out of the bathroom. "Let's fuck them up. The dwarf; why, I submit to you, should he be allowed to breed? This city has reached a Malthusian saturation point with his kind. So let it come down. They are creeps and we have the light. It seems to me that I've been waiting for this moment all my life."

"This is great," said Reese, sitting down on the couch. "The Harvard drug dealer and the homicidal divorcé—what a team. Give me a shot of that."

Weatherly handed him the bottle.

"Okay, right now they're casing the place," said Weatherly. "They've probably jumped the garbage gate and are around back. That's what I'd do. I'd get off the street and go around back. Everybody take off his or her shoes. I'm going upstairs."

Reese took off his glasses. His eyes hurt him. They were bulging from the back. With his right palm he pressed in on his left eye.

"How do you know Asher?" Reese asked Julie.

"I am the reason he's in Cambodia. For a while there, we both lived in L.A. Then we fled each other. Now we're coming back together again."

"Jesus Christ," said Reese. "I think I'm going to get drunk. But first, why don't we call the police because I'm not sure I want to be a party to this."

"I see now why Asher picked you," said Julie. "He said you were a citizen. I just didn't know you'd be so straight."

"Straight," said Reese, getting up and going for the phone on the coffee table. "Straight. That's really something. Straight."

Julie yanked the phone line from the wall socket.

"No cops," she said, reaching into her handbag and withdrawing a joint. "Not tonight; tonight we work for a different man. Tonight we are all in this house employed by the Old Man of the Mountain. We get high. We become Assassini. Are you familiar with the eleventh-century secret society? They were very big in Syria, the entire Levant, as a matter of fact."

She sucked on the joint and offered it to Reese, who declined.

"They killed at night on the fumes of hashish. Then, if successful, they were brought up to see their guru, the Old Man of the Mountain. Up on this mountain the men were rewarded with the most exquisite of pleasures."

"You've lost your fucking marbles," said Reese.

"Marbles, who said anything about marbles? I am shortly due to leave this country, and I am stoned. I have become," she said, exhaling smoke into a shaft of moonlight, "unhinged, a Manson chick. Just call me Sexy Sadie."

Weatherly came downstairs with a hockey stick and a long black flashlight.

"Did you guys hear anything?" he asked.

"No," said Reese. "We've heard nothing at all. I'm not having anything to do with this. I'm going to sit on this couch and get drunk."

"I," said Julie, snatching the flashlight from Weatherly's hand, "will be the keeper of the light."

The flashlight was cold and felt wonderfully substantial in her hand. It was the kind the cops used.

"As you can see," continued Weatherly, "the light doubles as a weapon. You could cave a skull in with it, no problem."

Julie slapped the handle of the flashlight against her palm and followed Weatherly down the stairs. The narrow wooden staircase creaked beneath their feet, sending shudders of fear and pain through her system. As they arrived at the landing, there came the sound of shattering glass.

"Penny's room," said Weatherly.

They ran down the hall, through the kitchen, and came to a closed door.

"Okay," said Weatherly. "Game time. When I open the door, shine the light. Ready—one, two, three."

Stuffed animals on a bed came into savage focus. They were foreign animals, animals of another generation from alien cartoons. Then came the eyes of the dwarf. His head was poking through the broken window. Weatherly's hockey stick flashed upward, but the blade hit the low ceiling and came down, missing the dwarf's head. As the dwarf's hand reached up for the window latch, Julie let out a terrible scream. From the doorway she rushed forward. The beam of the flashlight arched upward, lit the ceiling, and then came thundering down upon the dwarf's head. She felt the give, the crunch.

"You miserable weasel," she screamed and turned off the flashlight.

"Get out of here," she hissed.

They ran out of the room, through the kitchen, and back up the stairs.

"The guy he's with has a gun, but I doubt he'll come after us. He hates his boss almost as much as I do. He had to come along for the ride. It was an appearance thing."

She snatched the bottle of tequila from Reese's hand, took a swig. Then she walked over to the top of the stairs, cupped her hands to either side of her mouth, and screamed, "Dwayne, the cops are going to be here any second. I won't give them the make of your car if you get the fuck out of my life right now. Do you hear me?"

The Upper East Side was silent. Across the street the neighbors were having a late dinner in a sunken kitchen. A window sash partially eclipsed a bottle of wine.

"I want another grand for my troubles. I know where you live, bitch."

"Fine, come by tomorrow at noon."

"You better be there."

"You can count on it. Now get the fuck out of here."

Reese took up position by the window. Shortly he saw the hefty frame of the man they called Dwayne run across the street, get into his car, and peel out.

"He bought it."

"Thank God," said Julie, collapsing on the couch.

"What happened to the other guy?" asked Reese.

"She crushed his head like an eggplant," said Weatherly. "He's going to be all over my daughter's bed."

"We better go see," said Reese.

"I don't know if I'm up for that, boys," said Julie. "Why don't the two of you go down."

Weatherly and Reese went back down the stairs and turned on the main power switch. The rooms were suddenly flooded with light. Julie ran about the library turning off overhead lights and lamps until she was alone with the moon.

Downstairs the dwarf was dead. His throat had come down onto a piece of jagged glass at the bottom of the window frame. Blood was pulsating from his neck, turning Penny's bed into a pond of blood. Blood was trickling from both ears.

"Don't touch him," said Reese.

They stood in the room, mouths wide open.

"We better get our story straight," said Weatherly. "Because now the cops *are* going to have to be called."

From upstairs came music. The two high school friends were at first startled and then haunted. Julie had put on "American Pie."

chapter ten

Asher was awakened with a smack to the face. Someone was leaning over his futon. He was smacked again and sat up in bed. It was very early in the morning.

"What," said Asher, blinking. "What?"

The intruder wore a red Adidas sweatsuit and he had a disturbing buzz cut.

"Money," said the boy. "Mr. Hawk. Money."

"Okay, money, right," said Asher. It was one of the kids that hung around the Apsara, an employee of Mr. Hawk's. Asher now recognized him from his haircut. Years ago he'd worked behind the bar at the Apsara, and then later been promoted to lingering thug. He was on the national kickboxing team. Once quite drunk and with friends now all vanished from Phnom Penh, Asher had called this guy Flat Top after the Dick Tracy villain. No one had gotten the joke. Now Flat Top was in his apartment. Asher crawled over to his shoe box and withdrew the last one-hundred-dollar bill he owned. He held it up for Flat Top.

"That's all I got, kid," he said, standing up.

There was a tremendous blow to his chest. Flat Top had delivered a lightning-quick kick. Asher was picked up off his feet and sent sprawling back onto his futon. He thought his heart would stop. Then once he realized his heart might still work, it came to him that he could not breathe. Gasping for a breath he could not find, he watched as Flat Top ripped the bill in half, threw it on the floor, and exited the apartment. When his breath began to come back, he went to the window. Flat Top was wheeling the Dream onto the street. His landlord stood there doing nothing. Asher was infuriated.

"No," he screamed. "Get your hands off my Dream!"

He threw on a pair of boxers and was halfway down the stairs when he stopped himself. The Dream would have to wait, wouldn't it? It was good collateral. The Dream, it would buy him some time. He returned to his apartment. An awful morning sun sliced through his bedroom window. Asher quickly threw down the shades and fixed himself a line of heroin from his desk drawer. It was the first time he'd done the drug as an eye-opener. It was not a good sign, but neither were these good times. There were nerves to consider. Slowly, methodically, he packed.

At the taxi stand, the morning rides to Battambang and Siem Reap were being haggled over. There were three cars going, two Toyota sedans and a pickup. Asher asked the driver of the pickup how much it would be to Siem Reap and was pleased to find him-self not grossly overcharged. The driver spoke about as much En-glish as Asher spoke Khmer. This had helped him with the price. Twelve dollars to Siem Reap, not bad. A plane was seventy-five or eighty. The driver of the pickup showed him to the shotgun seat. The country folk, many of them probably from Siem Reap, were already in the back payload waiting patiently. It was nearly seven o'clock and already getting hot. Asher sat in the shotgun seat and watched as the driver haggled with more potential passengers.

Even through his morning line of smack he was growing impatient. The will to flight was with him now and, mixed with his hangover, it was making him impetuous and antsy. He'd left the remains of his smack supply in his apartment. He'd go to Siem Reap, visit with Alex, make phone calls to Julie, and kick his habit before it grew into a monster.

A boy selling sweet morning buns in plastic bags passed the car and Asher flagged him over. He bought some buns and a bottle of water. The driver was now in a heated argument with a policeman and then, after an exchange of chits and money, in another argument with what was either another driver or a potential customer. Asher couldn't tell. His anxiety grew. Mr. Hawk was known to have very good police connections, and the police were at every taxi stand, checking out who was coming and going. Asher took out his blinders, poured cold water over them, and placed them on his forehead. Departure was being delayed in order to maximize the number of human beings who could possibly be rammed into the vehicle.

"Come on, man," screamed Asher at the driver, pointing emphatically at his watch. "Let's go. Let's get the fuck going!"

The driver ignored him. He was now negotiating with another customer, apparently a valued one, and from the looks of it a gem merchant. He had the briefcase and jewelry of a gem merchant. After five minutes of negotiating with the driver, this fat gem merchant lumbered into the cab next to Asher, forcing him to relinquish his coveted window position. The gem dealer was a big sweater and clutched feverishly at his briefcase. Asher was forced to place his left leg on the driver's side of the stick shift, imperiling his privates. Finally they set off, through the market traffic in a blare of horns, through the city. Here the truck gathered speed as the road widened. There were no lanes and the morning mayhem was unsettling. The truck weaved through a throng of students on *moto* bikes and honked at the hybrid diesel cars of oncoming farmers, and through it all there was this tremendous morning light. Asher put his head back and closed his eyes in order to escape the wheeling city he had come to love and despise so. Yet even with his eyes closed he could not avoid its kinetic energy. He felt the city in his gut. The thousands upon thousands of tiny transactions that kicked up a thin film of red dust mixed with diesel made him car sick. He broke one of his buns in half and offered a piece to the gem dealer. The man twitched his head in refusal. He was tightly wound, this gem merchant, filled with the avarice of the urban middle class. Asher munched on his bun and considered the city he was leaving. There were just too many parts, too many parts. The whole, it was impossible to contemplate. Of course, this was true of any city, but somehow Phnom Penh was different. The energy was more hectic, naked, and disguised.

Shortly the traffic began to thin and the road to disintegrate. The scars and the ruts of municipal malfeasance began to show. The driver slipped in a cassette tape of contemporary Khmer dance music. Asher winced. It was way too early in the morning for this relentless electronic beat. He turned the volume down.

"Sorry," he said to the driver. "In the hour of need, passengers' rights must be asserted."

Just outside Udong, they waited for a ferry to take them across a tributary of the Mekong. It was a short ride across the muddy river and Asher was the only passenger to leave his assigned vehicle. He was glad for the air. Once on the other side, they were headed north up Route 6.

"Okay, boys," said Asher, swallowing a ten-milligram tablet of Valium. "Siem Reap or bust."

He shortly passed into a semiconscious, drooling lull. It was impossible to sleep, really, since the car bounced and shook and alternated between extreme speed and near inertia. They were headed north on a road with which Asher was not familiar. In the past he'd flown to Siem Reap. Now his circumstances had changed. When he awoke, he found himself in a traffic jam deep inside the country. To his right came the electric green of a rice field spotted with tall, slender jackfruit trees. It was jackfruit and Cambodian coconut harvest season. A nearly naked boy was somehow climbing a limbless tree, hacking at an invisible fruit in the distance. Ahead stood a line of cars.

"Where are we?" he asked the driver.

"Bridge," he said. "Broken."

Asher slightly elbowed the gem merchant and got out of the car. The peasants in the back were covered with dust from sitting on their corn sacks, *kramas* wrapped around their heads. A few wore cheap tinted sunglasses that flashed Asher's reflection back at him. He nodded to them and moved on. His back ached. He looked at his watch. It was one in the afternoon and blistering. Asher bought a green coconut from a woman who had set up a stall. She'd kept the fruit in a large pail of ice, and the milky liquid was cold and refreshing. The coconut was the jewel of the countryside. He'd heard somewhere that when blood was short, the milk was often put in IV drips to keep blood pressure up. The local woman's child clung to her side, regarding Asher with terror. She said they were outside Kampong Thum. Asher had never been to Kampong Thum. It was in the middle of the country, less than halfway to Siem Reap.

His taxi was nearly a dozen cars back. The road over the bridge had been rerouted to a muddy area through a thicket of trees growing by the river. Asher walked down to the banks with his cold coconut and straw. Luckily it was the dry season. If this were the rainy season, forget it. The river did not look formidable, only muddy. Nominally in charge of the operation was a country militiaman in faded green. If not for the belt buckle, the man could have been Khmer Rouge. Perhaps he was or used to be Khmer Rouge. The pants looked Khmer Rouge. They were the color of a lima bean. This militiaman was collecting a toll from each vehicle waiting to cross the river. Before each car crossed, there was a haggle over the fee: a five-minute interview, and an argument followed by a handful of filthy notes being flung into the man's hand. The price for crossing was what you could pay for it, depending on where you were from and what cargo you were carrying.

Local teenagers in shorts and wet T-shirts were pushing a pickup across the shallow river. Asher's head hummed with Valium. He sat on the stony banks of the river and watched the kids work. What the fuck, he thought, he'd help. He'd help for free. Asher took off his pants, unbuttoned his shirt, and hid his wallet beneath a large stone. The wallet had $350 in it, plus a few thousand riel, all he had left in the world. Slowly, Asher waded into the river. The water cooled as it deepened. There was something here he wasn't fully understanding, something vaguely baptismal. He had lost weight. There was an emptiness in his sense of lightness, an emptiness that was vaguely holy. He considered his raised white arms as the river's current gathered tepid strength against his hips and legs. He was ready to be of use and was in waist-high water with the kids when a white Toyota honked and came rumbling down the banks and into the river. Asher joined the cluster of Cambodian youth. Together they heaved at the back. The Toyota began coughing black smoke, but they managed to keep it moving. Shortly its front tires caught the far side of the bank, and Asher watched as it churned through a muddy gap in the trees. He felt unduly triumphant. Slowly he turned and waded back into the river for the next vehicle. After three more cars he was feeling less triumphant. His lungs wheezed and he decided to quit. He went back and sat by the river and considered his situation. A hangover, wet shoes, and no word from Julie. He'd spent a lot of money on phone cards, leaving increasingly irate messages on her machine in Brooklyn. Now he was in the middle of nowhere, observing a typical Cambodian fuckup. Short-term measures taken due to infrastructure rot, and of course the problem had a price. He watched the local militiaman haggle. Asher wondered if the boys in the river would get any of the money. They were a tireless and merry band, healthy village kids, temporarily the center of attention. The big road had come to them.

He walked back to the taxi carrying his pants. The sun was so hot his boxers had almost dried by the time he reached the pickup. The taxi driver shook his head. A rich *barang* in the river. It made little sense. The driver made the peasants in the back cross the river on foot. It was a front-wheel-drive vehicle and he needed weight in the cab. Asher and the gem merchant sat very still as the driver revved his vehicle and descended the banks. They crossed with little problem. The driver honked his horn in celebration. The gem merchant rolled down the window as the peasants scurried to get back in.

They were back on the road, but hadn't gone more than ten kilometers when the roadblocks began. Now they were deep in the country and there would be soldiers to contend with.

About twenty-five kilometers outside Siem Reap Asher began to see bodies taking form in the light. The driver twitched. Now there was no mistaking it: a gang of soldiers was in the middle of the road. It was getting a little late to be traveling; the delay of the broken bridge had cost them. The scenery was lethal in its beauty. A low sun burned through the side window, elongating the shadows of the ruts in the road.

"Martians," said Asher and then, to the driver, "I'd speed up if I were you. Speed up, goddamn it."

Asher drew a ten-dollar bill from his wallet and then put his wallet inside his sneaker. The water had stretched his sneaker, and he was able to step on his wallet with impunity. When he came back up, he was glad of his move. The soldiers were coming into focus. There were five of them. One carried a bad sign. It was one of those wonderfully slender, delicately thin Chinese-manufactured rocket launchers that was not the B-40 rocket launcher of the government soldier. It looked, frankly, Khmer Rouge.

"Khmer Khrohm?" he asked the driver. It was what some Cambodians called the Khmer Rouge.

The driver shook his head. The soldiers, they had not been paid, he complained. It was hurting his business. He was sorry for the discomfort but it was the government's fault for not paying the soldiers. The soldiers, they must be paid. It was not good, intoned the driver. It was a bad scene to have unpaid soldiers on the loose, on the roads, interrupting commerce.

The gem dealer was shading one side of his face from the sun and squinting at the men in the distance. If it was Khmer Rouge, it would be a splinter group, possibly defectors. The main force of the Khmer Rouge was well to the north of here. There was no sign of black pants to be seen, but then again, Asher had never seen Khmer Rouge actually wear black but in photographs. The problem with this rocket launcher was that it was the same kind he'd seen a few years ago when Khmer Rouge strays were known to walk for miles just to go shopping for condensed milk in the Siem Reap market. These guys seemed to be a mixed bag of marauders. Asher could tell by their tired stance and the way they held their armaments. They menaced the red road with their presence. One of them, possibly a leader of some sort, was flicking his hand down in the Khmer gesture to stop.

"I'd speed up, bud," said Asher. "Just ride. Ride into the sun."

None of them had their guns pointed directly at the car but that did not matter because now Asher could make out their faces, serious and scowling, bitterly drunk or bitterly tired; bitterly something. He was reminded of the night in Phnom Penh when the whistle had sounded. Suddenly he did not want to stop. He felt it quite necessary that the driver pass by this one, take a shot or two but not stop.

"Don't stop," he hissed. "Keep going. Go."

The driver downshifted. It was maddening. The threat was impossible to judge. The uniforms were tattered and mixed. Two soldiers had rolled up their wet pants into makeshift shorts. As the pickup rolled to a stop, the one who had been flicking his hand downward came up to the driver's-side window and began speaking in a quick, clipped Khmer Asher could not make out. Asher looked straight ahead and in doing so caught the eye of a soldier sporting a green Mao cap and carrying a car battery. His gun was discarded at his feet, sitting there on the road with its curling clip. The soldier next to him cradled a bottle of Johnnie Walker Black and was sitting on a case of Tiger beer. They were bandits, most probably deserters of mixed Khmer Rouge and regular army. They looked to be looters of the Cambodian night. The commander at the window drew a pistol and pointed it at Asher's temple.

"Breathe," said Asher. In his left hand, wedged between a Churchillian victory signal, was a rolled ten-dollar bill. He felt it taken from his fingers. Then the commander began yelling at the peasants in the back. He fired a shot into the air. Asher could feel the pickup lurch as the peasants scrambled. The soldier he'd made eye contact with picked up his gun. It was a very old gun, a veteran of Cold War struggles, now put to personal gain. Asher fell quite in love with the gun. In the light, the rust on the clip was splendid. The feeling was of past ownership. Several rounds rattled away on the road. The peasants fled with what they could carry. They scattered, some taking to one side of the road, some to the other. Then the bandits got into the back with their gear, their mood suddenly alive with plundering laughter. They pounded on the roof with rhythmic abandon. The commander got in next to the gem dealer. Thankfully, the driver and commander seemed to know each other. Asher trained all his listening skills on their conversation, internally cursing his loss of Khmer nuance. The gem merchant beside him tensed. He'd placed his briefcase beneath the seat.

The driver and the commander were speaking of a woman. That was good. From what he could make out, she was someone's cousin. A woman. Asher closed his eyes and breathed out in relief; a discussion of a woman. There was safety there. Still, he had taken another gun to his head. If the commander had pulled the trigger, it would have been banal enough. A bullet in the head, blackness, his body an obstacle for other cars to avoid. And all of it determined by the mood of one commander of bandits. Cheap. There was something in its cheapness to admire and loathe. As the car rumbled toward Siem Reap, he closed his eyes.

There came a pounding on the top of the cab. The driver skidded to a stop and two bandits jumped off the back. They disappeared down a side road. After another kilometer, there were more raps on the roof, and the guy with the car battery was joined by the holder of the case of Tiger beer. These two were drunk. They lurched off into the woods. Then they drove in silence through the outskirts of Siem Reap as the sun disappeared and night swiftly began to fall.

The taxi stopped at the market. There were no good-byes. The driver wanted three more dollars from Asher. The trip had been a costly one for him, he complained.

"Bat srai," said Asher. "Good evening, and fuck off."

He walked away and was not followed. The gem merchant had disappeared.

The bar of the Grand Hotel D'Angkor was actually doing business. There were months on end when Alex was his own best customer, and coming through the reception area, Asher was comforted by the spoken word of his native tongue and the T-shirts and postcards of the tourist trade.

"Well, I must say," came a voice behind him. *"That* is a first."

He had ordered a shot of tequila and an Angkor beer with which to chase it. Faced with its outrageous price, he'd been forced to take off his sneaker. In the mirror was an American woman perhaps five years younger than he. Asher looked her over.

She had bushels of thick dirty-blond hair and a reassuring East Coast demeanor. She wore a spaghetti-strap summer dress and expensive, minimal sandals with a square piece of silver on one toe.

"Hey, Andover," said Asher. "Could I borrow, say, five dollars from you?"

He fixed on her everything he had. He went down into his obscenity, stirred, and kicked out stardust. He went after her with his eyes.

"Well," she said. "Why not?"

"Exactly," said Asher. "Why not?"

The bartender was a Khmer homosexual, a very passive and loyal man, good to Alex. The bartender stood looking at the woman, waiting for her to pay. He had served Asher before.

"Fat here is a master," said Asher of the bartender. "A master of fornication and disaster, aren't you, Fat?"

"Mr. Asher, you come from Phnom Penh?"

"I have."

The American woman threw back a section of her hair, went into an actual purse, and pulled out a five-dollar bill.

"Could I have another vodka tonic, please," she said.

"And another," said Asher. "Tequila."

He wondered if she might know Reese. They looked vaguely equivalent. He thought he might ask her, launch into the name game. The name game in improbable places was the best. It was what made the name game sing, but then he realized that he did not know Reese's first name. In the mirror he realized that he had not shaved for some time and that it did not become him.

"I'm sorry to hassle you, Andover," he said to her in the mirror. "But it's been a long journey."

"Stop calling me that."

"A very long journey," he continued. "Of days and now, of course, of nights."

"Stop it."

Already he'd found her breaking point. Well, wasn't that something? It was time to rid himself of the road, to get loaded, and for that he would need Alex.

"Fat, where might I find Mr. Alex?" he asked. "Where is that slithery little Paki keeping himself these days?"

Here Andover laughed. It was a wonderful, deep-throttled thing, the best sound he'd heard all day.

"You look to be one of those boys," she said, "who believe that being sent away to boarding school is a form of detention, you know, like reform school."

"I did, yes," said Asher. "We stay close to home in Chicago."

"You're mean," she said.

He realized that she was drunk, and with that, he was disappointed. He hadn't seen that before, her drunkenness and vague stupidity.

"That is the first accurate thing you've said tonight," remarked Asher.

"You're mean."

"Stop saying that," he said. "What's your name?"

"Emily Sterling."

"Nice to meet you, Emily."

They shook hands.

"What are you doing in Siem Reap?" she asked.

"I'm here," proclaimed Asher, "to climb the Bayon."

"Why the Bayon?"

"Because it's beautiful," he said. "Beautiful and complicated."

"Beautiful and complicated."

"That's right. What are you doing here?"

"I'm with the World Monument Fund. I fund-raise. We're here from New York with a group. Everybody is adopting a Garuda. I dreamt up the program myself. Twenty thousand dollars and a Garuda is yours, spiritually, of course." Asher had never particularly liked Garudas. They were squat monsters, mythical guards of plundered temples.

"Spiritually, huh, well how's this for spiritual? I heard your guards mine the site at night. How's that for spiritual?"

"We do not use land mines."

"That's not what I heard," he shot back. "The Nagas and Garudas at Preah Kahn are so famous for being ripped off that there was no other choice. This is two-year-old information, but from what I hear, the river entrance is mined at night."

"How did you know we work at Preah Kahn, and where," said Emily Sterling indignantly, "did you hear this about mines?"

"I used to be with UNESCO. We did a lot of work here. I have my sources."

"Well, I don't believe you. Our director also happens to be on the board of Halo Trust. He's worked with Princess Di."

"Has he?"

"He has."

"Well, give him my best," said Asher. "Are you staying in the hotel?"

"Naturally. It's been a really great trip. You should come out to the site."

"Thank you," said Asher, who did not particularly enjoy Preah Kahn. "I will."

She took her drink and turned. In the mirror he tracked her.

In this part of the world she was a rarity. One shouldn't be mean to a rarity. He drank his beer and decided not to be mean to Emily Sterling. He decided to seduce her. He considered her money still on the bar. Abraham Lincoln. There was a man—Kentucky, Illinois. The beard, the man. It was nice of her to leave him with Lincoln.

"Look your emancipator in the eye," he said out loud.

He was a bit worried for himself now. The intonations of his own voice scared him. No one was going to get him tonight. He really wasn't to be gotten. He began to become vaguely drunk. Twice in a month now with a pistol to the head. That had to stop. Really, it was not good. Now it would be necessary to get a mission. Quickly he came up with one. Alex. Find Alex. But he did not have to find Alex because suddenly, as if summoned, Alex was with him. He was hovering right over his shoulder.

"The house," said Asher. "The house has arrived."

Alex kissed him on the cheek.

"You look terrible," said Alex.

"Yes," said Asher. "But I'm still not from Karachi."

Alex came from a rich family in Karachi. Instead of taking over his father's chemical empire, he'd joined UNESCO. Alex was informed and funny about his dislikes. He hated UN bureaucracy, the Khmer Rouge, the CPP, and more specifically, the CPP deputy governor of the Siem Reap province, Prince Ranariddh, French preservation archaeologists, journalists in general, and *Cambodia Daily* journalists in particular. In some ways the journalists were the worst. The only news was bad news. They wrote about art theft and the occasional death or abduction of tourists. They were bad for business.

"Can we go to the back office now?" asked Asher. "I'm in serious trouble and have many long distance phone calls to make."

"Splendid," said Alex. "I'm so glad you've arrived."

"It was," said Asher, "an extraordinary road."

"I supposed it was. You seem to have lost many things, weight being one of them."

"I am an expert in weight these days. Weight is what gets me by."

"Oh Lord," said Alex. "That bad?"

"Sadly so," said Asher, getting up.

They walked through the hotel and into the back office. Alex locked the door behind them.

Two days later Asher found himself roaring out to the monuments on the back of Alex's Triumph. Peasants and soldiers flew by, and the air was sprinkled with grasshoppers. It was Alex's thirty-fourth birthday. To celebrate they'd split a chilled bottle of Sancerre over foie gras and headed out. The road was wide and well paved. Alex, as the Buddhists say, was at one with his motorcycle, and for Asher it felt good to be in the hands of a friend on the way to frolic on the monuments that rarely failed to transport him to a state of near holy benefaction. The road narrowed, drawing shade from cypress and banyon trees, and over the whine of the motorcycle Asher could hear the pitched reverberation from the host of insects of the forest. There came a wide turn in the road, and the majestic honeycombed towers of Angkor Wat came into sudden view. Alex slowed. Naked children splashed about in the reservoir of water lilies nearby, and in the distance came the monument of all Khmer monuments, backlit by the descending sun. It took his breath away.

"Don't stop," he said into Alex's ear. "The mother of all frequencies is best seen moving and at a distance."

"You jaded fuck."

"Who me?" shouted Asher over the engine. "Jaded, never. I have goose bumps. Want to see them? Look, I've got fucking goose bumps."

A throng of Japanese tourists sporting identical white sun caps were climbing into a microbus. Now, who was jaded, thought Asher, he or the Japanese? It was difficult to tell. They were loyal. He was aimless. They were law abiding. He was . . . he was . . . it was difficult to admit, but he was a drug dealer. And yet he refused to believe he was jaded. No, thought Asher, I am a rugged individualist and Merchant Prince. The Japanese are the sheep. To follow blindly, to climb into those awful buses, to lump oneself together with other sheep, to aspire to the mind of bureaucracy, was that not more jaded than the life he was currently living? Or was he simply displaying his narrow racism to rationalize his corruption? What did he know about the Japanese anyway? Next to nothing. Akashi, a Japanese bureaucrat, had headed up UNTAC. He'd been passive and wildly unpopular. The Khmer Rouge kicked him around. Still, Asher vaguely knew two Japanese individuals, both photographers, and wasn't that what it was all about anyway? The individual and the family. He would go back to Chicago and marry a plump native of his home state. If she ever did arrive in Cambodia, he would not fall for Julie G-Spot. Not that, not again. No, his ends were still noble. *Nóstos*, the arduous Homeric journey homeward, was his end. But *nóstos* had to be *achieved*, did it not? It must be gained by certain means, and the means, the means, oh, fuck, he could not escape the means. They were rotten.

The road curved around to the west side of Angkor Wat and gave onto a long straightaway. At a dip Alex gunned the Triumph. Asher suddenly had to grab hold of his friend's waist. Usually this was a big moment for Asher. When the road rose up and the gates of the walled city of Angkor Thom could be seen in the distance, when the enigmatic face of the God King, frozen on the precipice of expression, beamed down on those who would pass beneath, when he sped through the gates feeling an equal dose of homage and transgression, that was traditionally the zenith of Asher's visit to the monuments. But now sunk in a morass of guilt over the means of achieving his *nóstos,* he saw only the face of an idol, and it was a face he'd seen many times before. A bad omen. Perhaps Alex was right. Perhaps he was jaded.

They came to the section of road that ringed the Bayon and circled. The sun was filtering through the trunks of trees, splashing spangles of orange onto the towers of gray stone heads. The Bayon was all about heads. There were hundreds of them. Heads staring south. Heads staring north, east, and west. All of them the same head, the same face. Alex stopped the motorcycle next to a contemporary Buddhist pagoda painted yellow with red trim. Young monks standing at a nearby well watched them enter the monument.

They passed through the east gate, which was flanked by two rectangular waterless pools. Asher passed his hand over the breasts of an Apsara dancer, smoothed by centuries of touching, and walked over to a relief portraying the opposing armies of the Chams and Khmers having it out with the help of elephants and tigers. The Chams were ethnic Vietnamese, mostly from the Delta area, who had briefly conquered Angkor and then been repulsed by Javahamran VII, the God King, who later built Angkor Wat. Angkor Wat: in its greatness lay the seed of destruction. It had sapped the empire of manpower and resources, leaving the thirteenth-century Khmers open to invasion by the Thais. Poor Cambodia, thought Asher, and to think the walled city of Angkor Thom, of which the Bayon was the center, had once been home to millions of people, more than any European city at the time. Farther down the line were scenes of everyday life, a pig being dropped into a cauldron, a monkey god dancing.

Alex handed Asher a skin of wine. It was a refreshingly cold stream that hissed onto the back of his throat. When he was done, he passed the skin back to Alex and was confronted, suddenly frozen by the stare of a god king.

"These faces," said Asher. "They're freaking me out. There are entirely too many of them."

"You feel they're judging you?"

"Something like that."

"They're saying, my dear Asher, in the next life you will come back as a hungry ghost."

"A hungry ghost?"

"Yes, it's worse than coming back as an insect. It's a kind of Buddhist purgatory, if you will. The hungry ghost runs about, ravished by his appetites. He eats. He drinks. But he can never be satisfied. Never."

"Look, Alex, I don't need your bad karma right now."

"Bad karma," said Alex, spraying wine into his mouth. "Bad karma. Who is guilty of putting out bad karma?"

Asher said nothing. His hands were trembling as he lit a cigarette.

"What goes around comes around, my friend," Alex continued. "You must be familiar with the most basic of Buddhist tenets. What goes around comes around. You put poison out there in the system, you get poisoned."

Asher was stung. The faces—he could not escape the empty eyes that bore down on him from every conceivable angle and height. Even with his eyes closed they stood witness to his shame.

"But what happens," he managed to get out, "if one is already a hungry ghost in this life?"

"Come on, man," said Alex, pacing about in a state of agitation. "Why did you do it? I mean, the other day a really rich Thai businessman came up to me with a series of Polaroids. They were shots of nagas and Buddha heads, lintels and so forth, all of them marked as to which temple, and he said if I could get some guys together to chisel the stuff out, he'd pay me an extraordinary sum, a lot of money. It would have been two nights' work, max, a few bribes, and I'd be well on my way to being a rich man. A very rich—"

"But you didn't do it because you not only didn't need the money but you didn't need the bad karma, right? You're Alex Kahn and you didn't need the karma, and now you're actually equating moving drugs with participating in the sacking of a culture. Look, people want to get high, okay? I did not invent that. It's an irrefutable fact. It's also an irrefutable fact that I'm broke. If I didn't help move the stuff, someone else would."

"QED," said Alex.

"QED," said Asher in disgust. "Spare me your Oxford debating society bullshit."

"A month after I was approached by this Thai, several of the artifacts in question disappeared. I knew they would. I knew if it wasn't going to be me, then it would be someone else. That's what the Thai said; he said if not you, then someone else, so why not you? I simply said, *not me,* my dear fellow, now kindly get the fuck out of my hotel."

"And that must have felt good," said Asher. "A Pyrrhic victory for the karma of Alex Kahn. It must have been wonderful. I can see you dining out on it too, am I right? You bought some insurance with that bit of righteousness, right? No coming back as a hungry ghost, not for little Alex."

"Fuck off, Asher."

"And I can't believe I'm hearing this from you," said Asher, putting his face in his hands. "I'm at the end of my string, man. Can't you see that?"

"I can see that, yes," said Alex. "It is what greets a man after walking the path of least resistance. You come to the end of that path and before you lies the gallows."

"Oh, Jesus Christ."

"How much is this Hawk into you for?"

"Two grand plus nearly five weeks of usury minus the Dream."

"Your dream?"

"My Honda Dream."

"I see, and now you've come to Siem Reap to beg money from me."

Asher stood up and grabbed Alex's face in his hands.

"I came here because you're my friend. I came here for shelter and rest before Julie G-Spot arrives in Phnom Penh. I'm not here for your unearned money, asshole."

Alex kicked Asher's feet out from beneath him. His head hit the stone pathway and then Alex was on top of him with a choke hold on his neck. Unable to breathe, his eyes bulged into the eyes of a god king hovering above him. Then he passed out.

chapter eleven

IN BANGKOK, JULIE boarded the nearly empty flight to Phnom Penh, scanned for the richest man in business class, and sat down next to him. He was a bejeweled tycoon in a silk shirt printed with black tiger stripes and gray lotuses. Julie pulled out a thick *Vogue* magazine and began to flick through the pages, casting the occasional sideways glance at the man next to her. Alligator loafers on white socks, gold bracelet, tiny rhinestones embedded in the frames of his large shades, greasy black hair with a razor-sharp part, thick gold rings set with rubies and sapphires. He was the full-on enchilada, decided Julie, Asian gangster wealth personified. As the plane pulled away from the gate and the little steaming towels were passed with tongs, he introduced himself. His name, he said, was Hang Boonma and he was going to make this airline pay. He asked her nationality and was given it. He asked her the purpose of her business in Phnom Penh. Julie said that she was a travel writer for *Vogue*. Was he familiar with the magazine? Naturally, yes, but of course, he said, but his answer was a touch too emphatic to be believed. Was she traveling alone? No, she was with her photographer, currently traveling in economy class. He seemed little interested in the photographer and came back to the airline. They actually had the nerve, he said, to charge him for excess baggage after they'd lost his luggage on a previous flight. Clearly they knew not with whom they were fooling. Royal Air Cambodia, it was enough to make him start his *own* airline. And this was not the first time he'd had a run-in with their sniveling incompetence. On his outgoing flight, they'd refused to hold the plane at Pochentong for three of his colleagues running only ten minutes late.

It was funny, a few years ago there was an airline called CIA, did she know, quite funny, yes? Cambodia International Airlines. Ha, ha, perhaps he would revive CIA, said Hang Boonma. She asked him the nature of his business in Bangkok. There were many interests, as many as there were petals on a flower. But as president of the Cambodian Chamber of Commerce, he would make the airline pay, she would see. She was looking at his ring, no? It was a fine sapphire, no? She could touch it if she wished. It came straight from the ground of Khmer Rouge–controlled Pailin. The plane took off down the runway and for a moment the tycoon was silent. As they ascended, Julie felt strangely drawn to this man's turbulent magnetism. She considered Asher and his wary anxiety. This Hang Boonma was a pig, and he would certainly be guilty of an unfortunate bedside manner, but at least he was flying on the wings of his own convictions. A strong power yen; not so long ago she'd found that an unalluring-enough quality in a man, but not now, not anymore. The plane broke through the clouds. Oh Lord, she half prayed, deliver me from the hands of weak men. Deliver me from their trembling, uncertain ways.

At cruising altitude the tycoon spoke up again. She must not worry about the Khmer Rouge, they were no longer to be feared.

Pol Pot was a dying old man. No, now most were coming out of the jungle and joining the government. They wanted to make money like the rest. She must come visit his office, then she would see. He put his hand on her knee. Where did she call home? For the time being, said Julie, Paris. Hang Boonma withdrew his hand and made his displeasure with Paris keenly felt. He had never been there, no. Too many of his enemies in the government, the Royalists from the FUNCINPEC party (he pronounced the last, *pec* part as if he were coming down on hard wood with a hatchet) lived much of the year in Paris. Weak men, more French than Cambodian, and guilty of nepotism. He would make them pay. She would see. The enemy of your enemy is your friend; she must never forget this. But then again, what is a man without enemies? No man at all. Some men said you could judge a man by his friends, but they were wrong. You could judge a man by his enemies and how effectively he dispatched of them. Just look at the way he'd been treated by Royal Air Cambodia, a property owned by the Royalists, thin-blooded men, his enemies. He would make them pay. She was a very attractive young lady. A lady with her looks could make a name for herself in his country, if she knew the right people. Would she like some brandy? He'd bought it at the duty-free. He yelled at the stewardess for cups and withdrew the brandy from a purple sack with a gold pull string. Ah, the best. It was top-drawer. She must understand that when you got to be a man of his age and stature, nothing but the finest would do. Julie had poured the stuff but never in her life tasted brandy. It wasn't her scene. It tasted fine. It tasted like a velvet rope, getting past it. Life was too short, said the tycoon. . . . Ah, but this airline, it was not the first time they'd crossed him. He would make them pay.

He gave her his card. She must stay at his hotel. He was leasing his land to the Inter-Continental. He'd make a phone call to the Swiss manager and make sure she stayed for free. Or she could stay in the hotel he preferred, the Holiday. There was a nightclub and a casino at the Holiday. It was as clean and well run as any hotel in Paris. She would see. The rooms had all the amenities. There was a satellite dish on the roof. Each room had approximately twenty-five channels. Impressive, no? He was going there, to the Holiday, after the plane landed. Would she like a ride? Might he have the pleasure of her card? She was sorry. This trip was on such short notice she'd forgotten to bring her card. The tycoon grunted and pulled out paperwork from his briefcase. Julie flipped through *Vogue*. She read a story about a model and her wild ways with her actor boyfriend.

The plane descended through the clouds, and a vermilion-colored earth shimmering in light and water rose up at her. She hadn't expected the flight to be so short, but already they were coming down on a strange land. Thin roads bisected great swaths of craggy earth interrupted by a small mountain range rising abruptly from flatness. Then the mountains were gone and three palm trees stood lonely and triangulated on the widespread land. Julie placed her hand over her mouth. She felt Asher out there. She felt him pulled in by the treacherous undertow of this country. Poor, poor Asher, she thought, a flame was that boy, a flame. Then there came a body of silver water reflecting light upward into her eyes and a village with a yellow-roofed pagoda and all of it red in the descending sun, red and deathly still.

Hang Boonma took no notice of his land. He fiddled with his jewelry and made snorting sounds of manly impatience and disgust. Now the plane arched over the outskirts of the capital. The roads became busy with darting commerce and there were tin-roofed shanties and concrete military installations with fenced-in drilling fields, soccer fields, and barracks.

"Well, here we are," said Julie, raising her glass of brandy after the plane had landed. "To your health, and to revenge. To a healthy revenge."

The bejeweled tycoon snorted and touched her glass.

"Come with me," he said. "You are my guest. There will be no need for customs."

As she descended the ramp, Hang Boonma waved at a cluster of men standing a few hundred yards away outside a building with mirrored windows.

Julie followed the tycoon. Shortly they found themselves in a white-tiled, air-conditioned VIP lounge with black leather couches and love seats. Baskets of fruit wrapped in cellophane sat on glass coffee tables. The tycoon began barking angrily in Khmer. Then he grabbed one of his bodyguards by the arm, withdrew a pistol from the man's holster, and walked back out onto the tarmac. The bodyguard followed, trying to restrain his boss. Julie walked back outside and shaded her eyes. Jet fuel and heat bloated the air in waves of distortion. The bodyguard was pleading with his boss, pulling on his silk sleeve, but there was no stopping the man. He shoved his bodyguard away and threatened to pistol-whip him. As the last of the economy-class passengers were disembarking, he walked beneath the wing, raised the pistol, and fired at the wheels of the plane. One shot, two shots, three. He unloaded the clip, the empty bullet casings retracted upward and back, glinting in the sun. A wheel of the plane gave way and the wing of the plane nearly hit the tycoon's head. Then he walked slowly back into the VIP lounge and gave the pistol to his body-guard.

"Welcome to my country," he said to Julie. "Now I must go, quickly."

Outside the VIP lounge the tycoon ducked into a black Chevy Suburban. His bodyguards leapt into the back of a pickup truck and tore away from the airport brandishing their arms.

"I love this place already," said Julie.

chapter twelve

Mr. HAWK PACED the lobby of the Apsara tallying sums in his mind. The month of April had found the man alone with his air-conditioning bills. Now it was nearing the end of May, and he was late on his rent for the first time in five years. If he had only collected half of what Asher and the others owed him, he'd be out of the woods. But he hadn't. Instead, a host of outside events had conspired to squeeze him into a peevish state of pecuniary distress. The grenade attack had slowed the stream of tourist dollars to a tinkle, foreign investment was drying up, and even though he'd shipped home nearly all of the Vietnamese girls, the Apsara's lingering association with Mr. Hawk's native country was beginning to haunt him. The army and police shunned Vietnamese women and had taken to frequenting a brand-new massage parlor out on Monivong Boulevard, owned and operated by Hang Boonma, Mr. Hawk's landlord. Then, to add insult to injury, he'd been down in the laundry room and overheard the girls gossiping. On the heels of the departing Vietnamese, a menstrual-cycle shift had taken place. In bewitching solidarity, virtually all the Cambodian girls had come on to the same clock. Those who did not complain of cramps were littering the trash with their bloody menstrual refuse. All of it was undermining Mr. Hawk's grip, and to make matters worse, Hang Boonma had just called to announce that he was coming over with some friends for a massage. The call had put the fear in Mr. Hawk. Hang Boonma did not have to go anywhere to get a massage. The girls came to him. Soon he would be arriving with his goons to push pressure points in person, which was particularly cruel because in the scheme of things Mr. Hawk was nothing to the Big Man. Nothing at all except . . . now he saw it. It was his Vietnamese blood. The Big Man would gain face with his goons if he was seen leaning on a truant Vietnamese businessman. But what was doubly strange was that, like Mr. Hawk, Hang Boonma was part Chinese. He couldn't remember whether it was through his mother's or father's side of the family, but the Big Man had Chinese blood, and still he was coming to persecute him.

Mr. Hawk went behind the bar and poured himself a stiff Johnnie Walker and turned on the microphone. Feedback filled the Plexiglas cage and the girls grimaced and glared at him. A special guest was expected tonight, he told them, a special guest and his associates. They were to give whatever was asked of them, and they were to give it freely. If they were tipped, they were tipped, but there would be no haggling over hand jobs. If asked to suck a dick, they were to suck that dick, and they were to do it with spirit, as befitted the station of the men whose dicks they were sucking. Did he make himself perfectly clear? These men were wealthy beyond their wildest imaginations. He asked each girl to imagine her father in his fiftieth human reincarnation. The total sum of each of their fathers' fifty compounded fortunes could not match what *one* of these men had made in *this* lifetime.

With that Mr. Hawk turned off the microphone, drained his

Johnnie Walker, and returned to tabulation. He found comfort in adding up the compounded sums he was owed, and with his calculator he punched out the numbers lovingly. Of course, with each rising sum there was a story. There was Chun Sophy from the central market. The old man had argued with the police, who had robbed him. Then there was Shy En, the Taiwanese businessman looking to start a Korean restaurant. He at least had made one payment. Mr. Hawk's wife had taken pity on their neighbor, a young *moto* driver who couldn't pay his wife's medical bills. There was Tun Chay, the compulsive gambler and CPP deputy governor of the Siem Reap province, three weeks late, followed by Sarun, a gun runner with connections to the Macao mob, to whom he'd lent money for protection. Po Rady, a manager of a Caltex gas station and the only borrower on time with his payments; three minor one-hundred-dollar loans, all of which were late; and Asher. Mr. Hawk paced the carpet of his massage parlor. Truancy and neglect; he felt it out there constricting the night. He walked the narrow hallway back to his office and opened his safe for the third time today. Perhaps he had miscounted? But Mr. Hawk was not one to miscount, and as he thumbed down toward the bottom of the paltry pile, his heart sank. A sum was a sum, and though he tried, he could not will the rent into existence. For the first time in five years he was late. Now *he* would be in Hang Boonma's ledger. He closed the safe and walked back into the lobby. A German motorcycle race was in whining progress on the Sky Sports Channel. Men in leather were taking a tight inside turn, one knee nearly touching the smooth pavement. Mr. Hawk went behind the bar and refilled his glass with Johnnie Walker. This was how it had begun with his father, borrowing on the street to pay late rent on the Cholon restaurant, followed by two bad months and more debt. He slammed his fist down on the bar. Could it be that his debtors didn't take him seriously? Or were they not paying him because he was Vietnamese? There was that to consider, the deep-seated Khmer hatred for the Vietnamese. Now the scotch fed his growing anger. It was a Tuesday night and only one paying customer had come through the door, a World Health Organization field coordinator, the man from WHO. That was it. Now he was alone with this menstruating mob. Through the Plexiglas Mr. Hawk considered his girls. They were lounging on one of three carpeted stairs; two were gazing into compact mirrors while the rest watched television, slivers of the motorcycle race reflecting off their eyes. Their collective lethargy and boredom was annoyingly infectious. He refilled his drink. A strange, hazy drunkenness that was unable to quell his anxiety ringed his thoughts. He was going to have to make an example of somebody. If he was going to collect, if he intended to get out from beneath Hang Boonma's impending usury, it would be expedient to send a message to the debtor community at large. He walked back behind the bar and scanned down his ledger. A *barang*; it could be a master stroke. Even Hun Sen avoided killing foreigners. Their occasional deaths were associated with paperwork and threats to cut off donor aid.

Through the doors came the first of Hang Boonma's bodyguards. He was a thin, watchful man with sunglasses, and upon scanning the premises for undesirables, he threw open the door for the rest of the entourage and took up position in a nearby corner. Mr. Hawk put his ledger down and came around from behind the bar. Standing alone in the middle of the room, he felt naked and lashed to a whipping post. And yet he summoned a smile. There were five men: three bodyguards, the Big Man's Singaporean accountant, and the Big Man himself. The room glinted with gold jewelry and pulsated to their swaggering haughtiness. Oh, how they hated him. With his palms pressed together in greeting, Mr. Hawk bowed before the Big Man. Hang Boonma clapped his tenant on the back and walked behind the bar, where he poured himself a water glass full of brandy.

"The boss," hissed the accountant into Mr. Hawk's ear, "is in no mood for you tonight."

"Ice," boomed Hang Boonma. "Some ice for this drink, now!"

Mr. Hawk scurried behind the bar. Luckily he had prepared for this moment and filled his father's nickel-plated ice bucket, a gift from a French gourmand of the 1950s, with ice. But now the tongs shook in his hand and two cubes fell to the floor.

"My accountant tells me that you are late with the rent owed me," offered the tycoon.

Persecution was all around him. It was only a month's rent and yet the shame hovered in every recess of his being. As he stooped to pick up the ice cubes, his bowels loosened.

"I've been trying to put my capital to use at ten percent a week," replied Mr. Hawk. "But times are difficult. Only one out of twelve makes his payments on time; the rest—"

"You have lent foolishly," Hang Boonma replied. "This is almost as fatal as borrowing foolishly."

"Yes."

"I'd like to talk to you about it some day."

"Yes, well, so would I."

"And you are still using Vietnamese women for massage?"

"No, sir, I sent them all back home."

"Still, it marks you," he said. "My men here, they do not want to fuck a Vietnamese. A *barang*, he can not tell the difference, but we *can*. We can tell the difference."

The accountant solemnly nodded his head and resumed his study of the women behind the Plexiglas. It was as if he were looking down at a menu after having already eaten.

"A Vietnamese pussy smells like the Delta," offered Hang Boonma. "From which it sprung."

"Yes, but I've sent them back to Saigon. These girls here are from Battambang and Samlot. I've got two pairs of sisters from Samlot, as a matter of fact. They're farmers' daughters fleeing the confusion up there. Can I interest you in one of them? The youngest of the four is two soldiers past her virginity, but still, she is a lullaby."

"I haven't come here to have my chisel screwed by some country bumpkin."

"But there are no Vietnamese anymore; why not relax and unwind yourself? It is on the house."

"It is on the house," mocked the tycoon. "What house? Whose house? This place still reeks of Vietnam Delta pussy."

"Hang Boonma, I would appreciate it if you would not repeat that to other clients. The—"

"I'm going to start you out on your own medicine," he replied. "Your foolish lending is going to cost you five percent a week. Now get my accountant the best of the Samlot sisters, and while he becomes her third soldier, I'd like to play checkers."

Hang Boonma clapped his hands together and a sliver of a smile passed over his face and was gone. Mr. Hawk scurried back into his office to fetch the board. How was it, he wondered, that he had rated a game of checkers with this man who seemed to register nothing but haughty contempt for him? Could it be . . . but of course . . . it was their common Chinese blood. Their financial affiliation was lent an antagonistic face due to Mr. Hawk being

Vietnamese and the tycoon Cambodian, but running beneath these flag-flying hostilities was the underground stream of their shared Chinese blood. It was the reason Hang Boonma had rented to Mr. Hawk in the first place. They shared a code, a secret bond that was above nationalism. They were both overseas Chinese. From Jakarta to Saigon, Singapore to Mandalay, if Asia were an airplane, the overseas Chinese occupied business class. They were xenophobic men, not easily given to marrying outside the circle of their own blood, and they shared an insular, cautious wariness.

Hang Boonma smoked, set up the board, and leveled with his tenant. Who was it exactly that owed him money and exactly how much? In tremulous whispers Mr. Hawk moved his men and ran down the figures. An example must be made, the Big Man agreed. When Mr. Hawk mentioned that a *barang* might send the appropriate message, Hang Boonma hesitated. A cigarette ash dropped on the board and he looked Mr. Hawk in the eye.

"What kind of a *barang*?" he asked.

"One no embassy will miss."

"It is dangerous."

"Yes, but so is my position. I am being taken advantage of. Soon it will not only be you to whom I owe money."

"What nationality?"

"An American."

"An American," repeated Hang Boonma, clutching his stomach as if he had just devoured shark's fin soup and was eagerly awaiting the second course of fried pork. "An American; that would be fine. If you were to make it the journalist Nate Thayer, I would forget all outstanding debts. I would forget your first son's debts."

"He still gives you trouble, this Nate Thayer?"

"I have sued him in Hong Kong for libel. My helicopters, they are all watched now. It is impossible to do business with this man writing about me."

"Sadly, it is not Nate Thayer who owes me money. It is another, more hapless American."

"Is he a journalist?"

"No, but I would not be surprised if he gives them the information. He used to come here with journalists and act as if he were one of them."

"No doubt he got in debt spending his time at that club of theirs on the river."

"No doubt."

"I will simultaneously arrange it so that Ambassador Quinn's men do not miss this American, and the others who owe you will think that he met his end at your hands."

Mr. Hawk studied the board. If he were to fall into the checker trap Hang Boonma had laid, would it be too obvious that he was letting the Big Man win? He considered the nature of the trap, the nature of his opponent. Clearly the tycoon considered his trap more clever than it actually was. The man sat across the board breathing heavily and rubbing his knees down in competitive agitation. It was not a bad trap, and no doubt Hang Boonma was already in love with its nature. In his drunkenness, he probably considered it a work of minor genius. The tycoon was temporarily leaving himself open so as to lead his opponent toward slaughter. As Mr. Hawk pondered he was only giving the Big Man more time in which to fall in love with the logic of his trap. Mr. Hawk fell into the trap, and three moves later made an admirable display of frustration at losing.

"You must always be seeing, forecasting into the future," Hang

Boonma announced. "Fax a copy of your loan records to my office in the morning. I will help find this *barang* for you and see that the message is properly channeled. There can be no forgiveness, Hawk. None. I will help you make him pay. Now let's set the board up again. I want to play."

And so as the chosen Samlot sister knelt inside her window-less room working the accountant in her mouth, as the body-guards' features slowly softened in slumber, the two Chinese businessmen in near priestly union fell to playing the ancient game. The room was silent but for the muted clicking of the wooden pieces, a sound not unlike that of rosary beads, all of it transporting Mr. Hawk to that happy time when as a child in Cholon he'd harnessed just enough gleeful cunning to defeat his father at this very game.

chapter thirteen

S HE AWOKE SUDDENLY and sat up in bed. Already the dream was leaving her. Asher walking into the sea, into the sun; the rest might as well have been sugar dissolving in tea. She found herself in a dark, bewildering room in the midst of an unknown night. Where was she, a man's apartment? The process of recollecting her location, the whirl of the remembering, scared her. She swung her feet squarely to the floor so as to assure herself she was not in a nightmare.

Then she crept out of bed, stubbed her toe on an invisible piece of furniture, and fell to the floor. There she sat Indian style and let her eyes adjust to the dim moonlight. She'd placed a bottle of duty-free vodka in the small refrigerator before plunging into this nap. She found the fridge, cracked open the bottle, and took a long pull. Then she went to the bathroom and took off her clothes. Looking down on herself, she was aware only of a disturbing distance between her head and breasts. It wouldn't be long now before the slight sag to her boobs took on a more inevitable droop. She had nice, full breasts, but exercise and push-up bras were no match for time and its coconspirator, gravity. For you see, it was the evening of her thirty-second birthday. Somewhere over India she'd flown into her oncoming anniversary quite asleep. Her parents would be calling New York from Lancaster, Pennsylvania. Each year on this date Julie's father granted her a financial relief from whatever corner she'd worked her way into. The only caveat was that she provide full disclosure as to the circumstances of her trouble. Julie's father was a lawyer. It was his way of keeping in touch. At first he'd performed something like a newly elected French administration, swooping down to annul her parking violations and speeding tickets. But gradually her troubles escalated to rent and then all that expensive dental work on her molars (read: abortion) until, well, what would Dad think of her situation now that she had more money on her person than she had ever seen but in the movies, and more trouble?

With a washcloth she stood beneath the tepid shower and scrubbed away the thin film of airplane travel. Then she wrapped her hair in a towel, and quickly dressed. She put on a pair of navy-blue corduroy pants and a paisley blouse. She hid the shoe box behind the refrigerator and put her room key, cigarettes, money, and lighter into a black fake Prada bag that she'd purchased from a Vietnamese counterfeit hawker on Canal Street.

Someone had left a tourist map of Phnom Penh open on the veranda table, but Julie's attempt to make sense of it was frustrated by the dangling remnants of her dream, which hovered just outside her mental reach. Before her was a horseshoe-shaped driveway lit by a floodlight and flanked by low-lying hedges that partially obscured the vines of a rose garden. Then came the gates of the hotel, a wide boulevard, and in the middle distance the walls of the Royal Palace. Julie took little comfort in her pleasant surroundings. She felt alone and referenceless. She'd left her watch in her room and the stillness of the night combined with the uncertainty of the hour drove her to a cigarette.

An explosion hit the night. She stood up and walked in its direction. There followed the *stut-stut-stutter* of small-arms fire. A night watchman at the gate tried to stop her from leaving.

"No," he said. "Very bad. You stay hotel. Stay!"

She walked past him and for half a block he followed, pleading in pidgin English. Stopping wasn't really a question. A flare threw orange stardust into the sky, lighting the tops of the foreign buildings. Julie broke into a run. The gunfire grew louder. At the far end of the palace she turned left onto a side street. Here she ran into Cambodians fleeing in her direction. Julie slowed to a walk. Suddenly she was joined by a group of English speakers. They were coming up the street behind her. One of them was talking on a cell phone, while the other two were adjusting their camera equipment.

"Bugger the Pol Pot story, mate," said the man on the telephone. "We might have a civil war going on right here in the capital. Hear that?"

The man held out his phone to the night, hoping for gunfire, but none arrived on cue.

"Well, they've taken a small break, but believe me, mate, Hun Sen and Ranariddh's boys are finally getting it on. It's been a long time simmering."

"Excuse me," said Julie when the man hung up the phone. "I'm looking for a man named Asher. Have you seen him around lately?"

"Never heard of him, but I'm just in from Bangkok. Roger Rollins, Reuters."

They shook hands.

"He was supposed to leave me a message at something called the Foreign Correspondents Club. Do you know where that is?"

"Now *that* I can help you with," said Roger Rollins. "It's right down this bleeding street here. That way, toward the river. Katherine is the one to ask about people. She knows everyone, don't you, Katherine?"

In the arc of a flare Katherine Coats studied Julie. She was the kind of promiscuous Yank men around town fell for. She looked to be good in bars, possessed large American breasts and bad American posture. Katherine's night with Asher had been a secret she'd kept bottled up inside, and though she tried not to admit it, his sudden disappearance had unduly intrigued her. A Khmer photographer had told her estranged husband, who had told her, that Asher owed a consortium of local businessmen a good deal of money. This had further piqued her interest. During their evening together she'd remembered being vaguely jealous of a Yank in Asher's past. Perhaps this was she. Gunfire rattled the street, punctuating her decision. Tonight she was gathering information, not disseminating it. Or might it be better to mislead?

"Asher has left town indefinitely," said Katherine Coats.

"Really," said Julie. "Where did you hear that?"

"From the horse's mouth," she replied. "He claimed that all his comrades from UNESCO, that knot, had all gone home and that he was becoming consumed with dangerous Hun Sen revenge fantasies. I'm sorry, I didn't catch your name."

"Julie."

Katherine walked on ahead. A typical Yank strumpet, she thought, refuses to give her family name. The informal sort; America was said to be full of them.

A crowd had spilled out onto the street of a nearby bar. They were mostly men talking in a manic state of gleeful agitation, screaming at one another or into cell phones. Inside, the bar was three deep and noisy. Fear's "Let's Have a War" was playing at full volume. Julie smiled to herself.

"What's going on?" she asked Katherine. "I just arrived here from New York this afternoon."

"Well, you certainly have good timing," said Katherine. "See that fellow over there? We call him Six-Pack, very American, very keen on the make of grenade launchers; fellow like that has been waiting years for a night like tonight, and you just happen to pop in."

"Who's fighting?"

"Ranariddh and Hun Sen's bodyguards. I can see Six-Pack's lead right now. 'After months of simmering tension, forces loyal to Cambodia's fractious coalition partners battled in the streets of Phnom Penh, full stop. At least five soldiers were reported killed and scores wounded as chaos swept through the capital late Thursday, full stop. Troops loyal to the Cambodian strongman Hun Sen launched a B-40 rocket attack at First Prime Minister Norodom Ranariddh's residence, full stop. The prince, who was eating sturgeon in his residence south of Arles, was heard by a source close to his entourage to be singing, *Je ne regrette rien.*" He is reported to be fielding phone calls from his father, King Si-hanouk, who was himself overthrown in a 1970 American-backed coup while being treated for obesity on the Riviera . . .' and so on and so forth. Well, hello there, Al darling, I'd like to introduce you to a fine new addition to our community. She claims her name is Julie and she's fresh off the plane from New York City. Julie, Al Rockoff. Al, Julie."

As Julie went to shake Al Rockoff's hand, the lights at the bar went out and the stereo droned to a halt. Cheers erupted all around. As in a concert, lighters were raised in the air, while down the street the gunshots echoed in irregular intervals. Long bursts were succeeded by short silences, broken by short bursts, followed by long silences, and so on, all of it forming an impossible, rhythmless staccato. Skull candles were lit by the bartender, and soon the red walls were flickering in a ghoulish light. Al Rockoff, two cameras swinging from his neck, offered Julie a joint, which she accepted. His mangy, dirty white beard lent him the Masonic air of a Greek Orthodox or Coptic priest, and his small eyes would have surely disappeared beneath the network of creases that textured his face had they not ceaselessly darted about their sockets as he spoke.

"Plenty of scenarios to be played out on this pinwheel, plenty, but of one thing you can be sure—is it Julie?—of one thing you can be sure, Julie, the narco-fascist Hang Boonma is behind the fighting tonight."

Julie reached into her bag and withdrew the business card given her by the man on the plane.

"Is this your man?" she said, handing Rockoff the card. "I think I sat next to him on the plane from Bangkok. He was looking filthy rich and angry with the airline. He was in business class so I went and sat down right next to him. He's the president of the Cambodian Chamber of Commerce, right?"

"How did you get this?"

"I sat down next to the wealthiest man on a nearly empty plane. Put it down to feminine wiles."

Heavy machine-gun fire startled Julie. It was a shade louder than before.

"Are you sure it's cool to stay here?" she asked.

"It's cooler than being out on the street shooting with a flash. Shooting with a flash down Norodom would not be wise. But back to Hang Boonma. He is Hun Sen's most powerful ally, right. Few years ago he paid for an entire dry-season offensive against the Khmer Rouge."

"How did he do that?"

"Her-o-in. When the Russians pulled out with UNTAC, he bought one of their helicopters. The man wants Ranariddh out so he can hopscotch between the triangle and Pochentong with impunity."

"I see."

"Of course he denies all this."

"Yes, I suppose he would."

"But he is behind everything."

And here Rockoff began to wag his finger in her face.

"Everything. Do you understand? Every round fired by a CPP soldier is directly or indirectly paid for by Hang Boonma."

"I believe you," said Julie.

For a moment she felt caught in the crosshairs of gunfire and Rockoff's rising fanaticism. Liquid candlelight shadows splashed upon the floor and climbed the walls. At the bar Julie ordered a vodka and tonic and asked the bartender if he knew Asher.

"Who's asking?"

"A friend."

"Yeah? I hear those are in short supply for him right now," he replied. "I know him, sure, but I haven't seen the man in at least a month. Someone said he owes some people some money."

"You know where he lives?"

"Right up the street, five or six doors. But I wouldn't go there without a flak jacket. It's in the wrong direction, you know what I mean. Maybe tomorrow things will have calmed down. His landlord is a painter, guy makes terrible stuff for hotels, but you can't miss it. Look for the first-floor gallery of bad Khmer art. But if I were you, I'd get yourself home. These people in my establishment right now are psycho warmongers. They're the only-news-is-bad-news types. Rotten, baby, rotten to the core, skilled body-count freaks, is all. You don't look like one of them. Get yourself home."

Julie tipped him and left. On the street a handful of the journalists were walking toward the fighting; two had television cameras on their shoulders, others held nothing at all. Julie was considering joining them when someone touched her shoulder. Asher, for a moment she felt it might be Asher, and in spinning around she felt a whirl of mounting excitement. Katherine Coats was standing in the middle of the street holding a drink.

"I'm awfully sorry to have stuck you with Al on your first evening," she said. "But a woman must cut her teeth somewhere."

"Oh, he was fine," said Julie.

"Yes, I suppose it could have been worse. He does rattle *on*, though. You were lucky enough to get a truncated version."

Her glass dropped from her hand and shattered on the street.

"Bloody hell," she said. "I always take that as a sign to go home. Would you like to come home with me? There's some argument as to who has the best apartment in Phnom Penh, the owner of the FCC or me, but I rather think mine wins in the end."

"Really," said Julie. "You know, I didn't catch your name."

"Katherine Coats," she said, holding out her hand. "Divorced, beheaded, died . . . absolved, beheaded, survived."

Heat lightning lit the distant sky.

"Now is the time for all good men to come to the aid of their country," said Julie. "Where do you live?"

"On the river," she said. "You do play backgammon, don't you? Asher was *so* very keen on backgammon."

Julie stood still in the street. Backgammon with Asher; now what in God's name would this woman know of playing backgammon with Asher? In California backgammon had been epic with them. They played for almost as many reasons as they smoked. They played so as to get drunk before going to a party. They played to lend their respective postmortems to the party. They played to unwind after an argument and to fight the boredom of unemployment and television. Now a pang of jealous desperation parked itself in the pit of Julie's stomach. What did this woman mean by saying Asher was *so* very keen on playing backgammon? Were they having an affair or had they fucked in the simple past? She'd spoken as if Asher would never again touch a backgammon board in Cambodia. This worried Julie. Did it confirm the unthinkable, that Asher *had* left Cambodia "indefinitely," that he'd somehow come up with the money and split so as not to face her again?

"Backgammon it is," said Julie. "Lead on."

An evening breeze off the river brushed against their faces and swirled street garbage at their feet. The city was silent now but for the softening sounds of gunfire, and as the two women walked in awkward silence, Katherine wished she had not invited this Yank back to her apartment. It had been impulsive and foolhardy. The Yank did not feel obliged to make small talk, nor did she seem honored by the invitation. Katherine Coats's apartment was a sanctuary. Some of her closest friends had yet to step foot in it, and here was this Yank on her first night in town witnessing what journalists waited months for, the eruption of high-level political violence. It would be front-page news tomorrow. Rumors of Pol Pot's death and/or impending capture had ushered in the big boys. CNN had sent a team from Bangkok. From Hong Kong came a *South China Morning Post* reporter. There was a correspondent from the BBC. The *New York Times* had hired a bodyguard. The price for handlers, drivers, and translators was skyrocketing. The parachute-press corps had arrived to cover Cambodia's iconic news item, Pol Pot, and instead had been thrown a bone. Now there would be no tramping up to the northern provinces, no waiting around in malarial jungle towns for misinformation about Pol Pot.

Katherine Coats kicked a rolling beer can down the street. The Khmer Rouge were dead. The vast majority had defected to the government, and it was disgusting to see how the CPP and FUNCINPEC whored themselves out for their allegiance. Anyone who knew anything about the Khmer Rouge knew that Pol Pot had been outside the circle of real power for some time. And still the Western press came running on any rumor about the man. No, the Khmer Rouge were pawns in Hun Sen's drive to finally bury the UNTAC election. If Hun Sen could not win the Khmer Rouge over to his side, he would attack FUNCINPEC for collaborating with war criminals. Tonight signaled the beginning of the end to any semblance of democracy in Cambodia. The struggle had finally come to Phnom Penh and of this she was glad. Katherine Coats did not like to travel. For years it had been the countryside that had been dangerous and newsworthy. Now the battleground had moved to her backyard.

At the river they took a left and the wind kicked up. Across the Tonle Sap sat an island where Buddhists had taken to flying huge

saffron flags in a call for peace. Now heat lightning briefly illuminated the huge banners and then plunged them back into obscurity. A block from her apartment, the wind suddenly died, and the
two women found themselves in a slipstream. They turned to face
each other.

"We're in for a good soaking," said Katherine Coats as the first
drops of rain swiftly grew to a torrential downpour.

chapter fourteen

F OR THE SECOND DAY in a row Julie walked to the FCC to
see if there was any word from Asher. Nothing. She'd tried
to reach his apartment but the police had cordoned off the block
in the aftermath of the street fighting. At night she gambled and
drank at the casinos. Then on the afternoon Asher arrived at the
FCC from Siem Reap, she missed him by three blocks. She herself had just taken a late lunch at the FCC and was on her way to
his apartment, which the police had finally opened up. As she
walked inland the streets became nearly impassable. The rains
had come early and the newspapers were filled with stories of municipal drainage problems. It was the season of the cyclo. All the
moto drivers were spending their hard-earned cash replacing spark
plugs doused into worthlessness by the rains. Now Julie found
herself in the vaguely uncomfortable colonial position of sitting in
a cyclo while a panting man wheeled her down a street that resembled a river. At one intersection there was a dip in the road.
Here two children in see-through slickers were pushing cars
through chest-high water. The children were being goaded on by
a grown man who collected money from the cars at a higher level
of the street a few yards away. As Julie's cyclo driver got down from

his perch to manually push her through this mess, a scream rose up from the street. A young boy, one of those who'd been helping push cars, had lost his footing and was being swept toward a swirling, circular eddy. Julie jumped out of her cyclo. She watched as the man, perhaps the child's father, pushed through the mocha-colored water, one fist still clenching the notes he'd collected from the cars. Through the water the man moved in ghastly slow motion. The child was slipping down, slowly losing his grip on whatever there was to cling to. Suddenly Julie realized what was happening. A manhole. The kid was being sucked into a manhole uncovered to facilitate drainage. She ran toward the child, each step a dragging agony. The child's head turned a fraction and caught her eye. She was the last mortal soul he would ever see. The father screamed something in Khmer, but he had too far to travel. The child's head disappeared, his body sucked beneath the miserable street. For a moment the father stood paralyzed with horror and fear. Then he dove. The street froze, hanging in anticipation. When he came up empty-handed, a Khmer woman let out a terrible wail. He dove again, and again came up empty-handed. Julie closed her eyes but couldn't escape the image of the young boy's death. Small enough to fit down the manhole, he would be sucked through some ghastly underground tunnel, dragged through the sewers of the city until he came spilling out into the swollen river. Now the man stood motionless in the street, staring down at the red five-hundred-riel notes caught in the eddy. Too light to sink, the money circled and circled and circled around.

It took him a long time to get into town. It was only after he landed at Pochentong that Asher realized he had nowhere to go.

His apartment was out of the question. The thought of Mr. Hawk and Flat Top filled him with foreboding. There was Katherine, but was she really a friend? It was difficult to tell. It had become for him a soiled city of compromised friendships, of weak links and petty betrayals, years of mixing business and pleasure, of crossing lines, of sharing women and information, of corrupt maneuvering, of tainted favors given and received, and through it all the nightly numbing of his nerves, the dulling of his wits and watering of his brain.

He took a cyclo to the FCC and called Katherine's mobile phone in the second-floor business office. A recording told him that he was out of luck. He ordered a drink and read a three-day-old *Bangkok Post*. The front page carried an AFP wire story about a shootout between Hun Sen and Ranariddh's bodyguards. It had all gone down three blocks from his apartment. He took a second drink to the balcony, where he sat on a stool and gazed out at the scenery. It was early in the wet season for the river to be this high. From his bag Asher withdrew his binoculars and leaned out over the balustrade to check the royal landing pagoda to his right. It was a small yellow gazebo with stairs leading down to the river. There were maybe five steps left uncovered by water. A nude child did a flip from the top stair, came splashing down into the water, and had to swim furiously against the current to get back to safety. If the river rose three more steps, the city's drainage pipes would be covered by river water and then things really would get backed up. It had happened during his first wet season; the Tonle Sap and the Mekong had begun draining into the city and not the other way around. Once he'd befriended UNTAC's municipal drainage advisor, Ulf, the Swede. When drunk, Ulf liked to walk down to the landing pagoda and count steps. Once he'd taken Asher with him on his quasiscientific baptismal ritual, the shorter Swede forcing Asher to wade deep into the river to count how many steps there were to the bottom of the staircase. The mighty Mekong; he would miss it. It was one of the few things Cambodia had on Vietnam. Phnom Penh's shit flowed with vengeance downriver to Saigon, where the Mekong's constricted estuaries bubbled with stagnant filth.

Someone tapped him on the shoulder. It was Katherine.

"Hello, Asher," she said. "I've missed you. People have been talking. Where *have* you disappeared to?"

She was wearing a baby-blue camisole and a beige linen skirt and flip-flops. Her dark hair had been cut short so as to curl around her ears, and her blue eyes had constricted pupils.

"Katherine, you've cut your hair."

"Yes, isn't it splendid?"

When high and in public, she became archly British and annoyingly coy.

"I was wondering if you've run into a girl, an American woman who's looking for me?"

"An American woman looking for you? Can't say as I have," said Katherine. She did not know why she lied. She just did. Perhaps it was the country. Here the only truth was power. His information was contagious. It spread like smallpox in the Sudan.

"Fuck," said Asher. "She's supposed to be here."

"Can you simply believe these water levels? I don't think I've ever seen the river this high, this early in the season. It must be runoff from logging in the north."

"Are you sure you haven't seen anyone out of the ordinary? She's blond and completely noticeable."

"Ah, well, an attractive American woman doesn't stay single in this town for very long, now does she? Perhaps she's taken up with some undesirables in your absence or fallen in with a knot of people who might encourage her to weirdness."

"Unlikely," said Asher. "The woman of whom I speak does the influencing. She is not one to be influenced easily."

"I see," said Katherine. "I didn't know you kept such influential company."

"Katherine, there are sides to my character which you simply will never experience."

"So it appears," she replied, placing her hand on his waist and moving him toward the balcony. A burst of withering rain sent street vendors running beneath the eaves of buildings, and the Tonle Sap suddenly seemed riddled with bullet holes.

"Seriously, though," he said. "You haven't seen anyone? She was supposed to have left me a note or be hanging around the FCC as of yesterday or the day before."

Katherine paused. There was something about his weary strength, his muscular, urgent fearfulness that drew her to him. The gaps between their fornication were splendidly timed. He was a hunger spot, a bountiful irregular pleasure. She wanted him again, and what this Julie was doing in town filled her with annoyance.

As for Asher, he sensed Katherine might be lying, but his pride kept him from prying. She was a tea bag, after all. One didn't grovel with the English. It was considered poor form. If his Julie G-Spot were in town, it would simply be a matter of time before she showed at the FCC. He pictured her coming up the stairs, her hair wet from the rains and her breasts bursting from whatever getup she wore these days. He could make the rounds of the hotels but the weather really wouldn't permit that. No, he would wait. He would sit in the FCC, see the *barangs* go by, get drunk on the two hundred dollars Alex had lent him, stay put until she arrived in her arms. A lyric from *You're Living All Over Me*, a favorite Dinosaur Jr. record of their love affair in L.A., came to mind. It went: "I'll be down. I'll be around. I'll be hanging where eventually you'll have to be."

Asher and Katherine refreshed their drinks at the bar and then reclined in leather armchairs at the far end of the room. For a moment an uncomfortable silence sat between them.

"Well, you certainly missed the spectacle," said Katherine. "Ranariddh and Hun Sen's boys finally went at it. The whole thing was practically kitty-corner from your apartment."

"Yeah?" replied Asher, not terribly interested in the news of the day. "They let off a bit of steam, did they?"

"I'd say a bit more than that, darling. I'd say the kettle is just beginning to whistle."

"You always think that," he said. "Has there been any troop movement from out the Tiger's Den way? If there's coup material brewing, it's going to come from the east."

"We've got Chea out there right now checking it out."

"Chea is going to get his throat cut one of these days."

"Chea," said Katherine, "knows how to take a calculated risk, unlike your fellow countryman Six-Pack. That sod drove his car straight into the firing line and caught a piece of shrapnel in the shoulder. CNN did a hospital-bed interview."

"Good for Six-Pack."

"And they found some FUNCINPEC MP out past Pochentong with his eyes gouged out. Did you know one can sell a pair of eyes on the body-part market for four hundred American dollars?"

"Jesus Christ, Katherine. Can we change the subject?"

"Fine, but I'm just saying I can feel it, darling. I really can. Hun Sen and that cop of all cops, Hok Londy, are going to find some pretext to bring the whole house down."

"He'll wait until after the elections."

"Perhaps."

"Have you seen Larissa around?"

Larissa Martin was the manager of the FCC and keeper of a great many communiqués and secrets.

"She's in Burma with Allen," said Katherine.

"Fuck," said Asher. "So who's running the place?"

"No one, really. Why don't you come home with me?"

"Because I've got to find out if this friend of mine has left me a message or not," he replied. "Besides, I'd be useless to you. I'm working my Merchant Prince nerve ending. Things have arrived at a critical juncture."

"And a wee bit of china wouldn't change your mind?"

Asher sighed. It would be nice to get high, very nice, and very stupid.

"Thank you, no," he said. "I'm going to sit here and read the paper."

"We can come back at eight," said Katherine. "Mr. Kim will be on duty then. He'll know."

He was at once annoyed and flattered by her uncharacteristic insistence. He kissed her on the forehead.

"You're not being very British tonight, darling," he said. "I like you when you're British; now leave me alone."

"Fine," she said, a flash of anger cutting across her complexion. "I will."

chapter fifteen

At the ground floor of Asher's apartment, Julie found a man gently swinging in a hammock.

"Excuse me," she said. "But I'm looking for a friend of mine. His name is Asher. Do you know? American man, Mr. Asher? I was told he lived here."

The landlord silently nodded in the direction of the stairs.

"It is top floor," he replied.

At the third-floor landing she came upon Asher's pillaged apartment. The door was open and the first thing she saw was a familiar tattersall shirt, one she'd often worn in L.A., hanging from a lamp. The lightbulb had burned through the back. She walked into the apartment and found herself standing among a mixture of broken glass and shattered record vinyl. They'd destroyed all his records. As a farewell gift, she remembered shipping his records out to him along with her turntable, the only component now left of the stereo. It sat smashed on the ground, partially wrapped in speaker wire. Slowly, Julie walked through the carnage. Record sleeves and album covers were everywhere. A bookcase had been kicked over and paperbacks rifled through and discarded on the floor. She recognized her own worn college copies of *The Congress-*

man *Who Loved Flaubert* and Bradford's *On Plymouth Plantation*, bookends of an American history and lit course, long forgotten. They'd been looking for money inside her college books. It was almost funny. In the bedroom the mattress had been cut open, and spray-painted red on the wall above the bed frame was $ OR DIE.

She put her hand over her mouth. Her knees buckled, and she shortly found herself sitting Indian-style next to a miniature honeycombed replica of the four-headed God King she'd seen in her guidebook. The base had been pried off. Julie kicked the head across the room. On a nightstand she spotted half a joint rolled in Asher's hand. Slowly she stood up and went out onto the terrace to smoke. Little mounds of earth darkened by rain commingled with fragments of clay, along with dead flowers and vegetation she did not recognize. She lit the joint and gazed out over the red roof of the National Museum. Middle-aged tourists walked in the garden, and for a moment she envied them. It would be nice to be a tourist, wouldn't it? To leave your expensive home and travel. Some of the tourists walking in the garden were couples. They looked to be European. Julie blew smoke in the direction of the tourists. The thing about these tourists in this garden, she considered, was they would shortly go home. Their trip abroad was all about refreshing the home perspective. She sucked hard on the joint, burned it down until it singed her finger, and then flicked it off the balcony. Altering the home perspective. It was not her trip. Now there was no home to alter.

"Well," she said to herself. "I'm going back to my hotel."

Asher hid behind his newspaper, half reading the news of the world while growing increasingly petulant. Where the fuck *was* she? Drinking didn't help things, either. Gin wasn't relaxing him in the least. It was making him sweat. Al Rockoff came into the bar, and Asher stood up and moved to a corner chair. Asher respected Rockoff's strange concoction of informed insanity but was in no mood for the man's rambling. He was reading a three-day-old *Bangkok Post*. A ferry had gone down in the North Sea. Where the fuck *was* she? The Thai Minister of Finance had been fired. Where the fuck was she? In Phnom Penh a gun battle had erupted between forces loyal to FUNCINPEC and the CPP. Where the fuck was she? He found himself head-butting the center crease of the paper in order to arrive at jump pages. Stock markets were down all over the world. He decided to take action.

On the second floor of the FCC there was a business office. A docile Khmer woman lent him a tourist guide to the city, and he began to call hotels. She was not at the Capital, a cheap and backpacked hangout. She was not at the high end Cambodian. Now the money on his phone card was running low. Nobody by that name had checked in the Royal or the Pailin. At the Renakse the desk clerk took his time. Asher stamped his foot and cursed the meter. He was down to fifty cents. Yes, she had checked in. Would he like to be transferred to her room? Asher hung up, bounded down the FCC stairs, and sprinted through the city. He did not see the city, he ran through it, until he arrived panting at the Renakse's front desk.

Her key was not at the desk; no, she was in her room. Asher ran down the hallway, heaving with excitement, 101 . . . 103 . . . He paused at her door. His temples pulsed and his eyes bulged from their sockets. He did not knock. He walked in and there she was, lying in bed reading Edith Wharton's *Glimpses of the Moon*.

He dropped his bag. Gently she lay the book over her breasts. She smiled at him serenely, with a loving familiarity. She smiled at him as if it were her birthday and he had dipped down to the corner store only to return to make her breakfast in bed. It was a wonderful smile, a smile that canceled time. In that one exchange there in the doorway, all the years that had separated them dissolved. It was magic. The years simply fell away and for one ebullient, shining moment, they were left with the root of their love. Asher threw off his windbreaker and vaulted onto the bed. They began cautiously, muttering exquisite little nothings, their flesh gently touching, taking them to a distant ritual of rediscovery until the touching led to the actual scent of things, which slowly and then quite suddenly drove them to madness. Afterward they lay side by side, gazing up at the ceiling fan until they both fell into a profoundly relieved sleep.

Asher woke first. Beside him Julie slept. It was all so improbable. Julie G-Spot in Phnom Penh. He crept out of bed, pulled on his boxers, and watched her sleep. She had coarsened wonderfully. In place of the milky-smooth complexion there was a darker pallor, with thin smoking creases down her cheeks and crow's-feet in the corners of her eyes. Julie, oh, Julie; finally someone had come along to brighten his days. From her icebox he withdrew a bottle of water and drank copiously. Then he took out her bottle of vodka and took a few slugs of that. On his way to the bathroom, he noticed a blue shoe box wedged between the back of the icebox and the wall. He took it out. He should have suggested a hotel with a safe. That had been stupid. This hotel would not do. Never mind, they would be leaving soon enough. Sitting in his underwear on the edge of the adjacent bed, he looked down on the baby-blue shoe box. Could it possibly hold eighty grand? Once a friend of his in L.A. had told him that a million bucks in the movies doesn't look like a million dollars because the *idea* of a million dollars simply doesn't match the actual size of the count. In the movies, they have to pad the briefcase to make sure a million matched the imagination.

The sound of a rubber band woke Julie. She stirred, opened her eyes slightly, and froze. Her old lover, skinny and gaunt, his eye sockets rimmed with black, was hunched over on the opposing bed. He wasn't on her bed, no, he was on the other bed, his bed, and he was counting her money. A bolt of betrayal cut through her. The avarice, the greed in his expression was more disturbing than the fact that he was counting the money without her. She'd hoped they would do it together. In her imagination she had seen him renting out a private room in a Chinese restaurant, ordering a feast and at the end wallowing in their success, throwing the cash about in an orgy of self-congratulatory abandon. Instead, she was forced to deftly close her eyes when he glanced her way. With her eyes closed it was worse. Paranoid suspicion engulfed her. God knows what had become of Asher in the years since they'd known each other. He was in debt, yes, but exactly how much, he'd never told her. What would happen if he owed money all over town? Now the lustful fondness she'd felt for him only an hour ago was tainted by the erstwhile feelings she'd had for him in L.A., the old wary distrust. She opened her eyes slightly again. Now he was placing the shoe box back in its hiding place. How much he'd taken out, if any, was a mystery she did not want to uncover.

When she sat up in bed, he came over and kissed her.

"I can't tell you how fabulously strange it is to see you," he said. "I'm overwhelmed. Really. It's just really, really . . . I don't know, just great to see you again. When I look at you, it's like I can see the finish line of the Boston Marathon."

"You're sweet," she said.

Nothing about the money. If only he'd told her that he'd found the money and had riffled through it; if only he had, but he hadn't. As for Asher, he *had* been on the verge of telling her but at the last moment had felt ashamed of his sneakiness. This was supposed to be a lovers' reunion, and it was. It was a lovers' reunion, for Christ's sake. What was he supposed to say, Where's the money, honey? And yet, the money was between them, a burning subtext of fallibility, salvation, and corruption.

Outside, the street was altered by her damp presence beside him. The years weighed heavily, making for an uncomfortable walk. They spoke of visas to Burma and the weather until they arrived at a dimly lit, two-story Thai restaurant. At the upstairs balcony they took off their shoes and were shown to a low-lying table surrounded with cushions. The waitresses were delicate women dressed in Thai silk. They were wonderfully sculpted and servile. Asher ordered a bottle of chilled vodka, and so they took to doing the one thing they'd always been really good at doing together. They drank. They drank the vodka straight, occasionally chasing it with soda water or ginger ale. Soon the candlelight began to brighten and Julie's eyes sparkle. Perhaps they both had never loved nor needed alcohol more than they did at that moment, sitting Indian style across from each other in the midst of a humid Cambodian night. At a short diagonal, a French couple hunched over their table, murmured barely audible missives in their native tongue, and at Julie's back sat three women, one of whom Asher recognized as a Swede from Médecins Sans Frontières. It was a hushed, intimate, feminine restaurant.

"I'm not going to say that you've aged," said Julie. "Because my memory of you in L.A. is kinda blurry. It's amazing, but I don't have a single photograph of the two of us, not one survived."

"That's because you sold your camera to Penicillin Polly."

"I did not *sell* my camera to Penicillin Polly," she said. "I lent it to her."

"Ah, yes, well," said Asher. "I stand corrected."

A waitress knelt before them, serving rice and green chicken curry from earthen bowls. The couple grew silent. Confronted with the food, Asher realized he was not hungry in the least.

"Penicillin Polly," mused Julie. "That's a scary one to consider."

"She hung the moon," said Asher.

"Someone said she'd moved out of the canyon to Malibu."

"She would."

Penicillin Polly went for men who were otherwise attached. She was into speed and sexual reprisal. The sink upon which Asher had once fucked her had fallen from its foundation and broken in two on the floor. She was a bad spirit to have conjured from their past. Asher lit a cigarette and exhaled down at the Médecins Sans Frontières four-wheel-drive parked on the street below.

"I went by your place," said Julie. "It's trashed, baby. They even broke your records."

"Yes," said Asher. "I suppose they would have. Before I left for Siem Reap, they took my Dream too."

"How inconsiderate of them. How much do you suppose you're down to these people?"

"You shouldn't have gone by my apartment. It might be watched."

"Oh, come on, it can't be more than five grand."

"I haven't done the math yet."

"Well, don't you think you're blowing things out of proportion?"

"People get found in the river for less."

He poured another measure into her glass and watched her knock it back. He liked to watch her drink. She had a manly, gruff way at going about it, and after she was through she flipped her blond hair behind her shoulder and slammed the glass back down on the table.

"So," she said. "Shall we? Shall we discuss what it is I'm doing here and what our plans are for the future?"

"That all has to do with the money. I'm assuming you brought the money with you."

She winced at his little lie.

"Do you think I would have showed without it? Yes, the money and I want to go to the beach. I am a wanted woman."

"Ah, and I'm a wanted man."

They touched glasses.

"Don't you find it exciting?" she offered. "To be wanted?"

"No, it is a great discomfort for me. How much did you get? I'm not saying that you aren't an enterprising young lady, but moving weight was why we brought your boss into this thing to begin with."

"I killed my boss."

"You what?"

"I crushed his venal little skull."

"Ouch."

"Eat," she said. "You haven't touched a thing."

"You killed a man?"

"Yep; your pal Reese was there too. I have no remorse. New York had reached a Malthusian saturation point with Glen's kind.

I've got something just shy of seventy grand, and I saw you go riffling through it, you shifty little bastard."

Asher leaned back into his cushions and folded his arms.

"I can't believe you're keeping it in your hotel room. Tomorrow, after I pay off Mr. Hawk, we are depositing that money in the bank."

"Oh, sweetheart," she said. "We're going to have fun now, aren't we? *Please*, tell me we're going to have fun. I want to take the train down to the beach. I want to take a long swim."

Asher was moved. Julie G-Spot, the sorceress. He'd forgotten about her eyes, how they flashed with drunken connivance. They were darts of excitement and hunger.

"Whatever you want," he said. "You just give the word. You want to go down to the beach, we'll go down to the beach. I'll pay off Mr. Hawk and we'll go down to the beach."

"Tomorrow," she said.

The French couple shot them a glance. The bottle was nearly half empty. A clap of thunder hit the night and then came the rains.

"The guidebook said the train cuts through some amazing country. I want to take the train. I'm not sure if I told you about AA Allen."

"No, you haven't."

"Well, he's dead now. I was with him in that miserable little Maserati he liked to boast about."

"I remember the vehicle well," said Asher. "How is it that you were in it?"

"I don't want to drive, Asher. I just don't, okay? It took them two hours to pry me out of the thing. I watched Allen die."

"Guess AA didn't pay off. Maybe if he was drunk he wouldn't have been driving so fast."

"Don't be a fucking asshole. He's dead."

"I'm sorry, I just never could get with AA Allen, but I'm sorry he's dead. I am."

"I don't ever want to see a car again," she said. "It was one of the reasons I moved to New York."

"Where did it happen?"

"On the PCH. We were going surfing."

The sunny picture of Julie and AA Allen driving the Pacific Coast Highway on a surfing trip momentarily filled him with hateful jealousy. AA Allen was a script doctor, an overpaid fixer of high-budget-production disasters. His sole topics of conversation were AA meetings and the "beats" he added into movie scripts. Asher wasn't particularly taken with the idea of the train. The system was unreliable and not particularly safe. Still, it might be fun. He'd never actually taken the train before, and he was sick of endless taxi rides.

"Some unfortunate shit has happened to people on the train, but that's usually when it's coming from the port at Sihanoukville, filled with *motos* and other imported goodies. There isn't much risk going south, not enough imports to rob."

"So you'll take the train with me."

"Why not."

"Fabulous," said Julie, clapping her hands together. She seemed to rise up out of her seat.

Later that night Asher walked into the Apsara happy, with money.

"These are good times," said Asher. "I have something for you."

Mr. Hawk was sunk in a black leatherette love seat. He saw

the sheen on Asher's face and wondered. Well, he said to himself, well, the *barang* has come up with the money. It was funny. The one debtor Hang Boonma agreed to make an example of was coming up with what was owed. Mr. Hawk took the envelope seated.

"Truancy," said Asher. "I suppose you thought I was going to play truant on you, but I didn't. I am a Merchant Prince. I deliver."

Mr. Hawk squinted.

"Aren't we supposed to have a discussion?" said Asher. "Aren't you supposed to say thank you for my servicing your usurious function?"

Mr. Hawk said nothing. Slowly he opened the envelope and began counting the money in his native tongue, lightly slapping the bills onto the Formica table. As he counted, he thought. Counting was easy enough; it was Hang Boonma that mattered here. Now it would be necessary to call him and say that matters vis-à-vis the *barang* had been settled. Or would it? The bills spilled were all crisp one hundreds. Then he withdrew his calculator and added up the interest. Asher's accuracy astounded him. The money was all there, and yet he had supplied one of Hang Boonma's thugs with a photograph of Asher taken from a back issue of the *Phnom Penh Post*. As he gazed down on the hundred-dollar bills, he wondered, should he call Hang Boonma and tell him Asher's money was in, or should he do nothing? It was always a source of great discomfort, contacting the tycoon or his people, unless it was absolutely necessary. The conversations were gruff and filled with a latent sense of recrimination and reprisals. He ran down a mental list of people who still owed him. It was still significant. Perhaps tomorrow he'd call the Big Man and tell him that Asher should only have a leg broken, or perhaps . . . well, one thing he'd do for sure is tell the kickboxer to lay off. Yes, that was what he'd do. He'd take care of his own people. What the tycoon chose to do was his business. It wasn't good to interfere in other people's business. He looked up at Asher.

"I won't ask you where you got the money," he said. "The serial numbers are not from this country."

"No, they are not," replied Asher. "It is New York City green, daddy. Clean, crisp, cold, hard cash."

"From the Big Apple?"

Asher laughed.

"Yes, sir," said Asher. "Don't mind the maggots."

The two men looked at each other in silence. Despite the usury, a well of departing emotion for Mr. Hawk sprang up in Asher. In all the years he'd been away from home, this massage parlor owner had been one of the few Khmers he'd been able to level with.

"I'm afraid this is going to be our last meeting," said Asher. "I'm going to the beach and then I'm leaving this country. I'm going back to Chicago."

"A massage," replied Mr. Hawk. "Number thirty-six, she is ready for you, free of charge. She is the only Vietnamese left. I have been hiding her."

"That's very large of you, Mr. Hawk, but I've got to go."

"Go then," said Mr. Hawk, rising from the love seat. "Go and prosper."

They shook hands.

"Thank you," said Asher. "I intend to."

chapter sixteen

THE TRAIN STATION had the unique Khmer sensation of busied inefficiency and languor. It was difficult to tell who did what. The ticket counter had temporarily closed down due to a birth in the counterman's family, and a replacement had yet to be found.

"Notice how the first two cabins in the front car are free," said Asher. "It's a mine thing. The rails used to get mined about twice a year."

"Don't worry, honey," said Julie, grasping the tickets. "The odds are with us."

Julie had purchased first-class tickets but the fans had broken and by the time the train pulled out of the station forty-five minutes late, their cabin was a miasma of discomfort. They'd been stuffed into a car with a chain-smoking hotelier and his wife from the southern town of Kampot. The couple had two children who howled incessantly, while the husband chain-smoked Embassy cigarettes and practiced his English on Asher. He had a good-natured, round, happy face, and he was proud of his hotel. He gave Asher his card. The wife, on the other hand, was not happy. Silent and pouty, smeared with lipstick, she had, according to her husband, purchased the latest gadget from Japan. It was a hand-held, battery-operated fan which whirled before her face. The children cried in near-perfect sequence: when one stopped, the other kicked in. Sometimes they sang a chorus together. As soon as the train left the city limits, Asher and Julie fled for the corridor and took to the roof. For a while the train ran nearly parallel to Route 3. Then it veered off and the train was alone in the countryside, chugging through rice fields or nothing much at all until a mountain would rise up suddenly in the distance. Then Asher, who had brought his set of Russian binoculars, would ogle the mountain and poke his head into his shirt to light the various things they were smoking. It was a fine time. Julie wore mirrored shades and a slutty halter-top that showed off her plentiful, slightly sagging boobs and powerful arms. She took pictures of him on top of the train with a *krama* wrapped around his head. From time to time Route 3 reappeared, running along next to the train like a momentarily lost friend.

They didn't speak much. They didn't have to. They sat with their backs pressed against each other, she looking out at the scenery past, he looking out at the scenery future. There was no rush to "catch up" and prick each other with petty jealousies, and so they kept things to the moment.

"What's the beach like?" she asked.

"What?"

"The beach, what's it like?"

"The beach is the beach because we are arriving there with impunity. We have money safely in the bank and on our persons. Mr. Hawk has been paid off. That's what the beach is."

"Come on," she said. "What's it like?"

"It's the South China Sea, okay? That means the water feels

like a baby pool, but we can swim out to the casino island that never got off the ground. There are boats too; we can rent out a fishing boat and scamper around. It'll be fun. There are lots of little islands."

"What's the hippie factor?"

"There could be a contingent, but after the grenade attack things have slackened off, touristwise. Still, there will be hippie backpackers, a brave lot. They make model ships and sail them out to sea at sundown. We'll have to watch ourselves, though. It's traditionally FUNCINPEC country, but the CPP is muscling in. The television station was rocketed to fragments a few weeks ago. The king's got a condo in Kep. I've checked it out. It's bad Miami Beach. The bars have mirrors."

"Cool. Can we have drinks with the king?"

"He's in Beijing; colon cancer."

"Too much foie gras."

"Exactly."

They turned and kissed.

"Sometimes, Asher," she said, "just a wee bit of a splinter of the time . . . sometimes, sweetheart, you're the champ."

The absence of bitterness lent the proceeding a wonderful lightness, a felicity, a playful candor. For a while the train again lost contact with Route 3, and mountains rose up on either side. Asher tensed but said nothing. Though most of the Khmer Rouge had defected to the government, there was still Phnom Voar, "Vine Mountain," to contend with a few kilometers on. It was an infamous Khmer Rouge–controlled mountain range, and for a moment Asher was glad they weren't traveling in the opposite direction in a train loaded with exports for sale in the capital. Suddenly the train slowed. In the middle distance soldiers were standing on the rails holding out their arms toward the carriages. Soldiers impeding movement; when would it ever go away? Asher watched as cigarettes flew out the windows.

"Cigarette tax, huh?" said Julie.

"I don't like this," said Asher, looking through his binoculars. There were about eight or nine soldiers, most sporting the red and blue RCAF patches of the government variety on their shoulders. Mixed in there were two older unarmed men of the local militia. With leathery, creased faces, worn uniforms, and flip-flops, they were the recipient of most of the cigarettes. There didn't seem to be a threat here, and the train began to gain momentum. Asher breathed out.

"You can't tell who the fuck is who anymore," he said. "The Khmer Rouge in these mountains have folded into the government, but they're still the Khmer Rouge. They're all cousins anyway. Even before the KR defected, they were cutting deals with their uncle so-and-so in the government."

They passed a limestone quarry where a section of a mountain had been carved out, and though the machines stood idle, the air was slightly dusted with limestone residue. The quarry gave onto a broad swath of barren, sun-baked land, the perimeter of which was dotted with the red and white skull-and-crossbones placards of a local demining unit. A lone cow wandered the mined field, and in the far distance a small group of village children waved their sticks and shouted in protest. They'd lost control of their cow and now it was in peril's way. It would only be a matter of time now, or perhaps, thought Asher, the unknowing animal might miss its death by a centimeter here, a centimeter there. Its ignorance might be a blessing. Umbrellas dotted the adjacent field.

"What," asked Julie, "is that?"

"CMAC," replied Asher.

"I can't believe this country," said Julie. "It's all one big fucking acronym. FUNCINPEC, CPP, CMAC, WHO. It's really kind of annoying."

"Cambodian Mine Action Committee," said Asher. "The umbrellas are to ward off the sun, but it's no picnic. See the legs sticking out from beneath the umbrellas, the blue pants. That's a CMAC guy digging up a mine. They pad their ranks like the army. Whoever reports back to the CMAC mother ship in Phnom Penh claims that he's got 150 guys working for him when actually he's only got, say, 110. The extra salaries go into the unit commander's pocket."

"It looks like slow work."

"It is," said Asher. "Slow and expensive. It isn't just mines either. There are UOs to take care of, unexploded ordnances. Bombs that fell but never blew up."

"Really," said Julie, "the bomb, huh? Kids in New York these days, when they say 'the bomb,' that means cool, elaborate, powerful."

Asher had no desire to get with contemporary American urban lingo.

"UO is technically an umbrella term," he said. "It could be a mine but usually when CMAC uses UO, it means a bomb dropped from a plane some years ago that didn't go off on impact. Their numbers rank well into the six figures."

Route 3 came back into view and they could see the white pickups and four-wheel-drives of CMAC at the side of the road.

Men were unloading surveying equipment and talking into black walkie-talkies.

The train rumbled on. It crossed a river fed by mountain water, and then the northern outskirts of Kampot could be seen in the distance. The tracks crossed Route 3 and headed west.

"We're fine now," said Asher.

"What do you mean, *fine?*"

"We're out of harm's way," he said. "Those soldiers on the tracks worried me."

"They were lonely," said Julie. "They wanted cigarettes."

"I know, I know, but I don't like it when the train slows down."

"You," said Julie, "are the most frightened man I think I have ever met. We're going to the beach, for Christ's sake. Don't you worry your paranoid pretty head. Your debts are paid. We've got money in the bank . . ."

"And shortly I will return home in triumph."

"Exactly."

She came up to him and wrapped her legs around his waist and hung her arms over his shoulders. They burned down the last half of the joint in silence.

"You can find yourself a nice Winnetka blonde who will do your laundry, and the two of you will breed and will live happily ever after."

"Thank you," said Asher. "That sounds nice. Don't forget to remind me to mow the lawn."

"I'll call every financial quarter," replied Julie, "to check up on how the little ones are doing."

They passed Kampot and arched southward toward the sea. On the left came a large coconut plantation. The trees formed a symmetrical field of lined alleyways that flashed in an orderly staccato. On the right was the benevolent Roulos mountain range. Green moss and thick vegetation partially obscured the rocks and runoff from a thin waterfall. Water caught the wind and sprinkled downward through a rainbow. It was lush, fertile countryside, a topographical cousin to the Vietnamese Delta. He pinned Julie down against the hot metal of the carriage car, ignoring the family of peasants and the sole representative of the train militia. They rolled to one side of the rumbling car and then the other, laughing and groping each other.

"No," she said. "Stop it. My tits are getting burned on the metal."

Their fornication was interrupted by the train slowing. Asher stood up. Again, there were troops on the rails. This he had not anticipated.

From a distance it looked like the same scenario, underpaid soldiers on the rails looking to cadge cigarettes, but as the train neared, something else began to take form.

"Fuck," said Asher.

The train slowed.

"Oh, come on," said Julie, lying on her stomach. "Just think of it as a toll wait. It's a fucking toll. People smoke here. They . . ."

A man standing on the rails lifted his Kalashnikov and began shooting at the train. As Asher hit the deck, he caught a glimpse of the man: a young bandit on full automatic spraying the train. Asher glanced over at the train militiaman. His neck tendons were standing out like a bodybuilder's as he returned fire. As the train continued to slow, a soldier leapt from a ditch. He had a round object in his hand that could be nothing else but a mine. For a moment the man disappeared beneath the train. Heavy fire now was being exchanged and Asher saw the militiaman sit down. A gut shot.

"Stay down, sweetheart, stay down," he whispered in her ear.

They suffered the explosion of the mine pressed against each other in senseless love and horror.

The locomotive moaned and hissed to a grinding stop. For a moment there was an unearthly silence. Crickets from the nearby wooden mountain chirped in the heat. Then a single pistol shot rang out and a Khmer voice began barking orders. Asher listened closely.

"What's he saying?" asked Julie.

"Something about identification," said Asher. "They want everyone off the train."

chapter seventeen

"Look, this story has incredible legs," said the bureau chief in Bangkok. "Incredible legs. I mean, talk about newsy drama."

"I know, I know, Frank," said Reese. "I've got to think about this one. Let me call you back."

"Don't call me back. Get down there. Get down there and dig up anything you can. There's nothing going on in Phnom Penh right now, right?"

"Well, the general assembly is meeting and—"

"Fuck those people, they're a rubber stamp, not news."

"Frank," said Reese. "It's impossible to file down there."

Frank Mackey was Reese's boss of two and a half years. He loved Bangkok and the life he lived there. Recently he had taken a Thai wife. He had a driver and memberships to various well-air-conditioned clubs. His interest in Cambodia was death. If there wasn't death, there wasn't news, not out of Cambodia. Anything involving the Khmer Rouge was good. Politics was good only if there was bloodshed involved.

"Reese, my man," replied Frank. "You can't believe the juice I'm getting on this story, back-channel shit. Two Americans and a missionary held hostage by the KR after the train they're riding in gets shot up? Come on."

"I've got to go, Frank," said Reese. "I'll call you."

"You better," said Frank. "I'm serious, there are times when I don't want to hear from you, Reese. I mean, I really don't want to take the call. All that copy you've been boring people with, 'Cambodia's fractious coalition took another turn . . . ,' that bullshit. No one wants to hear about how many assembly seats FUNCINPEC might win in the next election. This story has grit and serious news value. I want to hear from you."

"I got it, Frank."

"You got it?"

"Good," said Reese and hung up.

He threw his chair across the room. There was a footlocker for emergencies near the refrigerator. The footlocker consisted of a roll of high-speed Fuji film, a cassette recorder complete with tape, a secondhand camera flash, a list of important government and military officials' mobile phone numbers, and a bottle of Stolichnaya. It had been Reese's policy to institute the emergency locker. The rule was that if one of the items was used, it *must* be replaced so that the footlocker might be useful for emergencies over time. Reese went for the bottle of Stolichnaya and poured himself a glassful. Asher and that rip-off artist girlfriend of his up in Bokor. He drained his glass. The funny part was, before he'd left for vacation, he'd considered visiting the area. Theoretically, it was supposed to be safe. In the early '60s Bokor was said to be an abandoned mountain getaway for the rich and famous. Reese didn't put the bottle back in the emergency locker. For the first time in his journalistic life he left the bottle solidly on his desk for anyone to see. He looked at his watch. It was nearly noon. He'd first read the story during a layover in the Bangkok airport and had immediately come to his office to sulk. As the vodka burned his stomach, he wrapped his head in his hands. Tears came to his eyes.

"Goddamn it," he said.

For a moment he flashed to the police scene in Weatherly's apartment. The blood on the stuffed animals, the ghastly body, the police photographers, the white plastic gloves, the endless paperwork. The silent ride to the elegant precinct building. The fingerprints on the flashlight were not his. He had arrived at the apartment five to ten minutes after the incident. Weatherly had been nice about promising to back up that lie. There were hours of sitting in a holding room, waiting to be asked questions by different cops. Near dawn the plainclothes homicide detective named something-or-other LeMay sat down for a long taped interview. Reese asked him if he was related to Curtis "Bomb them into the Stone Age" LeMay. The detective didn't get the joke. Reese claimed ignorance convincingly. He'd walked into his old friend's apartment for drinks. Weatherly had just called the police. Weatherly had been in shock. He claimed this acquaintance of Weatherly's was in the kitchen when the guy tried to break in. Earlier in the evening he'd been drinking at the Gramercy Park Hotel bar, where, to the detectives' chagrin, he had paid in cash. Reese showed LeMay his press card and various other forms of identification. His fingerprints were not on the flashlight. How could he have seen the flashlight before since he'd never visited the apartment? It was a simple case of breaking and entering. If LeMay wanted to ask any more questions, it would have to be through his lawyer.

Weatherly had been nice about keeping his end up about the

timetable. They'd rehearsed that one before the police arrived. Weatherly promised that he would be the one who would tell them about Julie. And it was true, he didn't know her last name.

It ended with Reese giving LeMay several contact numbers. When he was finally released, Weatherly was still in the precinct building with his lawyer.

Then there had been his sister's wedding on three hours of sleep. A forty-eight-hour drunk, a sad, funny, wonderful ceremony involving Allison Graber in a back room of some mausoleum of an Upper East Side club, her bridesmaid's dress hiked up. That had been the second and most luscious encounter. The first had been an outstandingly passionate one-night stand in her apartment. Oh, and it had been wonderful the way their five-year age difference had melted away, had slowly shifted from an awkward, adolescent hindrance to mutual, all-out lust. He'd been funny and insane. They'd played more than footsie under the table during boring toasts. She'd been humorous, athletic, and most important, given his life in Asia, sane. She'd asked him to come sailing with her in Maine. If he'd really wanted to, he could be sailing in Maine right now, sailing with Allison Graber. But he wasn't. Now there was a tearsheet of the latest AP story on his desk that he did not want to look at again.

"Renegade Khmer Rouge guerrillas attacked a train outside the southern Cambodian town of Kampot Friday, killing 12 and holding three foreign hostages in the Bokor mountain range, government officials confirmed yesterday.

"The hostages . . ."

He couldn't go any further. Their names and ages typed out so cleanly repulsed him. How could this have happened? New York had circled the globe to come back on his fucking desk, coming back all the way around and washing up here! The trouble had moved faster than a plane, faster than he could handle. It was toxic and transcontinental, a soupy, sick mist that had crossed the world to envelop his beat.

"I'm going to excuse myself from this one," he said out loud. "It's done all the time. I'll say it's personal, that I have no objectivity."

He picked up the phone and called Frank.

"Reese, please, Asia is one large conflict of interest," replied Frank. "I know this Asher was a source of yours but I've got to tell you no. First thing you do is pin down the ransom demands."

Reese put his hand over the phone and breathed out. Fucking Frank, a what, where, and when man. His was not to reason why, his was to sit in his well-air-conditioned office and guard his standard of living.

"I still don't want to do it, Frank," he continued. "It's making me sick. The ransom demands will get political once TV gets on it."

"Reese, our job is not to forecast the news," replied Frank. "Our job is to cover it. Get it. If you can't handle this one, I'll get someone else to and you will never work for this organization again. It's a fucking story. Cover it."

Frank hung up on him.

"Pin," shouted Reese. "Get me all the fucking wire copy on this train thing outside Kampot from the beginning."

Pin came in from the other room. He wore a brown vest with mesh pockets over a black heavy-metal T-shirt. The ensemble gave him a vague military feel. "Catfish," that was what the local press corps had given him as a nickname. It had something to do with his whoring. Pin was an essentially happy man. He had a wife who nagged at him and who, he claimed, often got sick, but he had two wonderfully healthy children and despite his whoring, he was a fine, loving father and, most of all, a natural optimist. Reese supplied him with condoms.

"Hun Sen, he come back from Malaysia," said Pin.

"Fuck Hun Sen," said Reese. "I have to go down to Kampot."

Pin shook his head.

"It was very bad what they did there."

"Yeah, I know," replied Reese. "Notice how they shot all the Vietnamese first and on the spot?"

Pin was a great hater of the Vietnamese, and Reese used every opportunity to check his translator's racism.

"I thought all the Khmer Rouge in Kampot came over to the government," said Reese.

"They will be some who are soldiers still loyal to Ta Rin."

Rin had been a source of discussion with the human rights people and embassy personnel. Though he'd masterminded a 1994 hostage-taking of three backpackers, all of whom had later been bludgeoned to death, he still had been allowed back into the government. Hun Sen was big on "reintegration" and had offered amnesty to scores of Khmer Rouge sick of fighting in the jungle. They'd been trickling in for years. Rin now rode about Phnom Penh in a Land Cruiser, wore a government uniform, and held a decent rank. Besides the so-called "hardliners" in the north, there weren't supposed to be any Khmer Rouge left. It had been reported that Rin and all his southern Khmer Rouge had come over to the government last year. Clearly that had not been the case. Clearly there had been a few stragglers who hadn't "reintegrated," who, apparently, still lived in the southern mountains. Perhaps they were still in touch with their former commander.

Reese walked over to the fan and unbuttoned his shirt. The wind cooled his sweat, and in that moment of relief an idea came to him. What would happen if he got in on this one? What would happen if he used reporting the story as a cover? What would happen if he tried to save Asher and Julie's lives? There was little chance Fat Dave at the American embassy would go out on the limb. They were quite Israeli when it came to hostage stuff. There were policies about negotiating with human-rights criminals and so forth. He poured himself another water glass of vodka and on impulse picked up the phone. Slightly drunk now, his plan appealed to him.

"*Regarde,*" said Reese. "Can we have lunch?"

"Reese, you are back."

"Sadly, I am."

"And you have been . . ." A pause to light a cigarette. "You have been in America? How was your trip?"

"I need to see you, Valery. I'm serious."

"Good. I see you at the FCC?"

"No, not there. Let's go to the Timali Tiger place."

"The one across from the billiards hall on Monivong?"

"Yeah."

"I cannot say I am in the mood for this food, Reese."

"Okay, I'll take you to the Rendezvous," he said. "That's how much I need you now. Let's make it early, say, twelve."

"*Génial,*" said Valery.

Valery had a soft spot for the Rendezvous. One could always get her to eat there. She was French and loved to complain about the food.

Pin arrived with the tearsheets. There was AFP, AP, and Reuters.

"It's fucking hot in here, Pin," said Reese. "When did you call the air condition guy?"

"He come day after tomorrow."

"Why not today?"

"He say his niece is getting married in Takeo."

"Well, fuck this country."

There were infinite ways Reese related to Pin. For months they'd go solely on need-to-know. Once they'd driven all the way from Battambang to Phnom Penh without exchanging a word, not one. Other times Pin would sit with his head in his hands and complain about his wife, about money, and about his neighborhood police, who extorted from him. Then there were times when Reese would sound off himself. He'd go on about the lack of white available women in Phnom Penh, about government lies, about Frank. Now marching around the steaming-hot cement bunker of an office with the clattering fan as partial accompaniment, he launched into a litany of complaints. He vented.

"I'm telling you, Pin, I don't like it. I don't like this fucking story; this Asher tried to set me up once. He gave me a big package, claims it's his life's work, a screenplay, you know, for the movies; the thing weighed a ton and guess what? It wasn't filled with white pages, it's filled with something else. The guy, who for some weird reason I still like, ruined my vacation, and now I come back to hear that he and this slutty girlfriend of his, this woman whose unfortunate company I had to keep in New York, is not only *here* in Cambodia but is being held hostage by the Khmer Rouge. Which leads me to believe it can't be only the Khmer Rouge behind this train thing. There's got to be government collusion in

l i g h t n i n g   o n   t h e   s u n   245

there too, but that will be impossible to print. Remember '94 in Phnom Voar, those poor fucking backpackers? Once the story got on CNN, notice how the ransom changed? At first it was a local thing, damlungs of gold or something, and then Ta Mok sees the world is paying attention. The government wants to get tough on what's left of the Khmer Rouge. They start shelling the mountain, and the poor stoners are used as political pawns. It went from a few grand in gold to 'All foreign devils must leave Cambodia.' And believe you me, that will happen here. And it's going to be hot as hell down there and impossible to file. Thank God they just got mobile phone coverage down there, but it's still going to be a bitch. I'm telling you, Pin, I don't like hostage stories, not one bit, and Frank's going to fucking fire me if I don't get down there and file. But there'll be nothing to file. It will be some monstrous waiting game. But we got to break this thing before television gets there. They're already probably sending crews from Bangkok. When did this story break . . . ah, yes, day before yesterday. So we have maybe a day and a half on the television people. The hardliners in the north, Ta Mok, Pol Pot, that crew, they might not have access to the *New York Times,* but believe you me, they have satellite dishes and they'll be watching the tube to see how this plays out. Pin, do you know anyone in Kampot?"

"My uncle," said Pin. "He live there many years. He is manager of the cement factory, very good friend with the deputy governor. We go see my uncle. He give us good information, for sure."

Reese was glad of that. Pin had uncles all over the country. They were tough men and good sources. He considered telling Pin his plan of embarking on a brave new frontier in journalism.

"Boss," said Pin. "You should take a Xanax."

"Don't call me boss."

"Here, boss," said Pin, holding out a pink Xanax pill. "You take and I'll get the car ready."

Reese swallowed the pill and looked at his watch. Half an hour until his lunch with Valery. He took a seat behind his desk and closed his eyes.

"Pin," he said. "Get me the spoons."

When faced with moments of stress and/or hangover, Reese kept a pair of spoons in the freezer. Pin arrived with the cold spoons, and Reese lay on the floor. Pin placed them over Reese's eyes.

"Okay," he said out loud. "Calm thyself."

Valery Lane was a Parisian who had married and divorced a British import/export magnate with outstanding connections within the CPP. She used bottled water to wash her hair and she had a fencer's nose that flared at unsavoriness. She was the deputy director of the Phnom Penh branch of Bank Indo-Suez. It was the most reliable bank in town, was said not to engage in the washing of counterfeit, and had branches throughout Indochina. The UN had banked with Indo-Suez, and though it had recently been robbed, it was still considered the safest place to put one's money. Valery sat across from Reese in the shade beneath a canopy. Though she had given birth to two children, there was still that maddeningly trim French body with which to deal. She wore a dark blue skirt and a white linen blouse and a conspicuous lack of any jewelry whatsoever.

Reese wore beige Wrangler's and a dark gray button-down

shirt, which he put on for hot days so as to not make it quite so evident that he was given to sweating through his shirts. He gazed at the menu, uninterested, wondering, pondering, fearing what he was about to say. Of course, if he were to go through with what he was about to propose, it would be a great dereliction of his journalistic duties, but that was what drew him to the idea in the first place. Their coffee arrived and Valery looked over at him sternly.

"You seem . . . how do you Americans say it? . . . hot and bothered."

"Definitely hot," said Reese. "Definitely bothered. You see, there is a story I have to cover, and I don't want to do it."

"Then do not."

"Sadly, I don't have a choice. My bureau chief thinks the story is 'sexy' and, I quote, 'has a lot of legs.' "

"What is the story?"

"Are you familiar with that fellow Asher who used to work for UNESCO?"

"Certainly; for a while there he was impossible to miss, but I haven't seen him in at least three months. He bought me several drinks once at the Heart and was very kind. Also, I see him once in a while at the bank. He has a very old account."

"That's why I called you," said Reese. "Asher and his girlfriend have been taken hostage. The news came over the wires day before yesterday. They're somewhere outside of Kampot. It may be Khmer Rouge. It may be government. My guess would be a mixture of both."

"Yes, and that ghastly Rin who had those backpackers killed. I understand they gave him a nice rank for coming over to the government."

"Well, I've made some calls to my embassy," Reese lied.

"They've got this policy that's very Israeli, no negotiating with terrorists, that kind of thing. They won't help."

"Sometimes I do not understand your country."

"Believe me, neither do I."

Valery paused. Her coffee cup lingered up by her throat. Then she squinted at Reese.

"You want me to give you Asher's money, what he has in the account?"

"That's correct."

"You want to play Rambo."

"Don't give me that, Valery. I want to save a man's life. I might be the only one who can do it."

"I see."

She put her coffee down in its saucer and ordered from the menu. Reese looked her over. She was stalling, pondering, mulling the thing over. It was nice to see an attractive French woman think hard on something.

"I could be fired," she finally said.

"Look, Asher isn't at the bank to sign for himself. But believe me, he's spiritually there right now, hoping someone is going to help him at the window."

"He made a fairly big deposit the other day," said Valery. "I was surprised."

"He would have."

"Oh, it is bad. I do not like hostage situations. They are, how do you say . . . messy."

"Messy is a good adjective, yes, but I've got to go soon, and I can assure you, the man's life as well as his girlfriend's are in your hands. I don't know about the third guy. Apparently he's a missionary."

"But you are a journalist," she said. "Not a fixer."

"That is why I'm counting on your silence on this matter. I know you can fix it. It just takes the will to do it."

"You are not a journalist, Reese," she said. "You are playing Rambo."

The French loved to rag on Rambo. It was becoming a cliché.

"Fine, if you want to see it that way, you may."

Hungrily she dug into her Croque Madame, the egg spilling out onto the bread. The sight was making Reese sick.

"All right," she said, pushing her plate away. "But if you say one word to anyone, if you use your mouth with all those other journalists, I will have you fired. I'll call *le chief de bureau*, eh?"

"I won't tell a fucking soul. It wouldn't really be in my professional interests anyway. It's just that I'm getting sick of . . . sick of. I don't know, not actually *doing* anything for anyone anymore."

"But how will you get him out?"

"I'll find the go-between and negotiate."

"A good story, yes?"

"I'll file but minimalize."

"What does this Asher and his girl mean to you?"

"I don't know," he replied. "They're fellow taxpayers."

Here Valery laughed and took off her sunglasses.

"You have not touched your food," she said.

"I'm not hungry. I'm angry."

She finished off her Croque Madame and wiped her mouth daintily.

"I can be fired for this."

"You've already stated that, Valery, but covering your tracks will be easy enough. Doesn't Claude love you?"

Claude was her superior at the bank. They were often seen together. The gossip was that she was sleeping with him in order to get transferred to the Saigon branch, where the accounts were bigger and the air-conditioning more reliable.

"I will have my boy come to your office in two hours. I am to empty his account, yes?"

"Empty it."

"But you keep your mouth shut, eh?"

"You don't have to tell me that," said Reese. "You keep yours shut too."

"You take me on a date when it is done. You will buy me Campari and sodas and the best bottle of wine I can find. Oh, I'm so sick of the Algerian rot we have here. It is giving me an ulcer."

"That sounds fine," said Reese. "Can I put vodka in my Campari, vodka and Orangina?"

"*Comme tu veux.*"

"Thank you, Valery," he said, leaving a ten-dollar bill on the table. "You've taken a leap of faith. You've always had guts. Thank you."

She said nothing. She watched him leave and replaced her sunglasses. As he walked out onto the river road, he cast one more glance at her. The French, he thought, so awful, so wonderful, so goddamn inscrutable.

Hang Boonma was famous for the large sums of money he spent on surveillance in and around Phnom Penh. He had people in banks, at the airport, at nightclubs, and, as it turned out, at the train station too. On the morning Asher and Julie departed for the beach, there had been a man at the station. He was one of many who worked for the tycoon, and his job was to keep an eye out at the ticket window of the train station and report back to his boss about the comings and goings of a list of people of interest. Naturally, he was also with the police. Asher was on the list. In his hand he held passport photographs of people the boss needed to see. Some of the passport photos had been bought off the visa police at Pochentong; others had been obtained from the municipal police. Standing in the shaded entrance, he spotted Asher and immediately called Hang Boonma's office.

"Wake him," he said. "Tell him the *barang* Asher is fleeing by train."

Hang Boonma woke to the company of his favorite prostitute and to the news that Asher was fleeing. The man who owed Mr. Hawk and therefore owed him was fleeing south, and on the train, of all things, which meant he had very little money and in all probability had not paid Hawk. Perhaps he was trying to escape to Vietnam. Only peasants traveled on the train. The tycoon sipped his black Chinese tea and called Mr. Hawk's mobile phone. The number was turned off. Over his breakfast soup, he hatched a plan. If this Asher could not pay back Mr. Hawk, then his family or his government would have to pay. In his office, Hang Boonma opened his cell phone and called his cousin's number in Kampot.

"Sarun," said Hang Boonma. "You lazy cow, I have a job for you. It's the train again. Ready?"

"Ready," said the tycoon's cousin.

"It's the train coming from Phnom Penh."

"Oh, that is no good," said Sarun. "They have nothing on that train. It is filled with peasants and no *motos*."

"This is different. There are two *barangs* on the train and their lives are worth more than many *motos*. You understand? Their families will pay the cost of many, many *motos* for their lives. You rob the train today. Get in touch with your contacts. Make it look Khmer Rouge. But do not kill the *barangs,* you understand. Tell your men not to kill them. They are worth their weight in gold."

"In gold?" said Sarun.

"In gold."

"Where do you want me to touch the train, cousin?"

"I don't know, wherever I can still reach you by telephone. Take them into the mountains."

"How much do I ask for to begin with?"

"Fifty thousand for one. Twenty-five percent goes to me, later."

"Fifty thousand," said Sarun. "They must be very light *barang.*"

"Sarun," said Hang Boonma. "Demand fifty thousand and you'll get it. You ask for more and things will get difficult. What can a train robbery cost you? Three bribes, a meeting with whatever bandits are still around, and a mine. The train is coming now. They left the station an hour and a half ago. You do the usual. Have your men stand on the tracks begging for cigarettes and then, *boom, boom.*"

"*Boom, boom,*" said Sarun. He liked that. He was the deputy governor of the province.

The tycoon's favorite whore, who had now raised herself from a deep, financially favorable slumber, began to massage her boss's shoulders.

"Okay," said Sarun. "I do it."

"Make it look Khmer Rouge."

"No problem, cousin. Twenty-five percent. You have your man drive to Kampot once it is over. I know a place. There is very good communications."

"Good, you call me when you have them, but don't shoot them, cousin, you understand that?"

"I'll give the instructions but the men in that area are very undisciplined. Some are still Khmer Rouge. There are about a dozen of them who did not come over to the government with Ta Rin."

"Can you work with them?"

"Yes, but at a price. Rin, he still comes down here from Phnom Penh and gives them gifts. He wants to make sure they are not angry with him for coming over to the government. Some are still loyal to Rin and will not speak to me. I will have to offer more than usual."

"Pay it."

"I'll call you when it is done."

"You do that," said the tycoon. "Good-bye."

Hang Boonma grasped the whore's waist and took her back into his bedroom. He would finish his breakfast of noodle soup later.

"They try to run on Hawk. They try to run on me. No one runs on me, my flower. No one. Now come here," he said. "Come here, my flower, and sit on me like you did last night."

chapter eighteen

THEY WERE THE MOST beautiful flowers Julie had ever seen. On either side of the path they sprang up in violent pinks and whites, blues, yellows, reds, violets, a miasmic kaleidoscope of natural beauty. There were no roses, no tulips. She knew the name of not one of them. As they walked she occasionally picked one and put it in her hair. At one point she put a flower in the gun barrel of her guard. He smiled at her.

"I wouldn't do that again," said Asher. "This isn't Kent State."

"He likes me already."

They were a party of ten. There was Asher and Julie and a Danish Seventh-Day Adventist, who recited sections of the Bible in his native tongue. He heaved himself up the mountain and sweated profusely. He was a huge, beefy man, and though the path was well shaded by overhanging vegetation of every variety, he was sweating as hard as Julie had ever seen a man sweat. His white short-sleeve shirt was so translucent, she could clearly see his pink flesh and nipples. Behind and ahead of them were their captors. Most had rolled up their pants above the calf. They wore sandals and had rusty Kalashnikovs strung across their backs. Their pockets were stuffed with money stolen from the train's passengers. After being robbed, most of the passengers had been allowed to flee. Those that were carrying Vietnamese papers were lined up against the train and shot. They'd put their Kalashnikov on full automatic and sprayed them dead. One woman died holding her child. Asher had put his hands over Julie's eyes.

During the first hour of the climb, Julie wept. As Asher tried to comfort her, he inwardly cursed himself for taking the train. He'd let himself be swayed by Julie's automobile phobia. Fucking Allen and his Maserati, that AA bum; a car accident on the Pacific Coast Highway had a hand in this. Only his baseline fear kept him from lingering on the gruesome improbability of it all. Held hostage by Khmer Rouge and government bandits. This was supposed to happen to other people, to dumb-ass backpackers, to risk takers who traveled on the roads at night. It was not supposed to happen to him, but it had. The stone he kicked in his path struck the soldier marching ahead of him in the calf. The man turned, drew his pistol, and squinted at him.

"Go ahead," said Asher. "Do it. Off me, baby. Off me."

"Be quiet," said Julie.

It was a steep, serpentine mountain path that at one juncture, many, many years ago, had been paved. Now it was mostly rubble leading to a section where the old road was fairly well intact and then disintegrated back into a rutted mishmash of pavement and dusty earth. Above them was a canopy of palm and banana trees, and the only sounds were that of the Seventh-Day Adventist's prayers accompanied by the staccato rhythm of invisible tropical birds.

After another hour a light mist rolled in from the valley below and enveloped them. Their captors drew closer. Asher asked one in broken Khmer where they were going. He was a boy of perhaps eighteen, sinuously thin and mean, with a Mao cap.

He called Asher a "Yuon," which was racist slang for a Vietnamese person.

"That's the problem with you guys," he replied. "You really think the country is still infested with Vietnamese agents. But it isn't. Not anymore. They pulled out in eighty-nine, you loser. Visit Phnom Penh sometime and you'll see. The only Vietnamese left are whores."

They walked on and on. Asher took Julie's traveling bag, which consisted of cigarettes, a bikini, birth control, *Glimpses of the Moon,* a pack of playing cards, tampons, and the gin journal, a score sheet of nearly all the games of gin they'd played together in various locations. Asher had come somewhat better prepared. He had a change of clothes, a flashlight, a large bag of grass, two lighters, rolling papers, a carton of Camels, Xanax, a paperback thriller, and water.

Suddenly the Seventh-Day Adventist sat down.

"I'm not going any farther," he said. "I can barely feel my legs."

The eighteen-year-old with the Mao cap kicked him in the stomach, but was reprimanded by his superior. It was decided to take a cigarette break. They all sat off to one side of the road on a large black stone, partially obscured by a myriad of vines from neighboring trees.

"We're all going to die," said the Seventh-Day Adventist, breaking into heaving tears.

"Are you kidding me?" said Asher. "Your church will have you out of here in no time. Have you ever heard of Melissa Himes? Well, she was with the Seventh-Day Adven—"

"She was with the Latter-day Saints," said the Seventh-Day Adventist.

"Ah," said Asher. "Well, she got out for a few bags of rice and a tractor."

"The devil is strong here. I can feel him."

"Can you?" said Julie. "What does he feel like?"

"Okay, you two," interrupted Asher. "Let's save the big eschatological questions for later."

"What do you do in this country?" asked the Seventh-Day Adventist.

"I used to work for UNESCO," replied Asher. "Currently I'm engaged in the private sector."

"I don't think you'll find a convert in Asher here," said Julie, lighting a cigarette. "See that face? You are looking at decadent nihilism personified."

"Everyone has been saying that lately," said Asher. "Stop it. I'm a spiritualist and a Merchant Prince."

The mist suddenly rose above them, leaving the party in spangled sunshine. Through the trees Asher could make out the valley below. There were shimmering pools of water, a field of coconut trees, and rice paddies that stretched out to the rim of a hazy sea.

So as not to be immediately robbed of all his cigarettes, Asher gave two to each soldier. They nodded their heads and thanked him. The leader of the pack was an elderly man with a huge crescent-shaped scar on one cheek. He was shirtless and wore faded green pants. He handed a bottle of water to each of the three hostages.

"You try run," he said to Asher. "You think it possible to fly, fly away, we shoot you. We shoot you and wife."

"He's not my husband," said Julie.

Asher was glad to see Julie back in the world. The first few hours had been bad. She'd wept and wept. She'd cried out for her father, and her face had grown puffy with hysteria and fear. Now she had settled into the situation and her tongue was back. Asher took his *krama,* poured water on it, and wiped her face. Then he slung his arms around her and whispered, "Don't you worry, sweetheart. Your daddy is going to hear about this in the morning paper and be on the next flight to Bangkok with a suitcase of money. Don't you worry. All these guys want is money. We'll be back in Phnom Penh in five days, max."

In the distance came the whining of a motorcycle.

"I don't like the look of Scarface over there," she said. "He's going to rape me."

Asher looked over at the shirtless commander. He was speaking into a powerful transistor walkie-talkie known as an ICOM. From around a bend in the road came three soldiers; two were on dirt bikes, the other was on . . . well, if it wasn't a Honda Dream. They were ordered to get on the back.

"I'll take the Dream," said Julie. "Since you lost yours."

The three hostages whined up the mountain road on the back of motorbikes. Suddenly they were above the mist and into the brilliant sunshine. As the road leveled off there arrived a series of bombed-out houses and then, in the distance, came, of all things, a church.

chapter nineteen

IT WAS THE THIRD day of their captivity, and they were being held in the casino room of a ruined hotel. There was a smashed roulette table in one corner and a ripped piece of baccarat felt in another. The bats were everywhere. They hung from the rafters. They hung from partially shattered mantels and cracked cornices. They hung from wires. They hung in silence, black witnesses to the scene. The casino room was on the third floor of a hotel that at one point had been a mountain getaway. Asher vaguely knew the place's history through a Magnum photographer who had shown him aerial photographs. It was called Dokor, or Bokor; he couldn't remember. King Sihanouk used to enjoy a week or two here each year. Now it was graffiti-filled disaster. There were two stairs that led up to the casino room, one intact and the other a broken spiral staircase. On the first night, Asher had almost walked off it to his death. A ghastly sinking feeling had accompanied his ghost step into nothing. Luckily he had been treading lightly and was just able to pull back.

"One step, my man," he'd said. "One step."

When he got back to the casino room, he was reminded of a scene from a book he had not thought of in years: *Kidnapped,* with the stone spiral stairs that descended to nowhere, that led to death; that, and all the other N. C. Wyeth illustrations that had hooked him as a kid. *Kidnapped.* He shook his head and laughed to himself. No wonder they only guarded the other exit. They'd posted a boy there. He was young, narrow-faced, vicious, well armed, and utterly silent. He was either not a smoker or he refused, for hostage-taking etiquette's sake, the offer of Asher's cigarette. Asher called him Kid Silence. On this particular afternoon on the third day, Asher and Julie sat on the floor of the casino room playing gin rummy.

"It's like I have a low-grade fever," said Julie. "A low-grade fever that is a constant. It's real fear, sweetheart, and it's not going away. It's kinda terminal."

"Don't talk like that," said Asher, discarding.

"Well, how do *you* feel?"

"I try not to feel," said Asher. "Sometimes I think."

"You're a lucky man."

There was an old piece of burned wood that resembled charcoal which they used to keep score on the wall. Next to their markings was a self-portrait of a Khmer Rouge soldier in a Mao hat.

"The Vietnamese and the KR had it out here," said Asher. "I found bullet casings when they let me go take a piss."

"Really," said Julie.

"Yeah," replied Asher. "Just look at this place not from a luxury standpoint but from a military one. It's got a commanding view of the entire province and good cover. I remember hearing about it from a photographer. The funny part was the Khmer Rouge held the church and the Vietnamese held this hotel."

"Why is the church so structurally sound on the outside then?"

"I don't know. Maybe it was small-arms stuff."

"Maybe the photographer was full of shit."

"Maybe."

The Seventh-Day Adventist refused to play cards. He said that it wasn't a religious thing. He said it was just "against his sensibilities." He was like a beached albino walrus. He had a mustache. He'd never been to Cambodia in his life. Sihanoukville was to be his first posting. This had all come out on the first night as they lay awake beneath a kerosene lamp trying to build solidarity. Julie had been quite harsh and pretentious. She'd quoted Henri Bergson and ragged on the "myth of the afterlife." Asher had sat pretty much silent, sussing the guards, considering the situation, wondering about the ransom. When it came to their captors, the older the better. That was a solid rule. They laughed at his Khmer and he learned some new phrases from them, such as "When you pick the fruit, you kill it."

He'd never heard that one. Currently he was holding a terrible hand of cards, a pair of fives, a suicide jack, and four other randoms of varying suits with no numerical frequency. But there was something about the situation he now found himself in that helped his game. He picked up and discarded quite a lot, arranged things, focused, and eventually won.

"You son of a bitch," said Julie. "I'm sick of this. I used to be better than you."

"That was in L.A., sweetheart."

"So?"

"I'll say it again. That was in L.A. The terrain has changed."

It was beginning to be early sundown and with three guards in tow, they were allowed to go down to a small, fetid body of water that at one point had been a swimming pool. It was filled with rainwater the color of tea. In the former pool house Asher found two Dunlop tennis racquets and a dead yellow ball.

"Hey," he said. "We can play tennis. If they'll let us."

The racquets were warped and a few of the strings were broken, but beyond the pool there was a tennis court filled with weeds. There was no net.

Julie was wearing her tangerine bikini with flowers on it. The guards were impressed. They laughed and snapped at her bikini straps, then took turns guarding and swimming. The Seventh-Day Adventist did not swim. He was as frightened of the water as he was of his captors.

"I wish you'd come in," said Julie to the Dane. "With three we could play coin."

"Let's play anyway," said Asher. "We can teach the guards about free markets and the great money grab."

"Excellent," said Julie. "I've got a quarter in my bag."

From the edge of the pool she threw the American coin into the foreign water. Asher dove for it. In the dark water it was difficult to see, but not impossible. Soon he began to track the quarter as it shimmied and shook with the sunlight. Near the bottom, he snatched it and triumphantly rushed to the surface.

"Yes," he screamed. "Everyone is going to make everyone else a ton of money."

"You," said the Dane, "are a sick man. Your avarice and greed will get us all killed."

Asher got out of the pool and walked behind the Seventh-Day Adventist. Then he pushed him in the pool and dove in after him. When the Dane surfaced, he grabbed the man's hair, pulled his head back, and dunked him. Asher was kicked in the groin but did not care. Since he'd been in Cambodia, he'd seen the missionary population spread like smallpox. The Dane rose to the surface.

"I didn't come here to be insulted," said Asher. "If you don't watch yourself, I think I'll drown you in this pool."

The Dane was heaving. One dunk would be enough for this walrus. Asher had always been a little baffled by his personal misgivings concerning missionaries. He associated them with imperialism and overfunded expense accounts. There were so many of them now, they were driving up the price of rice in the countryside. Still, why the overblown anger for the man?

The Dane swam to the shallow end. His breaststroke was an odd, rhythmless flop. Julie and the guards were poolside, laughing.

"Honey," she said. "Back off the man, for Christ's sake. What has he ever done to you? Throw the coin and let's get on with the game."

"Sorry, sweets, looks like I lost it during the dunk. We'll finish our drowning games tomorrow."

The Dane slowly clambered out of the pool.

"Keep your God shit to yourself," said Asher. "Or I swear I'll cut your throat."

Water was spewing from the Dane's nose. He did not answer.

Asher climbed out of the pool. He felt wonderful. For a moment he felt cleansed of the boredom and stress of captivity. He and Julie began to walk back to the hotel accompanied by a guard. From a distance the hotel was a kaleidoscope of moss left to the weather. Yet there was something proud about the building. From the outside it was structurally sound, there on the bluff. Perhaps one day the Raffles hotels would fix it up and return it to its former glory.

"You are a very angry man," said Julie.

"I don't like missionaries."

"That's plain enough, but you see, there is something called cohabitation."

"That doesn't mean I can't abuse him."

A bit of Khmer came back to him and he told the guard that the Dane was a believer in God and that perhaps he should be shot.

The guard laughed and slapped him on the back.

"See," said Asher, "I'm gaining cred with our captors. They think I'm the fat man."

"You're as thin as a reed."

"I," said Asher, "am a Merchant Prince. Don't forget that."

"If you say that again I'm going to slap you. You're becoming annoying and obsessive with this Merchant Prince thing. We're both going to die penniless."

"What are our chances?" she asked as they entered the hotel.

"You want me to put a number on it?"

"We're staying in a fucking casino, why not? What do you think the odds are?"

"It's the ransom. Hopefully it's a straight money thing. If it's a straight money thing, it's much better than fifty-fifty. If it's not a money thing, if it's political, if the KR want something political, then, sweets, I'd say one in three."

He was lying. If it got political, they were dead.

"We happen to be American citizens," he continued. "We'll live. We are Americans. You got that? We're going to live and have children. I plan to spill my seed when this is all over and fuck the race."

Julie kissed him on the neck and took up her position in her hammock. Out of one glassless window the sun was coming down off the bluff and a thinnish moon, a very Islamic crescent moon, was rising out the opposing window. In the center of the casino room sat an as yet unlit oil lamp near a Bunsen burner, which was boiling a pot of water. The Khmer captors crouched, their knees bent at acute angles. Sometimes Asher took the same stance but he could never last as long as a Cambodian. They could squat for hours on end, doing anything—playing cards, gossiping, doling out ammunition, cooking.

Julie lit a mosquito coil.

"I wonder why they haven't robbed us?" she asked.

"Orders," said Asher. "It actually isn't a good sign."

"Why?"

"It means that someone who isn't here is running the show. Also, they robbed everyone they didn't shoot back on the train. I'm sure there are plenty of cigarettes to go around."

"Oh," she replied. "What do you think they'd do if we started fucking?"

"Shoot you in the head," said Asher. "We have to be very careful. Last night was uncool. I had to put a fist in your mouth."

The Dane came in from the pool still dripping, blubber hanging over his Speedo. He wiped his blond mustache, propped his knapsack up against the wall, and leaned against it. Asher lit a cigarette.

"I wish you wouldn't do that," said the Dane. "I'm allergic."

"Sorry," said Asher. "We're not in that kind of zone anymore."

"What zone," inquired the Dane, "is it that we are in?"

"We are in the land of the bats," said Asher, exhaling up to the rafters. "We are dark creatures of the night, paying for our sins."

"I see."

"Good. I'm glad you see."

They were summoned for a supper of noodle soup and a few shreds of fried pork. The sun had gone down now and the room was just barely lit by twilight. The sky was black and the sky was blue. The two colors had slept together. The guard lit the oil lamp and Julie and Asher began to play gin rummy. After a dozen games they retired to their respective hammocks and fell into a deep, untroubled sleep.

chapter twenty

THE DRIVE DOWN to Kampot was uneventful. In the shotgun seat Reese slept most of the way. AFP had hired a new
driver, who was impressive and fast. Pin sat in the back playing
with his cassette recorder. When Reese stepped outside the car,
the heat hit him like a body check. Quickly he walked into the
Kamrachi Hotel. It was a well-fortified place with reliable electricity. The driver and Pin took one room, Reese another. It was a
white room with air-conditioning and a television. Reese watched
CNN for fifteen minutes and then fell asleep. In his briefcase he
had held seventy-one thousand dollars, which he'd put beneath
his bed. The hotel room was without a safe and this worried him.
Still, he slept. He dreamt of his sister's wedding and Allison
Graber. She had arrived in Cambodia wearing a sarong that was
Caribbean sexy. There was a pool of water that led into a series of
caves which they explored with a limitless amount of dream oxy-
gen. When they came to the surface, they kissed. The kiss was the
bad part of the dream. They kissed as Reese imagined a vaguely
unhappy married couple might kiss. When he woke, he mastur-
bated, thinking of her all the way, and in various places on land.

The declining sun was coming through his hotel window. He checked his watch.

"Goddamn it," he said. "I could be in Maine now."

The hotel supplied a small fridge with a bottle of water. Very thirsty, Reese quickly downed most of the water and lay back on his bed. He would have to start drinking with the generals and sourcing out the town. Yawning, Reese stood up and looked out the window. There was a dusty traffic circle with spoke roads leading out in different directions. In the middle of the circle was a small fenced-in garden with a statue of King Sihanouk in his younger days. From his computer bag he withdrew a bottle of Johnnie Walker and gulped down a glass. Then he took a shower and took another drink out on to the narrow patio outside his room. What the fuck did these people do, really? he wondered. There were lots of coconuts. The province was famous for coconuts and gravel mined from the nearby mountains. Still, he saw no coconut or gravel or cement workers. He saw people on their *motos* zipping around to God knows where. He finished off his drink and refreshed it. The generals were said to drink heavily here and he would have to find out where they hung out at night. For that he would need Pin.

He found Pin listening to a Walkman, his door unlocked.

"Take that off," said Reese.

Sok Lida, the driver, was watching a Thai soap opera dubbed in Khmer. Reese turned off the television.

"Let's get going," he said.

"Where?" said Pin. "There is only one nightclub. The generals will be there. I have already spoken with my uncle."

"Tell me about it in the car," said Reese. "Let's go to the site.

You know, the place where the train got jumped. I've located it on the map; it's about fifteen kilometers east of here. The tracks are right next to Route 3. Let's get going before it gets too late."

Pin and Lida rose from their respective beds, upset and grumpy. This was just another story for them. Three *barangs* in the mountains; big deal. They liked the perks of traveling, though, the hotels and televisions, but Pin had said his mother was sick, a lie conceived to get back to Phnom Penh as soon as possible.

The drive at first was hilly and ran next to a shallow stream obscured by trees. Then the road flattened out, running through happy countryside. There were coconut trees and men making home improvements. The sun was changing from orange to red and it splashed its odd light onto the green reeds of a passing rice field. It was a healthy countryside life here. From the mountains there was wood and water, and though not far from the sea, the ground was fertile and forgiving.

Reese checked his map. It was a U.S. Army Corps of Engineers military product he was quite proud of for its quadrants and detail. They drove on. Reese put on a cassette of the Marshall Tucker Band's greatest hits.

"Oh, there's fire on the mountain, lightning in the air," sang Reese. "Gold in them hills and it's just waiting for me there."

There was no response. It made Reese miss America.

"Stop," said Reese. "The train tracks."

They'd missed the turnoff and Lida had to back up. At the train tracks there was a film crew, two men and a woman. Reese wanted nothing to do with them. His greeting was the gruff piece of professional bravado for which journalists are alleged to be famous. It turned out they were stringers from AP television out of Bangkok. For TV people, they were impressive. The cameraman didn't brandish his instrument like a weapon, and the woman he was with was articulate and attractive. They said they were getting stock footage.

At the tracks was a Cambodian policeman standing on the far side of a roadblock.

"Ask him if he thinks they've mined the road up the mountain," said Reese to Pin. "Ask that cop what the fuck the story is, Pin, charm the man, find out who the fuck is the go-between."

"My uncle, he already told me," said Pin. "I went and spoke with him. He lives very close to the hotel."

"Why didn't you tell me that earlier?" replied Reese. "See if you can get confirmation then."

Pin sauntered up to the guard. The guard shrugged. Pin continued the conversation and gave the guard a cigarette. Reese was unduly interested in what Pin was talking about but lay back. It was a Cambodian thing. He could be breaking news or talking about the bad luck of the guard's prostitute cousin. It was impossible to tell. Reese continued to observe. Ah, it looked like they were getting somewhere. The guard was smiling. Pin returned to the car.

"He says there is a man we should talk to tonight who goes back and forth," said Pin. "Same as what my uncle said. He doesn't know about mines but doesn't think so."

"Back and forth where?" asked Reese.

"The top," said Pin. "The top and back."

"The top of the mountain?"

"Yes."

"So there's already a go-between. He comes back and forth with ransom demands and so forth."

"Yes, up with supplies, down with demands."

"Where do the ransom demands go?"

"I didn't ask him that."

"How do we get in touch with this go-between?"

"He will be in Kampot."

"Where?"

"The nightclub. There is only one."

"Fine," said Reese. "Let's get out of here."

It was the kind of nightclub Reese had learned to loathe. The band was sad, terminally caught between East and West. The scotch he'd been drinking yellowed the lights. There were three singers got up in what Reese took to be red wedding dresses. As he took his seat with Pin, the band broke into "Hotel California."

"Oh, Lord," said Reese, placing his hand to his temples. "Please. Not again."

The song had been something of a youthful favorite for Reese. Now Asia had ruined it for him. To hear another disembowelment of "Hotel California" made him feel bitter and drunk.

The table sat in darkness. Waiters with flashlights came about serving buckets of beer. They ordered six Angkors and sat back in their respective seats. Pin was dressed in a white button-down short-sleeve shirt. From his shirt pocket he withdrew a pack of 555's, lit one, and slammed the pack down on the table.

"My mother, she is very sick," he said.

"I know, Pin, I know, but you gave your cousin the money before you left, so what else can you do?"

Everyone's relatives were getting sick. It fucked up schedules. Reese lit one of Pin's 555's, not his brand but a nice change. They were smooth, strong cigarettes, much like filtered Lucky Strikes, and they were favored by generals and the business elite. Reese's eyes began to adjust to the nightclub. There were three bored whores at one table, their dresses collectively gaudy enough to pick up the light from the stage. There was a table of the local military across the room from a table of local hoods, probably smugglers taking a break from the coastal town of Kho Kong. One of them, ridiculously, wore shades.

"What kind of physical description of the guy did you get?" asked Reese.

"Red shoes."

"What kind of fucking description is that?"

"The guard say he wears red shoes, red sneakers."

"I see," said Reese.

It seemed a reliable enough sign.

"I don't think I've ever seen a Khmer wear red sneakers, not even on the basketball court at Olympic Stadium."

Pin had no comment.

The band went into "Witchy Woman." Reese liked that. He had finished his first Angkor. It wasn't such a bad cover after all, but suddenly the lyrics of the song made him think of Julie. What was he doing trying to save that bitch? She'd fucked him over. But the night at the Gramercy had been fun, in a way. She'd been a great lay right when he'd needed it most. Still, what was he getting into here? This was not the news. Paying off a go-between was definitely not covering the news, it was making it. Still, if he could get them out before the ransom demands got changed, he'd have saved lives. Saving lives; that was a new one for Reese. They were useless at the American embassy; probably in a week or so someone like Fat Dave, the second secretary, some fucking chargé d'affaires, would waddle down here and try to negotiate a solution. He'd be faked out. U.S. taxpayers' dollars would be stolen.

A man walked through the dim light of the entrance. If Reese wasn't mistaken, those were red New Balances, of the mid-eighties variety, the spongy ones. Reese had once owned a blue pair in which he had won a Grove School running race. It was a victory of which he was still, sadly, proud.

"There he is," said Reese. "There's Red Shoes."

Pin slowly stood up.

"I think that's the guy," he said.

"Okay," said Reese, "tell him we want to meet him at the train tracks tomorrow at five in the morning."

"He will not agree to this. It is not in his interest to talk to us. It would be bad for his business."

"Tell him there's some money in it for him."

Here Pin paused.

"Money?" he asked. "Whose money?"

"Pin," said Reese. "Sit down. This is a weird one, and your discretion and silence are going to be absolutely required once we get back to Phnom Penh. Do you understand me?"

Pin sat back down. He looked at his boss, expressionless, waiting to hear what he had to say. Gossip and trade secrets weren't Pin's problem.

"I know two of the people being held hostage on the mountain. One is . . . well, what is she? She's an acquaintance. You know the word in English, an *acquaintance?* It's someone you know, *tic-tic.*

"The other guy you might even know. Asher. He used to hang

around the Heart when you were in love with that bartendress. Blond guy, kinda stocky, been around forever."

Pin shook his head. He did not know Asher.

"Well, I've got Asher's money. I had a talk with a lady at the bank and she gave me the money."

"Why did she do that?"

"Because she knows Asher, and she has a kind heart. She does not want to see him killed."

"The bank manager will fire her."

"He's in love with her, and she happens to be a very crafty French lady."

"Yes, boss."

Pin rarely called Reese *boss*. Mostly he called him nothing at all or just coughed.

"You are going to give this Red Shoes the money," Reese continued. "If he's for real. You think he's for real?"

"The guard said he was the one who has brought supplies. I think he wants to take a percentage of the ransom."

If there was one thing which Cambodians didn't know or care about, it was conflict of interest.

To Reese's great pleasure, he saw that Pin was getting excited. A thin smile came to his face and he opened another beer and lit a cigarette.

"How much Asher pay you if he come down alive?" asked Pin.

Reese rocked back in his chair. Fitful sleeping had been his only escape from pondering this plot, and not once had he considered his own pocket. Reese was not proud of this fact. Maybe Valery was right, maybe he was playing Rambo. At any rate, it would definitely not do to tell Pin he hadn't taken into account his own financial well-being.

"Tell you what, Pin," he replied. "If it all works out, I will personally see to it that Asher buys you a karaoke system."

It was Pin's dream to eventually run a karaoke parlor. He hung out at them constantly and spent too much of his salary on the whores who tended to linger about the parlors. Karaoke was Pin's real passion. Journalism was just a job.

"You want me to say that you will give him the money as ransom?"

"In so many words, yes."

"I'll talk to him."

"Make sure he's for real."

"I will."

Reese watched Pin approach Red Shoes. He offered him a cigarette, which was declined. Red Shoes lit his own. They sat down. Reese expected a long, drawn-out conversation, but it didn't go down that way.

"Shit," said Reese to himself. "He didn't go for it."

Pin came back to the table.

"He says the ransom is fifty grand for one. He will do it. He is for real."

"How do you know?"

"We are from the same province. He says he wants five thousand for himself. Fifty-five thousand. It is a lot of money."

The rapidity of the deal shook Reese, but it was typical, now that he thought about it. Negotiations either went slowly or quickly here.

"Well, fuck it. Tell him to meet us at the tracks tomorrow."

"He said early morning. First light. He has to pay the guards and they are sleepy then."

"*Prima luce,*" said Reese. "I like it."

"He wants to know if you accept."

Reese paused to ponder the brutality of the math. He had enough money for only one. Even if he withdrew all he had in *his* account, there wouldn't be enough for both. The two alternative options with which he was now faced—getting in touch with Asher and/or Julie's relatives residing somewhere out there in the great swath of America, or haggling with the captors and Red Shoes—were both beyond him. The first option would take up precious time; the second would be meddlesome and dangerous. If he tried to haggle, they might kill one of them or release neither. Pin was standing behind Reese's chair waiting to hear what his boss had to say. No, he'd give Red Shoes the going price, await the outcome, and hope that by the time he got back to Phnom Penh, Asher's portly American uncle or Julie's stingy godfather would be sitting at the FCC drinking gin after a troublesome day at the American embassy. Suddenly he felt Pin's hand come to rest on his shoulder. It felt light and reassuringly intimate. Perhaps Pin had already caught on to the dilemma. Then, ever so slightly, Pin squeezed his boss's shoulder. It was a signal not to linger.

"How about two for the price of one and a half," mumbled Reese to himself.

"I cannot hear you," said Pin.

"Tell him I accept," said Reese into Pin's ear.

Again Reese watched as Red Shoes and Pin spoke. It was a short one: a who, what, where, when, how much confirmation that took less than two minutes. Then, as Red Shoes stood up . . . It was odd. It was one of the weirdest moments in Reese's life. Red Shoes threw Reese a U.S. Army–issue salute.

chapter twenty-one

Asher and Julie were reading in their hammocks when they heard the sound of a motorcycle. As usual they were in the company of Kid Silence, the teenager with the three-legged stool, who sat where he always sat and did what he always did: sit, guard the entrance in silence. The Dane had taken up meditation in the corner. Asher stood up and went to the window.

"It's that guy again," said Asher.

"Who?" said Julie.

"The civilian," said Asher.

Asher watched as Scarface and two other high-ranking captors squatted outside the hotel, smoking and talking to the civilian who wore jeans and a black T-shirt. It was a long, drawn-out conversation.

"Something's going down," he said. "Something is definitely going down. A deal is being cut here. I can feel it."

"Great," said Julie, jumping to her feet and joining him by the window.

After a while the civilian went back to his motorcycle. He was thin and several years younger than the men with whom he'd been speaking.

"He kinda looks like a lizard," said Julie.

"I don't care what the fuck he looks like, but a gecko would be nice," said Asher. "A gecko is what we need. . . . Yes, he's coming back with a duffle bag. He's the money man. Yes!"

The group of men disappeared into the first floor of the hotel and Asher and Julie hugged each other. In her ear he whispered, "This is very good. Very good. Someone came through for us. I can feel them counting the money down there."

"Let's play some gin," said Julie. "I'm stressed."

From her bag Julie retrieved the deck of cards and her gin journal. On the top of each page was the name or nickname of the game's location—Delta Delay #167; Malibu Beach; Santa Barbara Sundown; Vegas Vagrancy—followed by the date. Below the location and date was a cross. Since Julie insisted on keeping score, the word *Me* and the word *You* were underlined and bisected at the top of the cross. Beneath were the falling vertical columns of opposing numbers. In the margin of some pages were telephone numbers and addresses of places to go or people to see later in the evening. Asher had been deeply moved when he'd first revisited the gin journal, and in captivity they both felt the superstitious need to honor its past with absolute accuracy and vigilance in the present.

In the middle of the fifth game, Scarface came into the room. They rarely saw Scarface anymore. He didn't eat with them. He slept down at the pool house and was in charge of the guards. He looked to be in his mid-fifties, his hair graying at the temples. The worn strap of his Kalashnikov ran diagonally across his shirtless chest. He walked straight up to Asher and held up his index finger.

"*Mooui*," he said in Khmer.

One.

Asher's heart dropped. The man's meaning was barbarically clear.

Asher pleaded.

"Bpi," pleaded Asher.

Two.

"Mooui," said the man, shaking his head.

Then Scarface barked something at Kid Silence. The teenager rose from his stool and squinted at Asher.

"Oh, fuck," said Asher. "Oh, please, why?"

He collapsed to the floor.

"What's the problem, honey?" said Julie, wrapping her arms around him as he began to cry.

"He says only one of us can go."

"Oh," said Julie and sat down herself. The Dane was still in the opposite corner meditating. He'd missed the whole transaction.

Asher and Julie began to whisper.

"Let's just send the Dane," said Julie.

"That's not funny. The Dane is not part of this calculus."

"Don't get mathy on me," said Julie. "And I'm *not* going without you."

"That's very romantic of you," said Asher. "I'm serious. I'm touched. . . ."

Tears were coming again. He would have to send her away. "I'm touched but there's a rule about sinking ships."

"This ship is not sinking," she said.

"What," said Asher, "you want to play eeny-meeny-miny-moe? You want to play She Loves Me, She Loves Me Not? That's not going to happen. You are going to walk down that mountain pass. You are going to swiftly collect as much money as possible from all your friends and family, acquaintances and relatives, and you are going to transport that money through that guy with the black T-shirt back up the hill. You understand me?"

"I'm not leaving you. Let's send the Dane."

"I don't even want the Dane to know about this."

Scarface ended the conflict. He grabbed Julie by the shoulder and pushed her toward the exit. Then he picked up her knapsack and threw it at her chest. Asher, surprisingly, was allowed to follow her out. They walked down the stairs and out into the sun. It was clear late morning with sun reflected off the swimming pool.

"Just get a lot of money," said Asher. "Go to the FCC and see what the press is and get lots of money transferred. Call my mom in Chicago. She's in the book. First name Jane. Who knows, they may all be in Phnom Penh by now with buckets of dough; your family too. It depends on the press."

"My family doesn't have buckets," said Julie, weeping.

Scarface savagely shoved her from behind. Asher put his fist in his mouth and bit down so as not to use it.

Then he watched her walk the winding path that led down to the church. It was a modest church, a nice terra-cotta red and structurally sound. At the church, she turned. Asher waved at her. She sat down.

"Don't do that, honey," he said to himself. "Walk, sweetheart. Please, walk."

Then he shouted it. He summoned everything he had in his smoker's lungs, cupped his hands, and screamed.

"Run!"

Julie stood up, passed the church, and slowly descended into a dreadful vanishing point.

Her only comfort was flowers. It had been three hours now and she was as parched and thirsty as she had ever been in her life. Earlier she'd dug into her bag furiously looking for a bottle of nonexistent water. Then she began to discard things she did not need: her bikini, her birth control pills (it was time to go off the pill), her toothpaste, her hairbrush. It was a Hansel and Gretel thing. Her hope was that Asher would one day find them.

As she walked she clipped flowers and twisted their stems together and placed the floral crown in her hair. Tears distorted her vision, and once she came very close to spraining her ankle. It was the hottest hour. Even the birds weren't singing. They were taking shade so as to not expend their energy. The road went on forever. With tremendous clarity she remembered the taste of an Italian ice she'd licked on as a girl on her first visit to New York.

If she had been a bit more with it, she would have covered her head with some piece of clothing, but she didn't think of it because she needed the flowers there. They were small flowers and she did not speculate upon their names. They ran the gamut, the whole spectrum of color, and picking them provided a break from the tedium of her march. She'd had no breakfast, no tea, no water. At four hours in she began to experience low-level hallucinations. The sun was high in the sky, beating directly down onto the road. Only with the occasional sharp turn came a sliver of shade. Off to the side of the road she sat down on a shaded rock. Then she made the mistake of smoking a cigarette. It was an incredibly stupid thing to do. But for Julie, time was smoking and cigarettes a great friend. When she stood up, a dizziness, a throbbing grid of pressure, enveloped her and she passed out.

She came to feeling much better. There was shade now. Her body felt cooler and her heart had slowed. Sluggishly she rose to her feet. Things were taking on the quality of a more focused dream than earlier in the march. Still, the snaking road was a nightmare, a brutalizing horror. She decided to use her hatred of the road for energy, and the good news was, she was getting to the part that was vaguely paved. The dark sections of road, rutted as it was, gave her a sense of impending civilization and she checked the flowers in her hair. She continued to walk, pause and pick, walk, pause and pick; that was the way Julie walked the trail.

The path eventually straightened and in the distance she saw a happy sight. It was a painted barber shop pole that hung horizontally across the road. A roadblock, and behind the roadblock she could make out people. Light was reflecting off camera lenses. She began to skip like a girl.

"The press," she said. "The fucking press. I can't believe it."

Richard Davies's zoom lens was broken, and he was reaching a breaking point with the lens through which he was now staring. It was a wide-angle. He did not need a wide-angle. He needed a zoom. Julie's skipping was just outside the range of a good shot. He could hear his competition, all with heavy zooms, firing away. For hours on end they'd been waiting around. Now the moment of news had arrived and Richard Davies wasn't going to get the shot. He badly wanted a photograph of Julie skipping. Suddenly Davies broke from the pack. He ducked under the roadblock and ran toward Julie.

"Get the fuck out of my frame," screamed CNN Bob.

Reese was furious too. Davies had confided in him about his

lens problem, but what the photographer was now doing was one of the most professionally selfish things he'd ever witnessed. Everyone with a camera was furious. Reese could feel the collective hatred as they hissed and bitched behind the roadblock. Still, Reese was not a cameraman and so he had the luxury of simply watching with his cassette recorder at the ready. Then an explosion rocked the road. Davies's body flew sideways into the bushes. A land mine—Davies had stepped on a land mine. Julie was down too. A silence fell over the press corps. Now Reese could see the blood. He didn't know whose it was but he could see it, red on the black bits of pavement. Suddenly he found himself running.

"No," screamed Pin. "There will be others."

That was not what Reese wanted to hear. He paused and looked for lumps in the road and saw none.

Davies was twitching in the road. His left leg was in the bushes. Julie was lying facedown on her stomach a few yards away. Reese scooped her up. It was effortless. As he ran with her, as he ran with her hot blood warming his chest, he prayed and leapfrogged to the small section of road that was still paved.

"Look down, look down," shouted Pin. "Look for *tic-tic* bumps. Look down."

Reese made it.

"Pin," he screamed. "Get the car."

Julie was bleeding from her left arm and leg. The leg was worrisome. A piece of shrapnel had caught an artery. In the car Pin tied a tourniquet with his belt. The driver flew. Not a word was spoken.

Luckily the Kampot hospital was familiar with mine victims. The doctor was old, spoke French, and said there was no blood.

"*Sang, nous avons besoin,*" he said.

"*Bon,*" said Reese, rolling up his shirt. "*C'est moi.*"

The doctor lay Reese down on a gurney while a nurse attended to Julie. As a child and all the way through adulthood, he'd been unduly terrified of needles. At Grove he'd once had a high fever and walked the halls of the infirmary inside a waking nightmare of needles with hissing sounds coming at him from all directions. Now, that fear was all over. He wanted it. He wanted the needle.

"*Allez,*" he screamed at the doctor. "*Allez, nous n'avons pas de temps.*"

Of course the doctor missed. His hands trembled. He missed again, then he hit. Reese watched the whole show, barely caring, wanting the pain. When the tubes were attached, he lay back on the gurney and wondered whether he and Julie's blood types could possibly match.

Then there was a video camera shining in his eyes. It was CNN Bob.

"I can't really go on record right now with you, Bob," said Reese. "See, I've lost a lot of blood. I think they really went for it."

"Just say something," said CNN Bob. "Please, say your full name. Just give me something, daddy. I got to get back to Phnom Penh."

"I'm retiring from journalism," said Reese.

The tape was definitely rolling now. Reese could see the bloodred eye on the front of the camera leering at him. He was transfixed by the eye. He and that evil eye were one.

"Is that because you'd rather save lives?" asked CNN Bob.

"I don't know," said Reese. "I guess you could say that I'm sick of the sidelines. I'm getting in the game now."

Then he fell back on the gurney and went to sleep.

* * *

Reese arrived back in Phnom Penh to a bonanza, an international feeding frenzy of a story. They hung it all on the Khmer Rouge and the Harvard graduate's "dramatic journey." The inaccuracies, small and large, rolled in. Reese refused all interviews, locked the door of his office, broke out the scotch and candy, and got disgusted with television news. But it was fun seeing himself carrying Julie in his arms as he sat there in his office drinking on blood loss. For hours Reese walked his office barely feeling the floor. For the first time in many moons he called his mother. When the sound of her loving voice came on the line, the sadness, the stupidity, the terror all welled up in Reese and he wept. She was his mother, after all, the woman of last resort. She said she'd send him a ticket home, and he said that would be fine, that would be great. He asked her to DHL it.

He avoided the FCC and interview requests. At night he walked around the palace walls and then went to sit alone at his favorite fruit-shake stand. He told Pin to go tend to his mother. Before he took the phone off the hook, he made two phone calls to other wire journalists, planting the lie that it was Julie's family that had paid the ransom demands. They told him that she'd been medevaced to Singapore and was on her way to L.A. She'd be fine.

The story gathered so much heat that the embassies started to make noise and the government arrested Ta Rin. Rin, who only days before had been seen driving around Phnom Penh in a Land Cruiser, was thrown into jail, a scapegoat to international pressure. It had taken one hostage crisis to revenge another. There were threats of cutting off international donor aid if "government and Khmer Rouge collusion against foreign nationals continued unabated." It had gotten political.

chapter twenty-two

ASHER AWOKE TO GUNFIRE. Immediately he looked for the light. It was just past *prima luce,* which meant the Khmer Rouge had jumped their co-conspirators. He couldn't see the fighting. It was all taking place below him. It was small-arms stuff, and from the sound of it, people were getting shot in their sleep. Asher had seen this coming. The third week had seen a growing tension between the so-called government troops and the Khmer Rouge. During the days Asher could hear the crackling of ICOMs transmitting Khmer static into the air. During the night arguments drifted up from the pool house. Now that fight was over. It hadn't been much of one, maybe one or two rounds returned in anger before death.

Asher rolled out of his hammock and walked over to the window. Last night the weather had been incredible. Some kind of system had rolled down the South China Sea. All night he and the bats had sat up with the lightning. Though the rain had not come ashore, the bats did not like the lightning. They could feel its electricity and could neither hang nor be quiet. They chirped and frittered about. They darted about the casino room, daring neither to rest nor depart for lower ground. At one point, while Asher had been waiting for another bolt of lightning to light the clouds, a bat had slammed into his neck. That had been unusual. All week long the bats had assiduously avoided physical contact with Asher. They were known for the sensitivity of their antennae, but this storm, distant though it was in the night, had upset their collective equilibrium. A rookie among them had come undone and struck him. Now the sun was rising higher, and the mountain came between the storm on one side and the sun on the other.

He'd spent an entire week in the company of Kid Silence and the bats. He did a lot of stretching, but mostly he wandered the casino room looking up at the rafters, trancing out on the bats. They were neither his friend nor his foe; that was what was so maddening. Oh, the bats with their little hideous claws and their black-velvet membranes for wings hanging there in orderly rows, oblivious to him. Oh, God, he didn't know what they meant. Bats in the belfry, batty; the little rats were a state of mind. Now all about his head they swirled as the storm approached in the coming light.

Asher, who had not particularly enjoyed the book he'd taken with him, had read the bastard three times. Now as the noise of the gunfight fell silent and the smell of gunpowder rose, he flung the book out the window. He enjoyed watching the pages flutter in the wind. Suddenly Kid Silence was walking toward him with a smile on his face and a pistol in his hand. Kid Silence took Asher's last pack of cigarettes from Asher's shirt pocket, plucked one out, and lit it. He had never stolen from him before. It was their first exchange in the week since Julie had left. During that time he'd read, stretched, rationed cigarettes, and played solitaire with the gin journal open by his side. The bats were good company for solitaire. From the rafters above they squealed as he slapped cards down against the floor. He'd heard stories that men in captivity kept records of days by scratching things on walls. Asher did not feel the need to mark time because he had the gin journal. It was a wonderful traveling companion. With it open on his lap he sat for hours revisiting a wide range of American vistas. He checked and rechecked scores of games past, finding comfort in addition. Only rarely had she cheated him.

They'd cut off his pool rights when Julie left. As for the Dane, well, that was a bit of a mystery. He'd disappeared. One day they'd simply taken him away. The Dane; perhaps he was dead, perhaps set free, perhaps in the church. Who knew? The Seventh-Day Adventists had a field headquarters in Kampot. Maybe they'd cut a God deal. It was impossible to know about the Dane, and Asher had to discipline himself from speculating upon the man's fate. The thought of the Dane made him angry and impatient. Impatience was the worst; it condensed time.

The storm continued to threaten, the sun to rise. Asher walked over to the window and watched as Scarface came out of the ground floor and onto the front lawn. He was laughing to himself. Then he shouted something up to Kid Silence. The teenager walked across the room and grabbed Asher by the wrist. They marched down the stairs and out onto the front lawn.

Asher studied the sky. He'd never seen anything quite like this. Morning lightning, morning sun. Then the clouds began to come in earnest. They came rolling in, the mountains unable to stop them. A bolt of lightning ripped across the sky and touched the sun. Lightning on the sun, the beginning of a new day. Then came the rain.

He was kicked from behind. Asher stood up. Kid Silence was holding a hoe.

"Oh no," he said, grabbing his face. "Oh no, not the hoe. Please, God, no, not the hoe."

Scarface came out with a pistol and his own hoe. He was in an old-school Khmer Rouge outfit now: black pants, threadbare green shirt, Mao cap. Through the wind and the rain he squinted at Asher and shook his head. At gunpoint Asher was walked down the winding path toward the church. The sun split the clouds, briefly illuminating the path ahead and pinking the steeple. It was a short walk and no one said anything to anyone. As they neared it, the Dane came out from the church accompanied by a young Khmer Rouge guard Asher had never seen before.

The earth in front of the church was quite soft, the grass healthy and green. Asher and the Dane were each given a hoe and ordered to dig.

"How deep will you make yours?" asked the Dane.

"I believe in cremation," said Asher. "I'm going to make it shallow as hell."

"Then you'll have to be patient," said the Dane. "May I at least ask that of you? I am going to dig myself a proper grave."

"I'll wait," said Asher.

"Thank you."

Side by side the two men worked, the Dane with angry, apocalyptic frenzy, Asher slow, pathetic, and steady. The earth was coming up nicely. It could have been a garden.

"You think something might grow out of us?" said Asher. "I mean, grow from our bodies?"

The Dane didn't answer. As his digging intensified in fervor, Asher's output decreased.

"I think," said Asher, "we're in synch for the first time."

Again, the Dane said nothing. His pink face had turned scarlet and his blond hair flapped in the wind. He was going at it furiously now and praying in his native tongue. Asher made his grave so they'd be forced to cover him up with a nice bump in the earth, Western style.

"To die with a Dane," said Asher, stopping work. "And never to be . . . never to be anything at all ever again."

"Why," asked the Dane, "will you not at least finish your final task? 'Wake up, and put some strength into what is left. For I have not found any work of yours completed in the eyes of my God. So remember the teaching you've received; observe it, and repent. If you do not wake up, I shall come upon you like a thief, and you will not know the hour of my coming.' "

"What is that, fucking Job?"

"The Book of Revelation."

"Is that the first or the last chunk of that tedious tome?"

"The last," said the Dane.

Asher returned to digging. He did not want to die angry, and the man was right. His grave was weak.

"It will be nice," he said when he was through, "to be relieved of you and your revelations."

It came swiftly enough, a hoe to the back of the head, the wind howling, their hands bound with twine.

"Kneel with me," the Dane had said, lumbering down to his knees.

"Sorry," said Asher. "I'd prefer to stand."

THANKS TO: *Gerry Howard, Chris Dechard, Sok Sin, Andrei Vesselovski, Ilia Olchanetsky, Jennifer Rudolph Walsh, Pip Wood, Ian Taylor, Michael Hayes, Daniel Pinchbeck, David Berman, my mother, Eoghan Mahony, Tom Beller, Sam Brumbaugh, Jessica, Paul Hare, Anthony and Kelly, Libby May, Stephen Malkmus, Joanna Yas, and the armed forces of the Kingdom of Cambodia, without whose impedance this book would not be possible.*

Robert Bingham *was the author of the short story collection* Pure Slaughter Value. *A graduate of Brown University, he held an M.F.A. from Columbia and was a founding editor of the literary magazine* Open City. *His fiction and nonfiction appeared in* The New Yorker, *and he worked for two years as a reporter for* The Cambodia Daily. *He died in 1999.*